The Curious Cases of

Sherlock Holmes

Volume 3

By

Stephen Herczeg

Paperback ISBN 978-1-80424-576-7
ePub ISBN 978-1-80424-577-4
PDF ISBN 978-1-80424-578-1

Published by MX Publishing
335 Princess Park Manor, Royal Drive,
London, N11 3GX
www.mxpublishing.co.uk

Cover design by Brian Belanger

To Mum

my biggest fan

To Steve and Sharon

For their ceaseless commitment

to helping others

Contents

Copyright Notices

Illustrations

The Case of the Left Foot ©2024 Stephen Herczeg

The Adventure of the Missing Journal ©2024 Stephen Herczeg

The Man from Moscow ©2024 Stephen Herczeg

The Adventure of the Tesla Coil ©2021 Thaddeus Tuffentsamer

The Strange Case of the Unicursal Hexagram ©2024 Stephen Herczeg

The Disappearance of Dr. Markey ©2024 Stephen Herczeg

The Demise of the Painted Devil
SHAKESPEARE: TEMPEST. Ariel (Act I, Scene II), from William Shakespeares The Tempest, 1611.
Wood engraving after Sir John Gilbert, 1856-60.
Obtained under licence from https://www.freeimages.com/

The Adventure of the Great Wyrley Outrages
Arthur Conan Doyle at his desk at Norwood, ©1894
Credit: The Arthur Conan Doyle Encyclopedia Private Collection.
Obtained under Public Domain licence

With thanks to:

Thaddeus Tuffentsamer
https://www.amazon.com/stores/Thaddeus-Tuffentsamer/author/B07BQMTHX1

Jeffrey McKeever
http://www.screamingceltstudio.com

Brian Belanger for the wonderful cover designs
Brian did most of the cover designs at mxpublishing.com from 2016 -2023, and does all of the covers over at belangerbooks.com.

Foreword

The world of Sherlock Holmes – as originally laid out by Arthur Conan Doyle – is one in which crimes and mysteries yield, albeit sometimes reluctantly, to logic, to deductive principles, and to common sense. It has strict rules, set character studies, and a certain steadiness. An orderly place, basically.

The world of Sherlock Holmes pastiches, on the other hand...

This latter, shadowed realm of pastiche, homage and re-imagining can be a fraught one, a sort of sandpit where rules are broken with each new tale by each new author. Strict adherents of the canon throw up their hands in horror (or at least mild dismay) when faced with texts which do not stick faithfully to ACD's version of Holmes and Watson, whilst steampunk adherents gleefully insert sleek fighting airships, mechanical computers and other retrofitted technology. There are crossovers with the works of ACD's contemporaries, or ruthless deconstructions of the original stories, and at the same time, writers who are aficionados of horror and the supernatural slide poor Holmes into situations ripe with actual curses, ghosts, demonic presences, and even Lovecraftian monstrosities, oh my oh my.

In this particular collection, Stephen Herczeg employs each and all of the above, though his Holmes and Watson remain fully recognisable and steady, like anchor points. Herczeg seeks above all else to entertain, and although I myself tend more towards a subtle tweak of the original material in my own pastiches, I find it hard to complain about some good old-fashioned entertainment.

Therefore although there are indeed some 'classic' tales here, prepare yourself also for H G Wells's warped science to emerge unexpectedly in a Holmes mystery, for a direct encounter with a subtle cosmic horror from the pages of H P Lovecraft, and perhaps most surprisingly, a distinct nod to Batman! ACD's villain Lysander Stark appears in a major role, as does the strange and arcane Simon Iff from the works of Aleister Crowley. Add in a touch of The Exorcist – or so it seems – and a wicker man, a mention of the real-life George Edalji incident, a serial killer with a gifted mother, and more… well, you get the picture.

Come not with too much canonical prejudice, but simply dip in and enjoy.

John Linwood Grant
Yorkshire, January 2025

The Case of the Left Foot

Christmas was fast approaching when I was finally able to begin tidying up my notes for a case from the previous February that would become known as "The Beryl Coronet". Sadly, for my good friend Sherlock Holmes, it had been several weeks since he'd had an interesting case, and he'd descended through that December into a worrying state of *ennui*, in spite of the approaching holidays. With winter and Christmas now upon us, my concern for him began to manifest itself.

It was then that fortune shone upon us, like the coming of the Biblical Star, when I heard the doorbell ring downstairs that morning. Within moments I could hear Mrs. Hudson, our wonderful landlady, climbing the stairs to our apartments.

Not wishing to seem too eager, I waited until she finished rapping on the door before crossing to receive her.

"Hello, Doctor," she said softly, handing me a small envelope. "Telegram came for him." We both glanced at Holmes's name printed on the outside. "I do hope it brings him out of his room. I know that people get glum at this time of year . . ." she added before retreating downstairs.

Closing the door, I turned and carefully opened the envelope, sliding out the folded sheet. Opening it, the message I read brought a smile to my face. Lestrade needed Holmes's services – something that generally led to some level of intrigue, or at least interest, in my friend's mind.

Reinserting the note into the envelope, I turned to find Holmes entering the sitting room. He spied the message in my hand and said, "What have you there?"

Handing the telegram over, I said, "Hopefully something of a worthwhile distraction for you."

Quickly reading it, he replied, "As you have seen, there isn't much detail, but Lestrade wishes us to join him at Dufour's Place in Soho."

"Strange location to meet," I said.

"Not if there's someone for us to see in the mortuary."

"Of course," I said, remembering the establishment of such in that very place some years back.

"Well, shall we away?" Holmes asked, disappearing from the sitting room to get ready without another word.

***

When I rejoined him mere moments later, Holmes stood unconsciously tapping his foot in repressed impatience. The sniff of a mystery had brought all his senses and expectations to the fore.

We were soon trotting through the streets of Marylebone and eventually into the more decrepit area of Soho. The contrast was striking. In the area near our Baker Street lodgings, the shops were decorated for the season. There was an energy in the air, and a marked cheerfulness as well. This seemed to dissipate as we travelled to the southeast, where there was less opportunity or reason for those around us to celebrate. And yet, if one looked closely, there were still small efforts made to acknowledge the holiday.

The driver turned into the somewhat grim area near Dufour's Place and stopped outside a three-storey Georgian building with a tired, run-down appearance to it.

The structure brought a sense of nervousness to my disposition. Even though I had never attended there, I remembered its history. It had been procured by the St. James Parish well over thirty years before, and a mortuary established to deal with the overflow of victims of the cholera outbreak of the mid-1850's.

I was merely an infant at the time, but part of my medical studies required research and re-examination of such outbreaks, and the lessons learned from their responses. Medical knowledge had advanced from those days, and I sincerely hoped that it was sufficient, but history shows that new variants of diseases are often encountered that force our knowledge and techniques to improve, generally at the cost of many lives in the early days of the process.

Standing before the mortuary, Holmes noticed my expression. "You look confused."

"I'm simply unsure why this building still functions as a mortuary. Surely there are better-resourced facilities."

"Ah, I have heard tell that the high rate of mortality for the area's inhabitants requires such a facility, even to this day. The Parish of St. James maintains the building as a way of helping those families that have suffered a death but have no means to pay the fees required at more salubrious establishments."

"That explains why it's so run down."

"Yes. I think the church's charity can only stretch so far. Renovations are probably well down the list of needs."

A short figure appeared in the doorway, rugged up with a thick coat and hat pulled down to his ears.

"Lestrade," Holmes called, receiving a nod and a wave of a gloved hand for us to join him inside.

Stepping inside the dim corridor, Lestrade's demeanour was dour at best. His responses were shorter than normal, giving me the impression that he was under great pressure over something.

"What do you have for us?" asked Holmes as we were led down the passageway towards a larger and slightly better-lit room at the end. A strong smell of decay and chemicals floated towards us, making my throat constrict for a moment, as it had been a while since my senses had been assaulted in such a way.

It wasn't until we entered the larger room that Lestrade finally answered Holmes's question. "This is a strange one, Mr. Holmes, and worrying." The room was large and rectangular, kept cold by the absence of heating. Several tables lined one wall. Each held objects covered in stained white sheets. I knew by their shape that they were recently deceased bodies, awaiting collection and burial.

My eyes then fell on the subject of Lestrade's despair.

In the middle of the room lay the examination table in question. Instead of the body of some poor unfortunate victim, a solitary shod foot sat in the middle of a clean white sheet. Even from where I stood, I could tell it was a woman's by the size and style of the shoe.

"My Lord," I gasped, stepping closer to peer at the dismembered appendage. It was a left foot, cut off just above the ankle, and wearing a shoe as if its owner had simply misplaced a body part as she strolled towards her place of employment, before being brought here to reside until she came to collect it like an item of lost baggage.

"We haven't examined it, Mr. Holmes," said the policeman. "I knew you'd want to look at it first."

Holmes stood nearby, a speculative expression on his face as he glanced down at the foot, gleaning as much initial information as he could. "Well, Lestrade," he said, "you have my attention. Do you wish to fill me in before I examine this item further?"

"I'll start at the beginning then." Coughing several times to clear his throat, and possibly loosen the built-up taste from the odours in the room, Lestrade reached into his pocket, starting to remove a notepad before shaking his head and simply telling us what he knew. "A little over a week ago, a young lass, Miss Elaine Waterson, employed as the personal assistant to Sir Lyndon Marsden, of Marsden's Fine Apparel for Women – "

"I know that place," I blurted out, receiving a withering look from Holmes. "It's in Mayfair, isn't it?" A harrumphing cough from Holmes stopped me speaking further.

"Inspector," he told Lestrade, "please continue."

"As Doctor Watson said, Sir Lyndon's business is in Mayfair. Very salubrious establishment it is, too, if I may add. I certainly won't be taking Mrs. Lestrade there any time soon. Anyway, Miss Waterson didn't come into work on the Monday of last week, and hasn't shown up since."

"Nothing untoward in that," said Holmes. "Possibly sick, or . . . ."

His eyes joined mine in staring at the foot upon the examination table.

"I'll get to that in a moment," said Lestrade. Pulling a piece of paper from his pocket and carefully unfolding it, he placed the page on the white sheet. "This was received on Wednesday of last week."

Holmes and I stepped closer and read the note. It was written in a thin scrawl, and I saw that it was in a woman's hand:

Sir Lyndon Marsden,

4

We have taken your assistant, Miss Elaine Waterson. She will come to no harm if you comply with our demands.

A personal advertisement will be placed in tomorrow's Times. The addressee will be Mr. Myron Betterman. You are to follow the directions indicated and deliver the sum of one-thousand pounds to the location mentioned.

If you fail to meet these demands, then the results will not be conducive to Miss Waterson's health.

Do not involve the police.

Ignore us at your peril.

I looked back at the dismembered foot and gasped.

"I presume that this Sir Lyndon fellow ignored them?" asked Holmes.

"Actually no. If it weren't for one of Miss Waterson's co-workers, we wouldn't have known about any of this."

Pointing at the foot, Holmes asked, "What led to this then?"

"Ah," said Lestrade, pulling a small piece of newsprint from his pocket and laying it next to the letter. "This is the personal advertisement as mentioned." I had to peer closer, but could make out the slightly smudged print.

Mr. Myron Betterman,

Happy to have made your acquaintance. Leave the item of concern in a satchel before the north face of the statue of the woman in Berkeley Square at mid-day Monday. Come alone. Don't be late.

"Sir Lyndon didn't make it to Berkeley Square then?" I asked.

"He did, but . . . ." Lestrade trailed off for a moment before continuing, "We were informed not long after the first note was received – the lady's co-workers found out, and were concerned. We

– a small contingent of plain-clothed constables and myself – spread out across the Square in anticipation of apprehending the kidnapper." A wry grin crossed Holmes's face as he turned towards Lestrade. "He didn't show, did he?"

"No," Lestrade answered with downcast eyes. "No, he didn't."

"So it is now Wednesday – two days after this aborted transaction, which seems to have been upset because of the police presence – and more than a week after the lady was taken. You should know, Inspector, that even London's finest look like policemen no matter what their dress – even to the uninformed."

"It would seem that way," Lestrade replied.

"What was Sir Lyndon's response?"

"His rage knew no bounds. My superiors were immediately notified, and that's why I'm now asking for your help. Then there is this," said Lestrade, pulling another piece of paper from his pocket. Unfolding it and placing it next to the other sheets, he added, "This arrived with the foot, early this morning."

"Before I read that, how was the foot presented? Surely not just left on the doorstep."

Lestrade shook his head. "No, no it wasn't. It was neatly wrapped, like a Christmas present, complete with a red ribbon. A gift card on the outside said it was for Sir Lyndon. Naturally, the first staff member to arrive had no clew, took it inside, and placed it on Sir Lyndon's desk."

A grimace crossed Holmes's face. "So the wrapping would be a useless place to search for information. Too many hands would have had the opportunity to touch it."

Nodding to a small table nearby, Lestrade said, "You can still have a look. It has been placed there for your inspection." Pointing to the third sheet he'd laid out, he said, "Read that."

It was neatly wrapped, like a Christmas present, complete with a red ribbon.

Holmes and I bent lower to read the note. I could see that the scrawl was certainly different from the original delicate scratching of a woman. This consisted of a much heavier set of letters, revealing that the author had found it quite a bit more difficult to manipulate the pen than had the person who prepared the first note:

> *Sir,*
>
> *You have involved the police. For that, you will pay, as has Miss Waterson.*
> *The sum is now five-thousand pounds.*
> *Deliver this amount to the same location in Berkeley Square by three o'clock this afternoon.*
> *Comply with our demands to the letter, or you will receive several more Christmas presents, each containing another piece.*
> *Come alone.*
> *If any policemen are detected, then you will receive all of your presents at once.*

"That is quite the definitive demand," murmured Holmes.

"Yes," said Lestrade.

"I assume Sir Lyndon wasn't happy with this either."

"Not in the slightest. I was called in directly and suffered several minutes of his cursing and red-faced fury before he finally stormed from the room. I had these items brought here as quickly as possible, Dufour's being the closest mortuary to Mayfair, and a sight more discreet for such an affair."

"Can we assume your superiors are not amused either?"

"That's an understatement."

"It's a good thing you brought me into it then."

"Can you find the kidnapper, before it's too late?"

"We don't have much time, and I have some questions that need answering, but I truly believe I can find the kidnapper and the poor unfortunate Miss Waterson."

I saw a slight frown cross Holmes's face as he was casting an eye over the packaging before he turned back towards the disembodied foot. Pulling his glass from an inside pocket, he proceeded to bend closer, examining the wound area closely.

Moving up next to him, I found my gaze drawn to the raw, meaty protrusion sticking from the top of the shoe. After a few moments, Holmes mumbled, "What say you, Watson?"

"The foot size is around six or seven, which for an average woman puts her height at around five-foot-four inches."

"Do we know Miss Waterson's height, Inspector?"

"As the Doctor said: She is five-foot-four inches in height, and of very slight build."

Indicating the amputation site, I continued with my observations. "The cut is clean, but shows a slight roughness, with some tearing. I would suggest it was made with something like a wood saw." Holding my hand out towards Holmes, I said, "Can I borrow your glass for a moment?" Taking the proffered instrument, I focused on the bones themselves. Each had been sawn through roughly, confirming my suspicions. Handing the glass back and pointing at the protruding tibia and fibula, I said, "See here? The cut across the bones is slightly jagged, I would suggest that my observation is correct, and the saw had been dulled before this horrid business. The roughness indicates a bluntness to the blade."

"Excellent. I thought as much myself." Taking back the glass and holding it in front of the Achilles Tendon, Holmes continued. "What do you think of this?"

It took me a moment to understand what he meant, but then I moved to one side. A dark shade ran along the back of the protruding segment of leg, disappearing into the heel of the shoe. "I need to see the foot."

"I agree," said Holmes, "and I would also like to examine the shoe by itself."

Delicately, I unlaced the shoe and prized the foot from within it.

"That was a little more difficult than it should have been, wasn't it?" Holmes asked.

"Yes, it was. I would have expected the foot to have become slightly smaller due to loss of blood."

"Quite, so, "said Holmes, picking up the shoe and studying it. "This is piquing my interest more and more."

Turning my attention to the foot, I rotated it and examined the heel and the Achilles Tendon, following the dark subcutaneous shadow.

"It was removed *post mortem*, wasn't it?"

Surprised by Holmes's quick summation, I nodded in agreement. "Yes. The body lay for quite some time, several hours, I presume, before the removal of the limb." Pointing to the dark shadow on the heel, and the discolouration by the tendon, I added, "Blood pooled here, as indicated by the lividity." Picking up Holmes's discarded glass, I focused on the wound itself. "Yes, I can see a thicker area of coagulation at the site of the cut, which would have been the exit point of the saw if working from front to back of the leg – not something that would occur in a fresh amputation."

"Any idea how long she was dead?" asked Lestrade, his curiosity showing at our discovery.

"I would have to say two or three days, but perhaps more. It depends on whether she was kept cold or not."

"In this weather? I can hardly get warm myself, even by my fire at night."

"Yes. So it could be anywhere up to a week."

"Still, that means it could be our poor unfortunate Miss Waterson."

Nodding, I said, "Yes, sadly."

"Then we've already failed."

"Not so fast, Inspector," interrupted Holmes. "We've only established the fact that the foot was removed from a corpse. Further investigations will be needed to confirm from whom – we have no proof that the foot belonged to the woman in question. It could belong to anyone."

Holmes returned the shoe to the table before pointing to the foot itself. "The owner didn't have regular access to the sort of bathing or grooming facilities one might attribute to an assistant working for a high-end fashion house." Following the direction of his finger, I saw that the foot's toenails were split, and could be called filthy, as well as exhibiting a marked fungal infection. I had been so intent on the wound and blood settlement that I had failed to observe that point.

"And I presume you noticed the slight swelling in the foot?" Holmes continued.

"Yes, I did. I put it down to the lass being a shop steward. Those poor girls are renowned for problems with swelling of the feet."

"Ah, yes, but our Miss Waterson is a personal assistant. We will have to confirm it, but I would expect her to be seated for the majority of the day, with short walking journeys to fetch items for Sir Lyndon."

"Right you are, Mr. Holmes. So if this foot doesn't belong to Miss Waterson, whose is it?"

"If I were to hazard a guess," said Holmes, gazing at the appendage intently for a few moments, "I would say it belonged to one of the streetwalkers who go missing or are found dead at far too regular intervals in our fair city." Turning his attention back to the shoe, he added, "This is where it gets interesting, though."

"Why?"

Carefully picking up the shoe, Holmes examined every side for a moment before continuing. "This shoe doesn't quite fit the foot – it's a bit too small, which is why we had trouble removing it. And it comes from Cobram and Sons of Oxford Street. Their mark is on the underside of the sole."

"That's a very expensive place to purchase shoes," I remarked. "Even for – no offence to Miss Waterson – a personal assistant."

A smile grew on Holmes's face. "Yes, it is quite an expensive item for Miss Waterson to possess. So that leaves us to our next port of call."

"Which is?" asked Lestrade.

"Miss Waterson's house. But first, one last item. Can you find me a sheet of paper?" When Holmes took the foot from me and stepped across to the nearby sink. He dripped some water onto the tips of his gloved fingers, then dabbed them gently onto the underside of the toes and ball of the foot before placing it onto a clean sheet of paper. Once satisfied, he returned the foot to the examination table and held the paper, showing the partial print formed from the dampened ingrained dirt on the base of the amputated appendage.

"And that's for what exactly?" I asked.

"Comparison," he replied.

***

Twenty minutes later, we stepped from Lestrade's carriage in front of a quaint three-storey terraced house in the middle of Chelsea.

"She has the lease of the entire building," Lestrade explained.

"Curious," I exclaimed, gazing at the beautifully presented streetscape before me. "This is an expensive house for a simple secretary."

"Personal assistant," Holmes corrected. "It seems to be the title afforded our Miss Waterson."

"Still."

"Yes, you are quite right," said Holmes, stepping towards the ground-floor entryway. "I find it quite bemusing that the subject of our investigations could afford such a lovely home." He turned toward Lestrade. "And a large home as well. How many servants?"

Lestrade shook his head. "None. All that space, and she occupied it by herself." He extracted a key from his pocket and all three of us filed into the entranceway. Without a word, Holmes headed upstairs, intending to search the lady's bedroom. I decided to linger downstairs and moved from room to room, hoping to gain a sense of the woman that lived there.

The house was sparsely furnished but showed an exquisite taste. I was extremely impressed by Miss Waterson's studious adherence to order. In the kitchen, there was no sign of any used dishes, all having been returned to their places once washed and dried. The parlour was neat and tidy, with no ash spillage from the small fireplace, and no half-burnt coal in the hearth.

Several photographs lined the mantelpiece, each sitting in exquisite silver frames. They showed a rather lovely young woman that I took to be our Miss Waterson, plus a pair of older folk with sour expressions. I speculated that they were possibly her parents. Another lone photograph showed the same pretty woman, but now dressed all in black, with the saddest look on her face. She stood before the doorway of a terraced house, different from the one we had entered. It took me a moment to realise the woman was likely depicted during a mourning phase in her life, possibly for her parents or someone close to her.

After gaining an appreciation for the presentation of the house and its almost museum-display quality, I was disappointed to find a lone ashtray sitting at the far end of the mantel. The stub of a cigar sat within, having burned down after the smoker placed it on the edge until only a small end remained. Sniffing the remains, I recoiled at the bitter stench. It had the hallmarks of an item smoked in the seedy dens frequented by lower-class workers and drunks, rather than something that would be found in such a beautifully appointed home.

Leaving the parlour, I made my way upstairs, joining Holmes and Lestrade in the lady's bedroom. Again, I was met with a well-appointed and neat arrangement. Holmes stood before a free-standing wardrobe, examining the clothing and rack of shoes.

Not wishing to break his train of thought, I stood silently in the doorway and made my own study of the room. Next to the wardrobe was a small dressing table with a mirror. An array of bottles sat before the mirror, with a small jewellery stand to one side, holding a single but striking necklace consisting of a thin chain of gold with a gold heart pendant. The pendant itself held a clear stone in its centre that must have been diamond. The necklace drew my attention almost immediately, as it appeared simple, elegant, and expensive, all at the same time – something that could never have been afforded on a simple assistant's wage. "Had she inherited money, perhaps – enough to explain the necklace and the large house?"

"Not at all," said Lestrade, in answer to my question. "She came from common folk, somewhere here in London. Where she obtained her funds has not yet been established."

Gazing at the contents of the table, I could see that indications that items were missing. Some of the fine facial powder that Miss Waterson used had fallen to the surface, leaving imprints of objects that had been removed. At least two larger items were missing. From my elementary understanding, I speculated that these might be a powder jar and bottle of facial crème. The table was also devoid of a hairbrush, comb, and hand mirror – items I attributed to women of all ages.

I was about to mention this to Holmes when he stepped away from the wardrobe and approached the table. "Items are missing," I said, jumping in to voice my observations.

"Yes. I observed that earlier," he said, leaving me slightly deflated. With his hand pressed to his chin and a finger pointing upwards, he continued. "There are two pairs of shoes missing, and likely some items of clothing, though I can't tell how many."

Joining him near the wardrobe, I spotted the vacant spaces at the bottom of the cupboard.

"She left of her own accord then?" asked Lestrade.

"It would look that way," said Holmes. "But whether that is because she planned a trip, or if she went willingly with her supposed abductor is another matter altogether."

Glancing back at the array of shoes, it was apparent that these sported the same mix of elegance and practicality as that accompanying the amputated foot. Pointing towards a specific pair, I said, "Those look very much the same as the shoe we saw earlier."

Holmes reached for one of the shoes, examining its underside. Nodding, he said, "Yes. Cobram and Sons, inscribed on the base of the sole."

"That's impressive. Two pairs from that establishment."

"Actually," said Holmes, studying the shoe, "we can only be certain that these were hers, but we do now have confirmation that Miss Waterson possessed at least one pair." Turning the shoe around, he held his glass up to the dark writing on the inside of the heel. "Yes, the same size as well."

Carrying the shoe to the table, he pulled out the paper with the foot's imprint on it. Then he removed a small folding knife from his pocket and proceeded to slit the top of the shoe, so that he could then pull it apart and see the inside where the foot normally rested. Then he compared it to the dirty imprint of the detached foot before passing the shoe and the sheet to me.

"Do you see it?"

Lestrade bustled over and leaned in as well. "I do," said the inspector.

All three of us had come to the same conclusion: The feet were completely different, but it wasn't really a surprise, considering the condition of the amputated foot at the morgue. The big toe on the paper imprint was larger than that impressed into the bottom of this shoe, and it appeared to bend towards the right, an indication of the beginning of a deformity from standing too long on rough, slightly uneven ground. The other toes failed to line up evenly as well.

"The shoe at the morgue," explained Holmes, "definitely belonged to Miss Waterson. The patterns within it conform to this matching shoe here – and neither of the Cobram shoes have the same wear as what we see from the amputated foot. It isn't much, but this, combined with the probable evidence that the foot was amputated after death, plus the condition and slight swelling of the detached appendage, allow us to be essentially certain that the foot does not belong to Miss Waterson."

"Then who?" asked Lestrade.

"And why?" I added.

"I think extortion is still our main *modus operandi*. And as to who the foot belongs to, I think I shall make some further enquiries."

"Where?" asked Lestrade.

"I'm unsure as yet, but I believe I already generally know the source of the limb in question. However, there is no haste to determine that at this stage. Our immediate need is to find the whereabouts of Miss Waterson, as there is every chance that she is alive and in good health."

"Marvellous," said Lestrade, his face turning quickly to concern. "But where?"

"Ah, that I do not know," said Holmes as he turned and almost darted from the room in his haste to leave.

Lestrade and I followed him downstairs more slowly, where Holmes was standing at the mantel, examining the cigar stub and photographs. Sniffing the cigar remains, he noted that it was Jamaican in in origin – something rather rare in England, possibly indicating that the owner had brought it himself from the Caribbean. From there, he moved from room to room for some time before ducking into a small nook near the kitchen. The tiny room contained a roll-top desk which clattered when Holmes opened it by the handles. A small array of notes and bills lay upon the green leather of the desk's interior.

Holmes picked up several and quickly read and returned them before holding one before him. "Was there ever any mention of the lady having additional premises in Rotherhithe, Inspector?"

Lestrade shook his head. "No, why?"

"Well, Miss Waterson has several letters and bills, all bearing the same Rotherhithe address. This one," he indicated the page in his hand, "is the latest coal bill." Reading it, he added, "Not very high, which would indicate that the heating isn't used very often."

"Strange," Lestrade noted. "Why would she have bills from another address?"

"Perhaps it's her parents' old house?" I suggested. "There's evidence in the parlour that her parents are deceased. If she has found the money to pay for a residence of this station, she may have been able to afford to keep the other as well."

"Good point, Watson," Holmes said. "It also makes me wonder if Miss Waterson spends some of her time there – perhaps on the weekends when she doesn't need to attend to her employer."

"That might account for the missing items," I said. "And there is the photograph of her in mourning, depicted before another house. That could be this Rotherhithe place."

"Interesting," said Holmes. "I think we should visit it, just to ascertain if our Miss Waterson is there. But first, I feel that we should visit the gentleman that has been maintaining this property for Miss Waterson's use."

"And who would that be?" asked Lestrade.

"Why, isn't that obvious?" asked Holmes, lifting one eyebrow as he turned to glance at Lestrade. "Sir Lyndon, of course."

***

Stepping from Lestrade's carriage for the second time that morning, we found ourselves before an impressive four-story, white-stoned Georgian mansion, taking up residence in the wealthy neighborhood of Belgravia. All around us, the houses were covered with Christmas decorations, but none could compare with Sir Lyndon's home – an enormous wreath upon the door, and smaller ones that matched on every ground floor window. Stretches of garland were draped along the front between the various upstairs windows. It was almost too much, but it certainly outshone the efforts of the neighbors.

"I'm in the wrong business," said Lestrade, glaring at the expansive premises before us. "There seems to be money in selling ladies dresses."

"I think you'll find that the work you do, Inspector," said Holmes, "far exceeds the amount of good created through Sir Lyndon's endeavours."

Lestrade nodded. "But it would be nice to treat the missus from time to time."

"Quite so, and I'm sure you will be able to work your way up to Chief Inspector or even Superintendent in the coming years, which should furnish you with more in the way of honest income to help supplement your lifestyle," said Holmes.

"Well, there's always hope, isn't there."

"It is a wonderful property, gentlemen," I pressed, feeling the nip in the air deep in my bones, "but it's also a bitterly cold day and time is of the essence. Shouldn't we move on?"

"Sorry," said Lestrade, moving up to the front door. The knocking on the door was soon met with a look of slight disdain from an elderly butler.

"Yes, may I help you?" he asked, his eyes peering down his nose towards the three of us.

"Inspector Lestrade of Scotland Yard. My colleagues, Mr. Holmes and Dr. Watson, and I would like to see Sir Lyndon. It is on a matter of urgency, and at his request."

"The master isn't in," began the butler, before a female voice broke out behind him.

"Who is it, Johnson?" the voice asked.

Before the man could turn, a woman that I presumed to be in her late fifties bustled to the front door, almost pushing the aging butler away. "Hello, gentlemen. Come in. It's frightfully horrid out there."

After we'd moved into the entranceway, decorated just as thickly for Christmas, Johnson took our coats and hats while the woman introduced herself. "I'm Lady Beryl Marsden." Indicating a nearby doorway, she added, "Please, let us adjourn to the parlour." Turning to the butler, she directed, "Johnson: Coffee, tea, and biscuits for our guests please." We left a slightly mystified Johnson and assembled in the adjacent room, a welcoming place where a warm fire glowed in the hearth. As we found our seats, I breathed deeply – somewhere in the house, treats were being baked for the holidays, and the odours from the distinctive spices filled the air. "Now," asked the lady, "what can I do for you gentlemen?"

Lestrade spoke up. "I am Inspector Lestrade of Scotland Yard, your Ladyship. Umm, I have been assigned to the delicate matter at your husband's workplace."

"Oh, yes? What matter?"

"Why, the case of a kidnapped employee."

"Oh, dear." Her face showed shock – I wasn't sure if it was from the newly acquired news or the fact her husband had possibly declined to share it with her. "Who? Not that lovely Mr. Benedict?"

"No, ma'am. It's Sir Lyndon's assistant, Miss Waterson."

At the mention of that name, Lady Beryl's face grew dark. "Oh," she said, with such disapproval that I was surprised she didn't rise and usher us from her house as fast as she could.

"You know Miss Waterson?" Holmes asked.

Turning towards him, Lady Beryl's face brightened, either through the application of a careful but well-rehearsed façade, or by way of a genuine interest in our presence. I was unsure.

"You would be Mr. Sherlock Holmes."

"That's correct."

"I'm happy to meet you, Mr. Holmes. I am a long-time friend of Honoria Westphail. I believe you would know her niece, Miss Helen Stoner. Honoria was most delighted by the way you helped her niece – I think it was four or five years ago now – and saved the young lass from a dreadful calamity. She was most effusive and described you in great detail," Then, turning towards me, she added, "And also you Dr. Watson."

Lestrade began to ask another question when Johnson arrived at the doorway. Lady Beryl turned towards him and said, "Ah, good – coffee and tea." Eyeing a small plate of pastries on the side, she thanked Johnson for his thoughtfulness and took the tray from him. Placing it on a nearby side table, she turned and asked us what we would prefer. Lestrade was becoming impatient at the delay, but I knew Holmes would be more than happy to engage Lady Beryl for some hidden details that we were unlikely to gain from Sir Lyndon himself.

Finally, after the coffee and cakes were served, Lestrade was able to ask his question. "Lady Beryl," he started, "we have come to apprise Sir Lyndon of our findings and ask him some more pertinent questions. He had asked that I make a report to him. Can you tell us where he has gone or when he will return? Time is of the essence."

"The last I saw of Lyndon was when he stormed back into the house earlier this morning, not long after the shop should have opened. Within moments, he left once again. He was in a frightful state, such that I didn't wish to even contemplate, let alone become involved. He has been in such a distasteful temper of late. We've hardly spoken a word."

"He hasn't confessed anything to you then?" asked Holmes.

"Confessed?" She gave him a speculative look. "About what? As I said, we've hardly spoken," Lady Beryl answered. "If there's something I should know about, then by all means, please tell me."

It was Lestrade who took the lead. "As we mentioned, there has been a kidnapping: Sir Lyndon's assistant, Miss Waterson."

"Most horrid, but that girl – " Lady Beryl started, but thought better of saying anything further and became quiet.

"Is there something about Miss Waterson that might be helpful?" I asked, assuming an air of innocence.

"Well," she replied, "kidnapping was the least of my worries where that girl is concerned."

"Why is that?" I prodded.

Lady Beryl stared into my face for a moment. Her eyes bore through me as if examining my reasons for the question before she relaxed and let the truth spill forth. By the end of her admission, my heart went out to this poor woman.

Dropping her head, she began to speak, slowly at first, and fighting her inner shame.

"It was around Christmas time last year – Can it have been a whole year? – that I first became aware . . . ." Then she gave a start and raised her eyes to stare at the far wall. "Lyndon and I have been married for many years. Our children are grown and gone off to make their way in the world. I had hoped that the time we now had alone together would re-engender a spark in our marriage, but . . . ." Stopping for a moment, she took a deep breath. I could tell that tears were welling behind her eyes, held in check through sheer force of will. "Last Christmas it was. One day I came home after Lyndon had already arrived, and as Johnson was busy, I put my coat on the rack. I bumped Lyndon's coat and noticed something in one of his pockets. Finding a small box, I almost placed it back without further investigation, but curiosity gained the best of me, and I open it to find

19

the most beautiful gold necklace – a delicate gold chain and a small gold heart pendant with a diamond in the centre. I couldn't believe it. Placing it back where I found it, I assumed that Lyndon had bought it for me, and when Christmas came around, I received a similar-sized box from him."

She took another deep breath and pulled a small kerchief from her sleeve, wiping at corners of her eyes before continuing. "My heart swelled as I unwrapped the little present, but then it sank into my shoes when all I found enclosed was a silk scarf. No sign of the necklace. He had bought it for another. It was then I truly knew that our marriage was nought but a sham."

"Oh, dear," I said.

"But that wasn't the worst of it," she added. "A week or so after Christmas, we had an engagement at the store – to welcome the New Year and congratulate the employees on a job well done for the previous year." Taking another deep breath, she finished off with, "It was then I realised who my 'replacement' was."

"Miss Waterson?" I asked.

Nodding, she continued. "Yes. There she was, as bright as day, dressed in a gown that she had no right to possess. And there around her neck – "

"The necklace," finished Holmes, already knowing the answer.

Turning towards my friend, the tears finally forming and sliding down her face, she nodded and dabbed at her eyes.

"We're so sorry," I stated, my concern for this woman trumping any care for the case at hand. "Have you confronted him?"

A small smile came to her face as she shook her head. "What else is there to do but accept it? I'm a matron, almost in my sixties. I have grown so used to this life. Over the last year, I have simply resolved myself to play the part of a loving, doting wife. I wouldn't wish to throw the spectre of scandal over the lives of my children, and I couldn't live with the shame in polite company."

This was something I had contemplated before. Even though the upper class live lives of affluence and influence, there is – even for them – a simmering underbelly of discontent within their ranks. In this house, it had been made all the more real by the events unfolding over the last week.

I was about to make such a comment when the bell rang. Lady Beryl moved to the connecting doorway to watch as Johnson attended to the newcomer. She must have recognised the visitor, as she sighed before stepping into the entranceway. Instead of waiting for the door to be opened, she turned toward the rear of the house and quickly walked away.

Within moments, a red-faced man appeared. He was portly, balding, and I made him to be in his mid-fifties. He was sweating profusely and breathing heavily from some unknown vigorous activity. As his eyes fell on the inspector, his thin voice bellowed out. "Lestrade, what in blazes are you doing here? Have you found her?" Taking a quick look at Holmes and me, he added, "And who are these two layabouts?"

"Sir Lyndon," Lestrade said, rising slowly to bring a sense of calm to the situation. "This is Sherlock Holmes and his colleague, Doctor John Watson. I've asked them to assist. I didn't think you would mind the added support."

"Holmes? The detective? You must be at your wit's end, Lestrade!" Anger began to bristle behind his thick eyebrows, countered when Holmes spoke up.

"Sir Lyndon, forgive our involvement, but we have already discovered an important fact."

"What?" he almost bellowed.

"We are extremely confident that the foot you received does not belong to Miss Waterson. She may be still alive – something that I believe may not have been the case if you had successfully paid the ransom."

Sir Lyndon's eyes opened wide in anger as he stared indignantly at Holmes. "What are you suggesting, sir?"

"In many of these cases, the kidnappers have no intention of returning their hostage. They merely wait for the funds to be given over, and then they execute the captive to remove any possibility of identification. Scotland Yard's involvement has prevented this occurrence, and probably ensured the continued health of young Miss Waterson."

"Nonsense. This is simply a business deal. This – " Sir Lyndon waved his hand through the air, searching for words. " – this *villain* has absconded with something I want. He has set his terms, and I am happy to meet them. Once I've paid up, he'll hand over Elaine. Simple as that."

"I beg you not to do that, Sir Lyndon," said Lestrade. "This 'villain', as you say, may not hold up his end of the bargain."

Sir Lyndon's face grew dire. "Of course that wasn't Elaine's foot – I never thought for a moment it was. And if you hadn't interfered, Elaine would be back in her rooms by now, and all this would be behind us."

Feeling the need to dissipate the ill feelings in the room and to satisfy my curiosity on one matter, I spoke up. "Sir Lyndon, you seemed very out of breath when you entered. I am a doctor – Is there any way in which I can help?"

His eyes fell on me, almost as if he hadn't taken account of my presence earlier. "I sped home from the bank. I'm afraid I'm a little out of shape. Too much work. Too much food. Why?"

"I had wondered if it was due to smoking. Cigars, perhaps."

I saw Holmes smile at my deftness at recalling the cigar found on the Miss Waterson's mantel. Yet the mystery deepened with Sir Lyndon's answer.

"Smoking? Filthy habit. I have never and would never smoke, and I'm incensed by your suggestion."

Holding my hands up in supplication, I said, "I do apologise. I am a medical man and simply seek to identify the most obvious causes of any malady. I congratulate you on such a stance."

Sir Lyndon's anger diminished slightly. He turned towards Lestrade and asked, "If the foot doesn't belong to Elaine, then who does it belong to?"

Holmes answered for the inspector. "That we don't know yet. But we have investigated Miss Waterson's Chelsea flat, and came here to report, but also to seek out further information."

"Yes?" The man seemed suddenly wary after the mention of the lady's residence.

"The Chelsea flat," continued Holmes. "You arranged that, of course, and you pay her rent and other bills."

Sir Lyndon looked shocked. He blustered his answer. "What? What do you mean? I . . . I don't know what you mean!"

"Come now, sir. It is certainly you who gives Miss Waterson an allowance for clothes, food, and other trivialities. You are a benevolent employer, but surely no one would expect that a mere personal assistant could afford the upkeep on such a residence. There is also the matter of how quickly you took it upon yourself to organise the monies to pay for Miss Waterson's ransom. That is something that any other employer would be very reticent to undertake."

Staring into Holmes's stoic expression for a moment, Sir Lyndon's face relaxed as he became resolved to his unmasking. He took a look towards the open doorway before striding across and shutting the door. Turning back, he answered, "Yes, yes you are right. I'm a damned fool, but have to admit I've fallen for the young lass. Things haven't been well between me and Lady Beryl for many years. I'm old, but still young enough . . . ."

He moved to a large, overstuffed chair and dropped wearily into it. "Elaine and I have formed a . . . a *relationship* over the last year or so. I moved her into the flat to . . . have a place where we can meet. When I found she was missing, and then that damned note arrived, I dropped everything to make sure I could get her back."

His downward gaze had hidden his expression, but as he lifted his face to us, I could see tears forming at the corners of his eyes. "When that God-awful thing arrived, I realised that it could mean the worst, but I still hoped she was alive." Reaching into his jacket he pulled out a thick wad of notes. "I spent all morning arranging for the new ransom. Regardless of what you advise, Inspector, I will happily give it just to have her back safe and sound."

"I hope we won't need to pay it," responded Lestrade.

Staring at the policeman, Sir Lyndon said, "I don't care. I will get her back, no matter what it takes." Abruptly standing, he indicated the doorway. "Now gentlemen, I won't lie, but I have matters to attend to.

By this evening I will have Elaine back, one way or another – with or without your help."

We shuffled out to find Johnson awaiting us with our coats and hats in his arms. As we prepared ourselves for the chill outside, Lestrade made one last appeal. "Sir Lyndon, I implore you to remain at home. Don't give in to these demands. It will not end well."

"Pish-posh!" was Sir Lyndon's only reply. He bustled us from his house, and that angry, red face that was the last sight I beheld there as the door closed quickly.

Holmes wore an expression of irritation before turning from the Marsden house and scanning the street. Then a grin grew on his face as he spied a young street urchin and hurried over toward him. Even from that distance, I realised that the boy must be one of his Irregulars – a fact that became clearer as the day grew long.

***

"He's just going to waste his money and get the girl killed," spat Lestrade, his impatience with Sir Lyndon spilling out from his normally calm but gruff exterior.

"Sir Lyndon will have observers of his own this time," said Holmes with a look in Lestrade's direction. "And they won't look like policemen." Pulling out his watch, he continued, "It's now just past one o'clock. We still have a good two hours before Sir Lyndon pays the ransom. Our next destination should provide some further intelligence as to the overall situation."

Some time later, as our carriage pulled into the more tightly packed and altogether unpleasant area of Rotherhithe, I started to worry that Holmes's optimism might be misplaced. Suspicious eyes followed us as we wound our way through the constricted streets, and I felt their stare stay upon me as we alighted before our destination.

The tiny, terraced house was worlds away from the two elegantly fronted addresses we had previously encountered. This whole section consisted of cramped three-storey buildings filled with various rooms let for lodging. Each of the buildings on this block sported yellowed and peeling paint with faded black trims to the windows. Unlike Sir Lyndon's extensively decorated digs, there was no sign of Christmas here whatsoever.

According to the information gathered at Miss Waterson's Chelsea abode, the apartment we sought was before us, at this address. Its darkened windows and worn and rotting woodwork gave it the appearance of abandonment, but I knew that it was actually a hive of local residents, as were the surrounding structures.

Thinking of the lady's fine Chelsea home, I asked, "Are we sure this is the place?" But I knew it was – this was the house in the photograph.

"This is the address upon the coal pedlar's bill," Holmes replied. Without waiting further, he led us up the stairs and tried to turn the door knob, but it was strangely locked. He tried again, and then knocked loudly. Silence greeted us until he repeated the announcement. Then the quiet was broken by a harsh voice from the basement alcove of the neighbouring house.

"She's gone out!" it cried.

The three of us turned and glanced towards the owner of the voice. There, below street level, sat the solitary figure of a woman, who I made out to be well into her seventies. She sat on a rotting armchair, surrounded by a cloud of smoke from the cigarette hanging from her lips.

"What do you mean, 'She'?" asked Lestrade. "How do you know who we're looking for?"

"Ain't but one lady lives in that building. She bought it somehow and kicked everyone else out – even the ones that had nowhere else to go. Keeps it locked up, except for when she comes by sometimes."

This was news. How could the lady have the resources to acquire this property – even as run-down and filthy as it was?

"Do you know when she will be back?" asked Lestrade.

"Why? What has she done now?"

"What does this lady look like?" asked Holmes. The woman was silent for a moment, weighing her suspicions, before relenting and giving a good description of the missing personal assistant."

"Do you know when she'll be back?" asked Lestrade again. "We simply wish to speak with her – to ensure that she's in good health."

"Looked pretty healthy to me. I'm more worried about why you men want to talk to her." Before anyone could answer, however, the old woman continued, blowing out a huge cloud of smoke. "It's none of my business. Her mother, God rest her soul, would turn in her grave, I tell you."

"And why would that be?" asked Holmes.

"Well, ever since Elaine started coming back, she's been – How d'you say? – not her mother's little girl."

"Elaine," asked Holmes. "Elaine Waterson?"

"That's her. Grew up here. That was her parent's house. They let the rooms until they died. Then she took it on. I kept an eye on it for her, but then a few weeks ago, she turned everybody out. I'm not surprised – she isn't much like her mother."

"A bit flighty?" I asked. "Irresponsible?"

"Umm, more a bit of a charva," she said. "And bringin' back the men? What would her mother think? It's like Kings Cross Station here, some weeks."

"Oh," I answered, suddenly taken aback.

"That new one's a big 'un though."

"New one?" asked Holmes.

"Gorgeous he is," the old woman said, a smile coming to her mouth, showing a severe lack of teeth. "Taller than all of you. Broad across the shoulders. Huge bushy beard, and the strangest thing – a length of hair at the back."

"Long like a queue?" asked Holmes. "Or is it tied up?"

"He leaves it long."

"Have you observed any tattoos?"

"I'm not the sort to stick my nose in, but now you mention it, I did. I bumped into them in the street a while back. The big fellow was holding a sack, but I saw letters tattooed on his knuckles. I could only make out an 'aitch on his left hand, but his right had the word *Sultan* on it."

"Hmm," murmured Holmes.

"What does it mean?" I asked.

"Well, the queue might be a tar, worn by Her Majesty's sailors, and the tattoo might be the name of a ship. Often sailor memorialize their first ship that way. Possibly his was the *HMS Sultan*. She was an ironclad in the channel fleet for many years. I think she's now in the Mediterranean."

Stroking his chin for a moment, Holmes finally said, "These new facts, added to the cigar stub we found, may mean that the man was in the Navy, but no longer. Possibly he's moved into the merchant trade." Staring upward into the clouded sky, Holmes thought for many moments, until Lestrade and I became agitated at his silence. I was aware that three o'clock, and the payment of the next ransom demand, was rapidly approaching.

I noticed the old lady gawking at us with a wry smile on her face as she puffed on another cigarette. Holmes finally broke the silence. "Inspector, you may need to send someone to the nearby docks to see which ships are leaving for the Caribbean today – possibly Jamaica."

"Why the rush?" Lestrade asked.

"Our quarry may be planning to leave England this evening, if the ransom demand is met this time. And the cigar is just the smallest indication that the man we seek has Caribbean ties."

Surprise on his face, Lestrade bustled back towards our carriage and spoke with the driver. Then he climbed aboard and they drove away. Holmes turned back towards the woman below us and said, "Thank you, Madam. As we said, we are here to see Miss Waterson. We shall bid you a good day and wait for her inside."

Indifferent, the woman simply continued to puff on her cigarette, adding, "I would take care around that fellow of hers. Big bloke. Seems to have a touch of anger about him too."

"Thank you," finished Holmes before moving again to the front door. Extracting his picks, he made short work of the old lock, and within moments we found ourselves inside.

The house smelled from a touch of hidden damp, and also the heavy tang of the same type of cigar that we'd found in the Chelsea flat. Holmes left me to bustle off toward the bowels of the house, seemingly with a singular idea front and centre in his mind.

I remained in the parlour, awaiting Lestrade's return. Soon he appeared in the doorway, a slight grin crossing his face as he spied me standing before him. "I assume that the front door was unlocked?" Understanding the intent of his question, I simply shrugged, causing an expulsion of breath and a slight shake of his head. "Mr. Holmes – what the devil is he playing at?"

When my eyes shifted to the passageway that Holmes had taken, the inspector started to move in that direction. I began to follow as he passed by, but a sharp retort from a female voice in the entranceway stopped us both.

"'Ere! What's the meaning of this?"

Lestrade and I spun at the sound of the voice and I spied one of the loveliest faces I had seen in my life. "Miss Waterson?" said Lestrade, to which the young woman nodded, tentatively. She was carrying a sack which, from the bit I could see, contained something wrapped in butcher's paper, and one or two green vegetables.

"Yes, and who would you be?" she said, her reaction to our impertinence strong in her voice.

"Inspector Lestrade of Scotland Yard, and this is Doctor John Watson. He is helping me with my investigations."

"Pleased to meet you, Miss," I said, my eyes dropping to her untouched left foot. "I'm glad that you are in full health."

Miss Waterson's eyes followed my gaze, before darting back towards Lestrade. She looked as if she might turn and bolt. "Why are you here? My Trevor will be very mad when he returns."

Presuming that "Trevor" was the fellow described by the neighbor, my retort was cut off by Holmes's arrival in the parlour. "That's if your Trevor returns at all," he said.

All eyes turned towards him. "What do you mean?" said Miss Waterson. "Why wouldn't he return? And who are you now?"

Stepping further into the room, Holmes took a slight bow and said, "I am Sherlock Holmes, consulting detective. I'm helping Inspector Lestrade in the matter of your supposed kidnapping." Holmes's eyes dropped to the woman's left foot, a wry grin came to his face as he said, "And you are Miss Elaine Waterson. It's good to see you fully intact."

"Why do you gentlemen keep saying that? And why are you so interested in my feet?" She glanced down and then asked, "And why won't Trevor return?"

"First things first, I suppose," said Holmes. "The condition of the bedroom seems to indicate that this Trevor, if that is his name, has removed both his items and himself from this abode."

"What?" Miss Waterson cried, before bursting past the three of us and heading into the rear of the house. Moments later she returned, a look of intense shock on his face. "All of his clothes. Everything. Gone. His bag – gone." Tears welled in the corners of her eyes as she glanced up at us. "Is he gone?"

I moved across, taking the sack from her, setting it upon the floor, and guiding the stricken woman to a nearby seat. As we passed, Holmes pulled out his watch and, checking the time, said, "Not quite, but it probably won't be long." Glancing at Lestrade, he continued. "Inspector, it's now two o'clock. We still have time, but it will be close thing."

"What's going on?" I heard the poor woman whimper.

"Ah," said Holmes, "now that's an interesting tale."

We related all that had happened so far. Miss Waterson's face remained placid during the story of the first ransom note, leaving me with a sense that none of that part was new. It was when Lestrade mentioned the delivery of the amputated foot that the lady's eyes grew wide in shock bordering on terror. "A foot? A real foot?" she exclaimed. "Who's was it?"

"Well, supposedly it was meant to be yours, but obviously," Holmes explained, indicating Miss Waterson's intact appendage, "it isn't."

"That's horrible. Why would Trevor . . . ?" Suddenly she went quiet. Her simple retort told Holmes and Lestrade almost everything they needed to know.

"It may be pertinent, at this juncture, for you to relate everything you know on the matter," suggested Holmes.

Miss Waterson seemed to deflate as the pent-up anxiety bled from her body. "It was Trevor's idea. He's lovely. I met him about three months ago. We had a bit of a fling before he was back on ship. When he came home to port, two weeks ago, he told me all about his idea."

"I can only assume that it was you who wrote the first ransom note," Holmes asked. When she nodded, he continued. "Does Sir Lyndon know about this Trevor?"

A shocked look crossed Miss Waterson's face. "No, of course not. Why would I tell him? He'd cut me off straight away." Her eyes grew wide, and tears began to form at the edges. "It's just that Sir Lyndon is kind, but . . . ." her face twisted into a little grimace. "I'm so much younger than him. I . . . I need to be with someone my age."

"Please tell us the rest," I said.

"Trevor wants to leave the sea life. That's all he's ever really known, but he doesn't want to stay in the city. He has hopes to buy a farm in the Cotswolds. We're going to live in the fresh air. Raise some sheep." She hesitated for a moment. "And some children." Looking from face to face, tears fell down her cheek. "I didn't think Sir Lyndon would miss the money. He's been so good to me, and he's so well off.

"He was so very angry on Monday, but I thought it was because his captain said he needed to do one more trip to see out his contract. So he didn't get the ransom?"

"He did not," Holmes replied. "That was when your Trevor devised his second plan – one that was all his idea." He looked at Lestrade. "The heavier script of the second note, with the intent of the Christmas present and the haste to receive the ransom."

"Must have been," answered Miss Waterson. "He's been so quiet since. Kept disappearing for hours on end. Once we sent the note . . . asking for the money . . . we agreed that I couldn't go back to Sir Lyndon. We've been here ever since, in my parents' old house. I woke up this morning and Trevor was nowhere to be seen. I had to duck out to get something for his tea. I wanted it to be nice when he got back. I bought a bit of beef. I thought he'd be here, but – " Sobs broke out of her, followed by a stream of tears. "He's gone!"

It took some time to calm the poor woman down. Holmes pulled out his pocket watch once again and I knew that time was passing. Somewhere Trevor was waiting to pick up the ransom, which would certainly be paid this time by Sir Lyndon.

It wasn't until a knock on the door that Miss Waterson came back to herself. Looking up, she exclaimed, "Trevor?"

It was Lestrade that opened the door to reveal his driver. After a few moments of whispered conversation, he motioned for Holmes and me to join him, away from the young lady. In hushed tones related his news. "There are two Caribbean cargo ships in port. Both are moored nearby – only five minutes away." He looked at his watch. "Nearly three. This Trevor will be retrieving the money now, and heading that way. We can be there well before he turns up." Nodding towards the young woman, he asked, "What about her?

Although we agreed that from a legal perspective, Lestrade had every right to arrest Miss Waterson for her involvement in the original kidnapping plot, we also agreed to defer doing so until we had dealt with the actual mastermind behind the crime.

As we left the house and drove to the docks, Miss Waterson gave us more information about her errant beau, as she now seemed to have turned against him completely upon realizing that he had no intention of returning to her once he had Sir Lyndon's money. The man's full name was Trevor Farnsley, and her description matched that provided by the old woman next door, and included a confirmation that the tattoos on Farnsley's knuckles indeed read *H.M.S. Sultan*. He had described his previous Navy service aboard that ship to her, and after he was discharged several years earlier, he'd found work plying his trade between England and the Caribbean.

The most useful piece of information that Miss Waterson provided was the name of Farnsley's current ship, the *Batavia*, whose home port was Kingston in Jamaica.

The trip in Lestrade's carriage was swift. We arrived at around a quarter-past-three. Leaving Miss Waterson in the custody of his driver, Lestrade went in search of additional reinforcements. After he returned, we went straight to the *Batavia*'s berth and consulted the Chief Steward. The man had the aged look of one who had spent most of his life at sea. A quick conversation confirmed that Farnsley wasn't yet on board, but was due before the ship weighed anchor at four o'clock.

As we deliberated on our next course of action, two more carriages appeared on the dock, filled with officers. Lestrade quickly instructed the constables aboard to make themselves scarce and wait for his signal. The carriages were driven away and hidden behind some nearby buildings.

A few minutes later, a small, filthy-looking lad appeared around the corner of one of the large warehouses. He glanced once behind himself, then over at Holmes before running for all his worth towards my good friend. A short, but agitated conversation ensued before Holmes motioned towards the opposite corner and followed behind the boy. As Holmes passed me, he whispered, pointing down the roadway leading onto the docks. "The lad was there when the ransom was retrieved. Farnsley is on his way – he's coming in a hansom."

"How did he know where to find you?" Lestrade asked.

"I told the Irregulars to deliver a message to any ships leaving this afternoon for the Caribbean. We were bound to be at one of them."

Following behind Holmes, we ducked down the tight alleyway and waited. Lestrade took up station at the closest point and kept watch around the corner. "Here he comes."

Just as the hansom stopped near the gangway, Lestrade hurried away, with Holmes and me hot on his heels. As we closed in, the hansom moved off, revealing a large cloud of cigar smoke circling the tall well-built figure of a man speaking with the Chief Steward.

Lestrade wasted no time, stopping only a few yards from the pair and speaking loud and clear. "Trevor Farnsley, I am Inspector Lestrade of Scotland Yard. We have reason to believe you are involved in the kidnap of Miss Elaine Waterson, and extortion of Sir Lyndon Marsden."

Turning to face the policeman, Farnsley's expression was a mix of horror and rage. He turned in an attempt to gain the gangway, but the Chief Steward swiftly blocked his way. Pointing at Lestrade, he said, "I think you should talk to the policeman first. We don't want no trouble on board."

Rather than talk, Farnsley threw his rucksack to the ground and balling his fists, strode towards the shorter Lestrade. "I've done nothing. Elaine is in her house in Rotherhithe. No harm has been done to her."

"There is the matter of five-thousand pounds that you have extorted from her employer," Lestrade said, keeping his eyes on the larger man.

Shrugging, Farnsley said, "What money? I haven't taken any money." Throwing his hands to the side, he continued, "Search me if you like. I got nothing but a few pounds."

"Ah, but that isn't quite true, is it?" said Holmes stepping forward, his hand grasping his revolver. "I had you followed from Berkeley Square all the way here." He nodded towards the little fellow peeking around the building corner that we occupied moments before. "My spies tell me that you picked up a small leather satchel at the base of the statue in Berkeley Square before hiring a hansom and heading here, with a brief stop at an address in Limehouse. I'm sure we could find the key if needs be, and at that address, a quick search should reveal the satchel, with its rich contents awaiting your return."

Farnsley's expression turned completely to rage, his eyes darting around for a quick exit. As he made to run, Lestrade pulled a police whistle from his pocket and gave two long blasts. Within seconds, the squad of blue-coated bobbies appeared from around several corners and headed towards us. The cigar fell from Farnsley's mouth as he gaped at the constables.

"You're knicked, Farnsley," said Lestrade. "We'll get all the details from you back at the station, but you aren't going nowhere for a long time."

The tall man bellowed with rage and started again towards Lestrade, but the sight of Holmes's revolver stopped him in his tracks. He swore and cursed under his breath until the paddy wagon arrived to take him to the Yard.

***

"So Farnsley confirmed that he never intended to take Miss Waterson with him?"

"No," said Lestrade, leaning back and taking a sip of tea. We were sitting in Baker Street, and around us were a substantial amount of Christmas decorations – holly and ivy and seasonal candles, all

33

brought in by Mrs. Hudson once she'd been able to make the effort while Holmes was away. I knew that he found them distasteful at best, but it pleased our landlady to celebrate the season, and therefore he would put up with it for a while.

"After we began to question him, it all came out. He met Miss Waterson several months ago, in a tiny pub down in Limehouse. His ship was in port. He was out with some of the other boys. They struck up a conversation and then a relationship. On the next voyage away, Farnsley came up with his plan and convinced the girl to go along with it."

"But not all of it?" asked Holmes.

"No. She agreed to ask for the thousand pounds, but knew nothing more about the rest of it. She had dreams of moving to the country – dreams that Farnsley used to his advantage. She thought that he'd already collected the ransom, and that they would leave London soon. But in the end, he only had eyes for the money."

"The cad," I exclaimed.

"Precisely. Well, he'll be at Her Majesty's pleasure for some time to come."

"I have one last question."

"Yes, Doctor?"

"The foot? Whose was it?"

"Ah," said Holmes. "I can answer that, and the inspector can correct me if I'm wrong." Lestrade nodded his approval. "I've made some enquiries, including at a similar building to the Dufour's Mortuary which is set up in Poplar near the parish church. As with many of the city's mortuaries, they overflow with the dead, from disease and the cold weather. I've had word that disreputable attendants have been selling off bodies to medical schools, and even individual students. Procuring a foot would not be difficult if one has the right connections.

"Given the proximity of Poplar to Farnsley's separate Limehouse residence, I'm sure that he had those. The original owner of the foot was probably a poor streetwalker or local resident, which will be easy enough to confirm. Hence, that's why the body had probably been dead for almost as long as Miss Waterson was missing. In order to add veracity to his trick, Farnsley put it into one of the Miss Waterson's shoes – which Sir Lyndon would recognize, since he saw them every day, and in fact paid for."

"Ghastly," I said. "And what of the lady?"

"I would think that she has been through enough," said Lestrade, surprisingly. "In this matter, she did intend to extort money from her employer – or lover, whichever term you'd like to use. But in my opinion, was that any more tragic than the situation she was already in? Indebted, and enamoured by a man twice her age, with no convenient way out of the arrangement? If she's honest with him, he will simply sack her and throw her out of the Chelsea apartment. I've left her to her own reconnaissance in this matter. Hopefully, it will be a lesson hard learnt."

He took another sip of tea. "And after all – it is Christmas. A little seasonal charity isn't amiss."

"Difficult," I said. "But fair."

"Agreed," said Holmes. "And this will stay with her as a Christmas to remember for many years to come."

"Amen to that," I said, staring into the flames burning in our little grate while the sound of carolers echoed up from the street below.

The Adventure of the Missing Journal

It was late one morning in the spring of 1886 that I returned to 221B Baker Street to find Holmes ensconced in his chair in our parlour, with numerous newspapers strewn about the place.

"Catching up on the news, Holmes?" I quipped.

"Yes, Watson, but sadly, the papers are so devoid of anything interesting as to make it hardly worth the effort."

It was then I noticed copies of the Argus and the Crawley Observer, both from far-flung Sussex lying on the settee next to Holmes's chair. "Brushing up on the farming news then, Holmes," I said nodding towards the two newspapers.

Glancing over at the discarded broadsheets, Holmes replied with a grin, "Ah, yes, when London is in such a state of civility, I like to delve into the activities of our neighbouring counties.

"Anything of note?"

Shaking his head slightly, he said, "Nothing in particular. Though there have been a rash of animal disappearances over the last few months. From reading the accounts, they occur singularly from several farms. I would suggest that the animals have broken free and wandered off, rather than the animated suggestion by the reporter that they have a rustler working in the area." Moving his eyes from the newspapers to rest upon my face, he asked, "Anything interesting in your morning patient?"

Removing my coat and hanging it on the nearby rack, I answered, "No, nothing interesting. An elderly lady injured herself in a fall last week. I simply attended to re-examine the wound for any infection and change the dressing. Almost as dull as your crime report."

"Quite so," said Holmes, picking up the next paper from his pile and poring through it.

As it was past ten thirty, I decided to organise morning tea with Mrs. Hudson. Just as my hand fell upon the doorknob, the front doorbell rang out. Hurrying downstairs, I met Mrs. Hudson as she emerged to answer the door. She eyed me with a puzzled expression and said, "Leaving again so soon, Doctor?" before turning the key and opening the door.

We were greeted by the tall, lanky frame of a young police constable. His face flushed red with shyness, he tipped his head, tapping his helmet with one finger and said, "Good morning Mr. Holmes, Mrs. Holmes, sorry to intrude, but Inspector Lestrade sent me." Accepting the small, folded note from the constable, I opened it and quickly read.

A smile came to my face.

"Oh, this should at least make Holmes a little happier."

***

After correcting the young policeman's two counts of mistaken identity, he blushed even more with embarrassment. I led him upstairs and into our parlour, introducing him to the actual Sherlock Holmes before handing the note across to my good friend.

As I had anticipated, Holmes's interest piqued with the location mentioned in the note. "The British Museum," he said, "What could have happened there that Lestrade needs my services for?"

Constable Dewes, as that was the name he introduced himself with, answered. "There's been a murder, sir, and a robbery."

My eyebrows rose at the information. "At the British Museum?"

Nodding, Dewes added, "Yes, sir. There's a very big kerfuffle going on. The Inspector was determined that I bring you with me. I think his words were, 'Bring Holmes here or don't come back at all.'"

Smiling, Holmes said, "It must have Lestrade in a tizzy then." Rising from his chair, he hurried off into his rooms, throwing a remark over his shoulder as he left. "Right then. Give me a few minutes and we'll be away."

***

Dewes' carriage drove up and stopped outside of the wonderful neo-Grecian frontage of the museum. The young constable hadn't expanded on anything during our journey, simply saying that the Inspector had instructed him to not taint the facts of the case. "He said something about Mr. Holmes preferring it that way." I glanced at Holmes to see him nod, a wry grin on his face.

We spotted Lestrade standing near the main entrance doors. A glance inside showed a lack of visitors, something strange for that time of day. It was then I saw another two Constables standing at the base of the steps leading to the main entrance, approaching any potential visitors, and politely directing them away from the building.

"Must be a rum bit of work, if they've closed the museum," I said to Holmes. He nodded in answer, but his eyes were already darting to and fro, seeking any clues they could or detecting anything that might be untoward in the area.

Our young chaperone took us past the two guardians and straight to Lestrade. "What ho, Lestrade?" asked Holmes, "What have you got for me?"

The short, slight frame of Lestrade looked even more withdrawn than usual. He shook his head, "I just don't get this one Holmes, don't get it one bit."

"Something must have happened out here, or else you'd be inside."

Pointing to an area between two of the tall ionic columns to the right of the doorway, Lestrade shrugged and said, "These johnnies they employ to guard this place. I wouldn't give you two quid for the lot. There's one that does the outside, two that do the inside. They are meant to relieve each other every hour or so, but we found one of them there. Dead. Don't know for how long. The two inside did nothing when he didn't show up to be relieved. They thought he'd just fallen asleep somewhere. Seems he does it all the time. It was only when the day guards were coming on duty that they found him." He shook his head. "Damn fools."

"Dead?" I asked, "Where is he now?"

"The Museum manager was here almost immediately. Wanted the body taken away as quickly as possible. I wasn't happy, but he seems to know the captain, same club, or something, so I did as asked. He's gone to the Yard, I thought you'd want to take a look before the coroner starts to examine him."

"Any idea what killed him?"

"I couldn't see anything untoward, just a mark on his face. In my opinion, he was slugged with something heavy. Hit his head as he fell. Poor bugger."

Holmes leaned in towards the area, inspecting a mark on the stonework with his glass. "Hmm. Yes, some hair caught on the stone here. A small amount of blood," He stooped to study the ground, "More blood and hair here. It may not have been the blow that killed him, rather hitting his head on the wall and ground."

"Poor fellow," I added out of sympathy for the man just going about his nightly duties.

After another few moments of examination, Holmes stood and stepped towards the entrance doors. A cursory glance showed them unscathed. "They broke in here?"

"That's the queer thing. No, they didn't. From what I can tell there were at least two of them. One broke in through an upper story window, then let in the feller that did the guard. The doors were closed as the miscreants left. The internal guards didn't even realise they had been unlocked."

"I would have thought that would be part and parcel of their rounds," I added.

"Yes, you would, wouldn't you," said Lestrade, huffing a veiled insult at his private contemporaries, under his breath.

Finishing his inspection of the doors, Holmes stepped into the impressive entrance hallway. Joining him I felt a chill run up my spine, something I had always sensed when glancing into the grandeur of the three-story-high foyer of this magnificent building.

"Where did they enter?" asked Holmes, looking for any sign of damage to the upper story windows.

Lestrade stepped next to Holmes and pointed to the high arched roof, with a line of skylights running around the top level.

In the far corner, a single pane of glass was missing, with only small, jagged pieces left in the frame.

"Impressive," said Holmes, moving into the foyer and hurrying towards the stairwell leading to the first-floor landing at the far end of the room. Lestrade and I struggled to keep up. The game was afoot, and Holmes didn't wish it to get away from him.

We caught him at the top of the stairway, glancing across the stone floor, searching for any piece of information that he could find. His head furtively scanned the area, jerking up towards the missing window pane, then down at the landing a full two stories below.

"You can't be serious, Holmes?" I asked.

"I'm not sure yet, Watson, but the journey from that window could only be achieved by the use of ropes or a ladder, which would beg the question of how those items came to be here in the first place."

"Then how did they climb down then?" asked Lestrade.

"That's why I asked. I think my learned friend is calculating whether they jumped, am I right, Holmes?"

"Possibly, but it would take a formidable athlete." He paused for a moment, before pulling his glass from his pocket, once more, and dropping to his knees. After a few seconds, he said, "Aha," and pointed at what I finally saw was a small patch of dust on the grey stone floor."

"What is that?"

"A footprint. Small and smudged," Holmes said, indicating lines of movement away from the initial impact, "But this is where the person landed." Looking to his left, he shuffled across the stone tiles. "They stepped here, then," he rose, examined the thick stone balustrade, before glancing at the floor below. Rushing down, he ducked towards the small archway from the foyer and dropped to his knees once more. "Yes, here, there," he added, pointing at the small dust imprints on the floor.

Joining him on the ground floor, I glanced up to the top of the stairway. "Are you saying our villain, jumped from that broken window, then leapt over the balustrade and dropped to the floor here? That's three stories in a matter of four or five steps."

"Yes, very lithe this fellow, I think," said Holmes. Following behind Holmes, he pointed out another few dusty prints showed the path our perpetrator took, as he made his way to the front doors. Examining the latches with his glass, Holmes murmured to himself, before standing.

"Anything further?" I asked.

Shrugging, he said, "There are small traces of dust on the latches, and several tiny scratches, but that could be from anybody that has secured these doors over the years. Regardless, it would seem that at least one of our robbers came in through that window, jumped down from the first floor, ran along the ground floor and unlocked these doors." Pointing at another set of smudges leading into the building, he added, "The second villain, waiting outside, followed him in. I can only assume, that one killed the guard." Turning towards Lestrade, he asked, "We have a probable means of entry, but now the question is, what did they steal?"

"Ah, that's where I can help," said a voice from beneath a nearby archway.

All three of us turned towards the source. Lestrade, recognising the figure, spoke up, "Ah, let me introduce my colleagues, Sherlock Holmes and his associate, Doctor John Watson. This is Sir Ezekial Zizza, the director of the British Museum."

Sir Ezekial stepped from the shadows and into the well-lit open foyer. He looked to be in his sixties but stood straight and proud. Following in his wake came a shorter and altogether smaller man, with a slight stoop, and wearing thick glasses. "Ah, the famous detective, good, good, I'd like this messy exercise cleared up quickly. Theft of any of our priceless antiquities is theft not against the museum but England herself."

"Was the missing object highly precious?" asked Holmes.

Sir Ezekial's expression showed confusion for a moment. "Ah, no, not particularly, but it was given to the museum and therefore part of England's heritage."

"What was stolen then?"

Turning to the other man, Sir Ezekial said, "I will let Kyle here answer that."

The smaller man stepped out of the director's shadow, his glasses making his eyes look enormous and lending him a frightened appearance. "Ah, hello, yes, um, it wasn't just the one. We had several, and they all seem to have disappeared." Turning, he indicated an archway at the far end of the foyer, "One was housed with the medical anomalies exhibit in the basement. The others were stored with other texts in the reading room below the library."

When the curator stopped speaking, I waited a moment before blurting out my question, "What were?"

"Oh," he said, his eyes growing even wider, as a look of stark terror at being questioned bloomed across his face, "Oh, I'm sorry, I presumed you knew."

"Knew about what?" asked Holmes, his voice gentle and more soothing than mine.

"The journals."

"Journals? Who's journals?"

"Ah, that is something that none of us knows for sure," Sir Ezekial piped up. "Last year, a doctor of anthropology, Herbert Magaziner, brought the journals to us. It seems that he procured them, of all places, in Fiji. He had been undertaking some studies of the local tribes, when the captain of a ship that plied its trade in the Pacific, met with him and offered the journals for sale. The good doctor read through them, and to quote him, 'Instead of burning such drivel, I decided to bring them to the British Museum as a curiosity.' We are always glad to accept new finds. They presented themselves as a slight oddity within the medical texts, and we thought the public might enjoy seeing them on display. Though we've only ever allowed one on the floor at a time. The rest can be read via the library."

"What makes these journals so valuable then, that someone would risk life and limb to steal them?" asked Holmes.

"Nothing I presume, but I am not well acquainted with the criminal mind," said Sir Ezekial.

The little man spoke up, "The language is English, and they talk about forbidden arts within the medical establishment. Vivisection. Of animals, something that has been frowned upon for decades, and virtually banned throughout the profession. Whoever wrote these journals was working outside of the influence and control of any medical institution. Which would be why they were found on an island in the Pacific. The captain told of finding the journals among the ashes of a burned down house and compound, but," the Curator's eyes grew wider, "he told of an operating theatre. Still intact. With one remaining patient on the table. Dead."

"Come now, Kyle, these are stories to tell children, not grown adults like Mr. Holmes and Dr. Watson."

"But they are probably true. The journals speak of such horrors. Of methods to reshape animal tissue to make them walk on two legs. Ways of restructuring the vocal cords to grant speech. Giving them opposable thumbs, and even redirecting their nervous system to increase their intelligence."

"Horrible stuff. Should be sold off as material for penny dreadfuls, not seen as any proper medical treatise." The director drew himself up and puffed out his chest. "Regardless, they have been brought into our collection for display and should be granted the proper security they deserve."

"Who wrote these journals?" I asked, "Surely he could not have been part of the British Medical Association. We have a proud history of staying with the bounds of plausible science, not fantasy."

"I am still unsure of the actual owner. I have read through a good many of the journals, but only one has any indication of a name. It was scratched deep into the leather with a knife or something similar. The style made it look as though the writer was indignant of the name they inscribed."

"What name?" asked Holmes.

"Moreau," said the Curator.

The name seemed familiar to me. Something flared in my mind, a memory from years before during my studies at the University of London.

Stroking his chin with one finger extended, Holmes paused for a moment before asking, "Can we see the display case and book store?"

***

Moving through one of the arches at the far end of the room, the Curator, Kyle, led us down two flights of steps into the relative dark of the basement exhibits. The gas lamps were set to a lower power, probably because the museum was closed to the public.

We entered a small room, filled with glass cabinets, arranged in an aesthetic display. Some were tall with multiple shelves; others were more or less glass boxes resting on wooden tables. Kyle moved away and went to several gas lights, turning the screw to adjust the supply and bring an increase of light to the room.

The display cabinets were filled with a disparate array of relics and artefacts all pertaining to the strangest aspects of the medical profession. Deformed foetuses floated in jars of formaldehyde. Skulls and bones recovered from bodies which would have appeared monstrous in life sat upon several shelves. Strange instruments, looking more like implements of torture, but probably used in ancient operating techniques littered other shelves.

Towards the back of the room, we saw the display case in question. It was of the tabletop style, with the main pane of glass shattered, the shards mixed amongst the items on display.

Holmes approached the cabinet and brought out his glass, stooping to examine the edges of the frame, but careful not to touch anything until he had finished his circuit. "How often are these cases cleaned?"

"Every night," said Kyle.

"Even in this room?" I asked.

"Oh, yes, the children are most fascinated with the morbid curiosities on display. We often find their little fingerprints and smears all over the cases, even though there are signs everywhere telling them not to touch."

Straightening, Holmes put his glass away before retrieving his thin, kid skinned gloves and a small paper envelope. Delicately, he picked something from one of the spikes of glass in the frame before placing it in the envelope.

"What was that Holmes?"

"It appears to be hair. It may be nothing, but I'd like to examine it under my microscope."

"That's where the journal was displayed," Kyle said, pointing to a small, and now empty, plinth in the rear corner of the case, "We generally turned the page every two weeks, to keep it preserved and ensure each received the same amount of light. Yesterday, it was open to one of the more detailed diagrams. I don't know if that attracted a visitor back."

Bending closer to examine the area, Holmes murmured before reaching in and picking out a piece of glass. Holding it up to the light, he turned it from side to side, before placing it back where he found it.

"Anything?" I asked.

"There was a smudged fingerprint on that splinter as if the thief needed to pick it up and move it away from the book."

"So?"

"Well, it indicates several possibilities. Given there are no other fingerprints on any of the shards of glass, I can surmise that there may have been more than one robber, but we already know that from the evidence of the person that opened the front door for another. Whoever broke the glass appears to have lost some hair, the coarseness of that hair indicates it was body hair. The absence of blood indicates that the arms were possibly thickly covered with hair. Again, these are suppositions rather than factual observations at this stage, I would need more evidence to draw a solid conclusion." Turning away from the display case, Holmes stared into space for a moment, before asking Kyle to show us the reading room.

A short trip down a dark corridor followed until we emerged into a large area sporting bookcases along the walls and a series of desks lined up in rows down the centre. Each desk possessed a small gas lamp which I assumed could be used by a person to provide illumination.

Intrigued at the room, I asked, "Have you ever been here before Holmes?"

"Oh, yes, Watson, many times. The museum boasts quite an impressive collection of archaic texts and volumes. The type of which cannot be found in any normal library or bookshop."

The Curator walked to one of the bookcases and pointed to a small spot on the shelf that was devoid of books. "The other journals sat here. There were nine in all."

"I'm intrigued; was their presence well known?"

"I don't think so. We published their reception in The British Medical Association Journal, many months ago, but apart from that their arrival was not heralded in any other way."

"Do you have any account of people interested in these journals? Has anyone read them of late?"

"No, we don't keep a record of that sort of thing. The volumes cannot be removed from this room." He walked across to a wooden box consisting of several small drawers and opened one. "This is the catalogue. The journals were entered under the name Moreau, and had numbers affixed to their spines." Sorting through the cards in the drawer, he pulled one out and held it up.

"The card, I presume," said Holmes.

Nodding, Kyle replied, "Yes. The only evidence that the journals were ever here."

***

"At least two people broke into the British Museum to steal nine journals. The scratching's of someone called Moreau, who supposedly was a vivisectionist, living on an island in the Pacific, working on ways of making animals more like human beings?"

"That seems to sum up part of the equation, Watson," said Holmes, "The other is the dead guard. We only know that he was supposedly killed by one of the intruders. We don't quite know-how and won't until we see the body." Staring out of the carriage as we traversed the streets to Whitehall, Holmes mused, "From what we saw outside the building, we are seeking two very different individuals.

One who is small, extremely lithe, the other, a large individual, who is very powerfully built."

Before leaving in Lestrade's carriage, we had walked around the outside of the building to the area beneath the broken window. What we found was an almost vertical climb of some fifteen yards. Within moments, Holmes was rewarded with the strangest sight. Several footprints were evident in the damp, slightly boggy grassed area at the base of the building. It was a small garden area, overhung with a thick canopy of trees, and therefore not receiving a lot of direct sunlight. The grassed area was damp, and the intruder had walked through to gain access to the Museum's wall.

Kneeling on the damp grass, Holmes brought out his glass and examined the footprints left behind by the perpetrator. Many murmurs echoed up from him, and when finally, he rose, to examine the wall itself, I asked, "What have you got there, Holmes?"

"Something most intriguing, Watson, most intriguing," he answered, before pointing to several dirty marks that rose up the wall on either side of a drain pipe. "The miscreant has tiny feet, which gives me the impression he may be either a midget or dwarf, but incredibly lithe with it." I took in one of the well-formed footprints on the wall, and almost gasped in the horror of the deformity of our villain. The toepads were tiny, ovoid in appearance, and very close together, forming more of a semi-circle rather than the natural straight line of a normal man's foot.

"Good Lord, the poor blighter, what would have led to that level of disfigurement?"

"I do not know, Watson, but it doesn't seem to trouble the fellow. There are no scratches or burns on the paintwork of the pipe, from any mechanical device or assembly of ropes. For all intents and purposes, the fellow seems to have simply shimmied up the drainpipe barefooted."

"Incredible."

"Quite so."

As the hansom pulled into Whitehall and stopped before Great Scotland Yard, I was snapped back to the present when Lestrade said, "Well, you won't have to wait long to see this unfortunate, I'll take you straight down to the room we use as a temporary morgue."

Lestrade led us into the building, then down two flights of stairs and along a narrow, dimly lit corridor, until we came to a large room, with several tables lining the walls. Sheet covered objects lay on a few of the tables, and in the centre was an examination table holding the body we were interested in.

The room was intensely cold but still held the unmistakable odour of rot. Several blocks of ice sat in containers in the corner of the room, providing an extra level of chill to the atmosphere.

"I apologise for this place, it's not what we would prefer, but the local mortuaries have been overrun of late and those upstairs want the costs dropped, so we set this place up. Any bodies we want to examine are kept here until the coroner comes to collect them."

"Damn chilly," I said, "But better that than have these poor unfortunates rotting away before your eyes."

Glancing at me with a slight look of disapproval, Holmes said, "Well, I suppose we should get on with this so that Watson can return to somewhere more comfortable." Stepping up to the examination table, Holmes drew back the sheet covering the body's face. He grimaced as he stared at the strange bruising on the man's cheek. Turning, he grasped a nearby portable lamp, lit the flame from a wall lamp and returned, leaning closer to study the area. "Obviously, this is where the larger man struck the guard," he said, pointing at the odd mark. It appeared to consist of two semi-circular teardrop-shaped halves that mirrored each other with a gap between them. Gently moving the man onto his side, he inspected the damage to the back of the man's head and nodded. "Hmm. Yes, a large wound where he struck the wall," he said before returning the man onto his back and turning towards me. "What do you make of it, Watson?"

"Astounding," I said, "Whatever it was, it hit him with incredible force. That would account for both the mark and head wound. The bruising would have occurred as he lay dying, but the clarity of that bruise is incredible. If I didn't know any better, I would say he was struck with something similar to a cow's hoof."

"That was my impression," Holmes said, "As if the assailant used the foreleg of a bovine as an actual weapon, or." He trailed off for a moment, a slight grin appearing on his face.

"No, you can't be serious," I said.

"Well, until we can eliminate the conjecture, it shall remain."

I shook my head, knowing what he was going to say next.

"This man may have been killed by a cow."

"Impossible," said Lestrade, "Must have been a club, surely."

Holmes was about to speak again when several harsh shouts echoed down the long, darkened corridor and filtered into the room.

"What in blazes?" asked Lestrade, before bolting from the room. Holmes quickly followed. I took one last look at the dead man's face, before pulling the sheet over his head and pursuing my companions.

Heading towards the noises, I found myself amongst the various holding pens set aside for the more detestable, or unstable criminal elements picked up by the bobbies. At the far end of the line of cells, Holmes and Lestrade stood with two uniformed constables. All four stared into one of the holding cells, the bobbies glancing around frantically, with expressions of horror on their face.

"Well, where did he go then?" I heard Lestrade ask as I joined them. I looked at the object of their attention and almost burst into a fit of laughter. Inside one of the tiny cells was a full-grown sheep. As if on cue, it bleated out in a pitiful voice filled with fear and confusion.

"What the devil is that doing here?" I asked.

"The question is, where did the man who was here before disappear to?" Holmes asked.

As I stared at the sheep, I noticed items of discarded clothing scattered across the floor. From my position, I could see that the shirt and trousers were torn as if hurriedly discarded, or burst apart.

Distressed at the lunacy of the situation, and the possible embarrassment it could cause, Lestrade berated the two constables. "Who was in this cell?"

"Ah," said one Bobbie, "He was a drunk, picked up on Great Russell Street, early this morning. The Constable, that brought him in, said he wasn't making no sense, and couldn't form no words. He was brought down here just in case he had a bad turn. Easier to clean up."

"But he's gone, and he left you this little present."

"Seems so, Sir."

"Good Lord man, we'll be a laughing stock if this gets out," said Lestrade, his demeanour becoming increasingly agitated.

"Inspector, if I may, the fact that this, um, fellow was picked up in Great Russell Street, which is near the entrance to the Museum, strikes me as particularly intriguing."

Confused, Lestrade turned back to face Holmes, "In what way?"

"Well, so far we have someone acting like a cat, someone with the strength of a bull, why not a sheep?"

"Come on Holmes, this is no time for games."

Chuckling, Holmes added, "Oh, I do agree Inspector, I do apologise, I wasn't trying to be funny, just pursuing a line of reasoning, as humorous as it may appear." Stepping up to the bars of the cage, Holmes hunkered down and peered in at the frightened sheep. "This little miss has a ring in her ear. It may be worth a look, plus I'd like to inspect those clothes."

"Constable, key?" asked Lestrade. The Bobbie brought out his set of keys and unlocked the door. Holmes stepped into the cell, slowly approaching the ewe which moved away, pressing herself against the very rear of the little room. Gently, Holmes reached out a hand and patted the sheep on the head, before lightly grasping her ear and examining the little brass band.

"Hmm," he said, "It looks like a registered farm brand, but I'll have to check the records to see where this little one comes from." Pivoting around, he deftly retrieved the items of clothing before making his way back to the door to join us outside. Examining the tattered shirt and trousers, a grin came to his face as he found something in one of the trouser pockets. "Aha," Holmes said, bringing out a small piece of paper.

Unfolding it, we found a hand-drawn map of what looked like streets, with an X marked in red on one corner. I immediately recognised the layout as the area we had just visited. A large rectangle was the Museum, and the X represented the corner of Great Russell Street and Montague Street.

"I believe we have found the lookout's clothes," Holmes said.

"What? The sheep?" asked Lestrade.

"Perhaps not the animal, but rather another member of the bandits, who had been stationed at this point," he pointed to the X, "And subsequently enamoured with his own success, may have celebrated a little heavily. How he then escaped and replaced himself with this ovine equivalent is anyone's guess?"

***

Leaving Lestrade at the Yard, I flagged down a passing hansom and told the driver to take Holmes and me to the Smithfield Markets. Stepping from the cab, the smell hit us with full force. Every manner of animal scent assaulted our nostrils, causing me to search the area in case I had stepped into a pile of manure.

"There's nothing quite like the sensory overload that one experiences at the markets, is there Watson?"

"I'm quite sure I've never suffered such an onslaught before. I can tell you that."

I was still a little confused as to our purpose at the markets, but it seemed we were in luck, the day was dedicated to the sale of sheep, cows, and goats. Holmes strode off towards the sale yard and stopped at a small table where a man took down names and numbers from a line of country folk, dressed in their finest for the day. Not wanting to seem out of place, we joined the queue, and waited patiently, glancing around at the hustle and bustle going on around us.

Finally, we reached the table and found a swarthy man, with the reddened cheeks of a heavy drinker, sitting before us. His watery eyes looked at us in suspicion. "This is for registrations. I think you gentlemen may be in the wrong place," he said.

"Ah, my good man, I do hope we aren't. I own a small property on the outskirts of the city of London, and I'm afraid that one of your sellers may have lost a sheep on his drive into the markets."

The registrar's face screwed up in confusion, "Oh, yeah, how'd you figure that?"

"Well, one appeared in my top field this very morning. I do not run any sheep, and neither do any of my close neighbours, so it was a surprise."

"Interesting, did it have an ear tag?"

"Yes, a small, metal tag in its left ear, inscribed with the numbers one, one, six and nine, and the letters D, F and C, written below them."

The man cocked an eyebrow. "Yep, that sounds like what you'd find." He reached beneath his table and pulled out a thick, bound volume, plonking it down in a cloud of dust, before opening and searching down several columns of numbers. "One, one, six, nine, you say?"

"Yes."

"Ah, here we are," the man said, his finger resting on one of the entries in the book. "DFC?" Holmes nodded. "That would be Drayford Fumey, down in Crawley. That sheep is a long way from home." The registrar moved his attention back to his current work and read down the list of sellers. After a while, he shook his head. "Nuh, he's not registered so far, may be coming in later today or might not even be here. Can't for the life of me figure out how one of his sheep ended up alone in London? I reckon someone's playing a joke on him."

"Do you have an address for him in Crawley?"

"Nah, just asks at the pub or Police Station. It's not that big a place, Crawley. Everyone knows everyone else."

Holmes pulled a guinea from his pocket and slipped it to the man. "Thank you, sir, you have done me a great service."

The man picked up the guinea, eyeing it greedily for a moment before it disappeared. "To be honest, if I was you, I'd find a good butcher and enjoy a nice lamb roast or two. Can't imagine it'd be worth your while taking a sheep back to Crawley."

Nodding, Holmes said, "Thank you, it is an idea, but I'm not sure I could dine on someone else's misfortune."

"Your loss."

Smiling, Holmes moved away through the throng of people and headed towards the holding pens. I assumed he hoped to catch sight of this Fumey character, or something similar. Instead, he took a direct path to the cow enclosures and took up a conversation with a rural looking chap standing next to the largest bull I had ever seen. Within a few moments, a coin slipped from Holmes' pocket into the man's hand. The farmer turned and pinched the bull on the rear, eliciting a loud low of complaint, and resulting in a wad of hair pulled from its rump which was transferred to another small paper envelope in Holmes's hand.

Confused, I broached the subject with Holmes as we exited. "What was all that with the bull?"

"Ah, I wanted to test a theory about that hair we found, and the easiest way was to have something sourced from the horse's mouth, so to speak."

"You've got a strange definition for horse's mouth," I remarked.

***

Back at our Baker Street abode, Holmes sloughed off his travelling cloak and hat and moved to his experiment table, slipping his microscope out of its corner, and extracting both paper envelopes. Within moments of placing the hairs onto a slide and studying them through the scope, he exclaimed, "Aha, come here Watson, let's see what you think?"

Stepping across to the table, Holmes moved away and indicated the scope. Looking through I could see three hairs through the eyepiece. The two longer, thicker hairs at the top of the slide appeared to be the same, the third was thinner and quite dark.

"The two top hairs are identical, except probably for the colour. One's a slightly darker shade. I would say that they were the ones you bought at the market. The bottom is from a different animal altogether, possibly feline or even human."

"Well done, Watson, well done. Now the reality. The top hair is from the market. The second hair is one of those I pulled from the broken glass cabinet at the museum. The third is mine, I pulled one from my forearm for reference purposes."

"Good Lord, are you saying that someone planted bull hair on the cabinet at the museum? Why would they do that?"

"Ah, that may not quite be the answer. I must cogitate on that a while longer. What I do find intriguing is that the farmer I bought those hairs from was from the Crawley area. I wanted to obtain hairs from the common species of cattle farmed around there."

"Crawley," I said, taking one last glance through the eyepiece, before moving away, "What is it about Crawley?"

"That I do not know yet, but we have a lost sheep with a Crawley ear tag, now we have mysterious animal hairs from a species of cow that originates from the same area."

"What does it all mean?"

"I think we need to take a little trip tomorrow," he said.

"To Crawley?"

"Yes. I believe there may be answers to be found in Sussex."

***

The following morning saw our plan begin to unfold. Mrs. Hudson fixed a wonderful breakfast that would hopefully provide us with the energy to complete our journey. The first stop was to find Lestrade and advise him of Holmes' findings. When we mentioned Crawley, he was both bemused and slightly confused.

"You'll want a local to help then?" he asked.

Nodding, Holmes agreed, "That may be appropriate. I've not been in the area for several years."

Pulling out a card, Lestrade wrote a small note on the back and then stared at it for a moment. "You should seek out Senior Constable Brandon Roberts. He's an old associate of mine. Moved back to Sussex after a few years on the beat here. Should know the local area at least." Glancing up at Holmes, he added, "Are you sure this is the best way forward? Everything's happened here in London, what would draw you to Sussex?"

"I can't put my finger on it, just yet, but as more evidence accrues, it all points to that area, as strange as it may seem," Holmes answered, accepting the card, and pocketing it straight away.

Our trip from Victoria station to Horsham was uneventful. I sat hoping to ask Holmes more about his theories, convinced that we were on a wild goose hunt, but remained quiet, accepting of my colleague's mysterious ways. The carriage we hired took us to Crawley and straight to the local constabulary. As I stood and paid our fee, the mid-autumn sun beat down from on high reminding me that the effects of the morning's breakfast were beginning to wear off in such a way that only a late luncheon would appease the gnawing feeling growing inside my belly.

Inside the police station, we found a bored-looking constable writing in a journal. His excitement at our appearance told me more about the lazy feel of the town than I had seen in her streets.

Showing the card from Lestrade, Holmes introduced us and asked about Senior Constable Roberts, but was told he was on a call to a local farm. "Something about a missing cow," the Constable mumbled, before realising what he'd said.

"A shame really," said Holmes, "We wish to consult with the senior constable about a lone sheep that has appeared in London. Supposedly from a nearby farm."

"A sheep?" the Constable asked, a suspicious frown crossing his face. "Do you know which farm?"

"We only have the identity tag in its ear to go by. It supposedly points to someone called Drayford Fumey."

The Constable's eyes grew wide, accompanied by a grin and a chuckle, "You've found Fumey's sheep? He's been going on about that animal for weeks. Badgered the senior constable for days over the lack of information about it." He smiled widely, "Wait till I tell the senior. Where did you find it?" Pulling a small pad of paper towards him, the Constable picked up a pencil, ready to write down some notes, "And who are you again?"

As Holmes told the Constable the details, he madly scribbled on the little pad, then reread what he'd written, chuckling once more. "British Museum? I didn't think the sheep was that remarkable."

"Oh, I think it might be, but not in any normal way," said Holmes, before changing the subject, "Is there a local pub that can put us up for the night? I'd be especially interested in the one frequented by the local farmers, we might be able to catch this Fumey fellow there."

"Oh, that you will, go straight down the High Street and look for the Ploughman, can't miss it. The outside stinks like a barnyard, 'cause that's where Roscoe, the publican, makes the patrons leave their wellies."

"Sounds wonderful," I added with a heavy dose of sarcasm that was lost on the young policeman.

"Please send Senior Constable Roberts down there when he returns. Regardless of the accommodation, we'll at least settle in for a pint or two while we wait," said Holmes.

"Right you are, then," said the constable, as we headed for the entry door.

***

Luckily, we saw the sign for the Ploughman swinging and creaking in the light breeze, moments before the undeniable smell of the country assaulted our nostrils. The source was lined up near the front door. I counted at least four pairs of boots, smeared underneath with all manner of farmyard detritus. A metal boot scraper sat well away from the door and was caked in the thicker muck, rubbed off by the farmers as they arrived.

The building itself was small and built of stones gathered from the nearby fields, locked together with lime mortar, with a well-worn thatch roof sitting atop. A thin line of smoke rose from the chimney, indicating that a fire burned within, which I thought strange on such a wondrously warm day, but soon realised it was from the kitchen out back.

Inside, a pall of cigarette smoke filled the front bar area, making it difficult to see in the dark room. Windows were few and far between, the main source of light provided by several candles sitting in holders along the outer walls and over the bar.

We found the landlord straight away, he was a large, ruddy-faced man and soon handed over a set of keys to a room at the top of the stairs towards the back of the pub. Holmes asked him to make sure that Senior Constable Roberts was informed of our presence, in case he arrived whilst we were upstairs. A quick question of my own found that a good luncheon was available, and I ordered a hearty meal that would welcome us when we came down.

My heart dropped when we were greeted by a lone double bed. I didn't wish to be delicate, but the thought of sharing with Holmes was not high on my wish list.

"Should we see if there's another room?" I asked.

"Later, Watson, later. We have more important matters to attend to first," Holmes answered.

Shrugging, I quickly relieved myself of cloak and hat and followed Holmes back downstairs. Within moments we were presented with a delightful midday meal, washed down with the local bitter. The relief almost made me forget about our sleeping arrangements.

It was as I drained the last dregs of my pint, that the entrance door opened, and the tall figure of a policeman stepped inside. Waiting a moment for his eyesight to adjust, he scanned the room, saw Holmes and me, and headed straight to our table. Removing his helmet, he looked both of us in the eye before saying, "Mr. Holmes?"

Nodding, Holmes replied, "Senior Constable Roberts, I presume?"

"Yes, Sir, I have it on good authority that my old comrade Lestrade sent you to see me?"

Motioning to the empty seat, Holmes said, "Yes. My colleague, Dr. Watson, and I are helping the Inspector with a rather peculiar matter at the British Museum."

"Smith, back at the station, mentioned that you found a sheep?"

A wry grin broke out on Holmes's face, "As I said, peculiar."

"And you think it might be Fumey's? Good, that fella has been pestering me for two weeks now. Probably mislaid the blasted animal on his last drive up to London."

A dry, crackle of a voice broke through the pall of smoke and addressed the senior constable. "Oi, Roberts, did I just hear youse have found my Dolly?" A hairless, old face approached from a nearby booth. He looked like he'd lived in the sun for the best part of a century, with well-tanned skin and deep crevices running across his forehead and beneath his eyes.

"Hello, Drayford," said Roberts, "These gentlemen have journeyed down from London, where they believe that have found your sheep."

"About bloody time," Fumey added, "Where is she?"

"Well, actually, she is in a cell in Scotland Yard, so she is perfectly safe," said Holmes with no hint of irony.

"The Yard? What did she do? I can't pay no fines."

"I'm sure that won't be necessary," said Holmes, "But once we have finished our investigations, I'm sure she can be returned to you."

Another voice piped up next to Fumey. I made out the face of another long-time farmer, but with much more hair on his head. "Have you found my bull then?" he asked.

From another direction came another question. "What about Neddy? My horse?"

"It's gypsies, init?" said another from the back.

Within moments, we were virtually surrounded by several older gentlemen who badgered the poor senior constable with a barrage of questions about missing animals, ranging from horse, bull, and sheep, through to a goat, at least two cats and a dog.

It was Holmes that stood and took their questions, answering with, "Now, now, please gentlemen, we are helping Scotland Yard with this matter. At this stage, we only know about Mr. Fumey's sheep. I'm sure once we track down the miscreant, if there is one, it will all become clear. Until then, I'm afraid no amount of questioning will elicit any further details." With an undercurrent of murmuring, the farmers broke away, returning to their seats.

Remaining on his feet, Holmes glanced down at the policeman. "Mr. Roberts, would you have a detailed map of the immediate area?"

"Yeah, back at the station. But why?"

"I believe there may be a pattern to these disappearances that may be worth investigating."

***

Within minutes the three of us stood around a table in the station's main room. Constable Smith joined us and lay down several maps of the area. Roberts pointed to one depicting the area just south-east of the town, a small stream ran through the area, with several ponds dotting it. To me, it looked like very good farming land.

Placing his finger on one of the small areas, outlined in a darker border, Roberts said, "That's Fumey's place there." Pointing to several others, he continued, "Bodie, the feller with the missing horse, Jones, the bull, Creighton, another sheep, a cat from Herring's, a dog from Dalton's."

"Do you mind if we mark off those farms?" asked Holmes, "Just the borders, I think there is already a pattern forming."

Roberts did as he was asked. Smith piped up and added a couple of other occurrences of missing animals. By the time they had finished, a good deal of the area was outlined in a darker shade. Holmes stood, his hand to his chin with one finger raised. "Do you see it?" he asked.

Extending my hand, I pointed to three farms bordering each other that were unmarked. "These three haven't made any complaints."

"No, I've heard nothing from any of them," said Roberts. Pointing to two neighbouring farms, "these are both sheep farms, but," indicating the farm furthest to the south, "I don't think that feller runs any livestock at all."

"Whose farm is that?" Holmes asked.

"A feller called Prendrick. Edward Prendrick. Been there nigh on ten years. Keeps to himself. Most folk around here probably have never seen him, let alone talked with the man."

"What do you think, Holmes?"

"I am unsure at this stage, Watson, but it may be worth investigating these properties. It isn't clear yet, but the evidence points to a connection between these animals disappearing, and the appearance of a sheep in Scotland Yard, which in turns seems to lead back to the break-in at the museum and the death of the guard. We must remember, the death is the main crime here."

"I'd be happy to accompany you," said Roberts, "Smith can come as well."

"There's probably nothing in it," added Holmes, "But if there is, it may be best if the constabulary is with us."

***

The first two farms proved fruitless. Neither farmer could identify whether any livestock had gone missing. Both ran sheep but had seen foxes of late and put any loss of lambs or ewes down to that cause. Although as we left the second farm, the man's wife stepped out and mentioned that the cat that lived in the barn hadn't been around for a few weeks. The old farmer shrugged and hawked a wad of phlegm into the dirt, suggesting a fox as the cause. The wife added another clue, which I thought strange in itself at the time, admitting that a few items of clothing had gone missing from her clothesline at her last weekly wash.

As the sun set, bringing a slightly chilly night with it, I began to lose faith that Holmes was on the right track. Roberts decided to end our search for the night with a visit to this Edward Prendrick, before returning to Crawley and regrouping in the morning.

It was as the carriage bumped its way along an overgrown track, that I noticed a bright orange light filtering through the trees. I prodded Holmes with my elbow and pointed towards it. "What do you make of that, Holmes?"

Glancing at it for a moment, he said, "Hmm. A fire. Out in the open." He nodded towards another soft glow in the distance. "The house is way over there. So, I doubt if it is our Mr. Prendrick."

Roberts stared at the glow as well, before thumping on the roof and calling out. "Smith, stop here. I think we've found those gypsies." As the carriage pulled up, he added, "I heard one of the farmers complain, and we've had some notice that there's a band of gypsies around somewhere. Lawless blighters. Steal anything that's not nailed down. Could be stealing the animals for food, or some such."

Roberts and Smith led the way, stealthily making their way through the thick underbrush towards a dry-stone wall that let onto the wide-open field beyond. From behind the wall, we could see the light came from a large campfire located on a small hillock, some thirty yards away. Several silhouettes, of varying sizes, sat around the flames and passed in front from time to time.

As we were about to vault over the wall and approach, one figure stood up and moved to one side. I couldn't see him clearly, but as he moved into the firelight, I caught sight of his hair, which was curled in such a way to look almost like the horns of a ram.

A low murmur began from the standing figure, answered by the others around the campfire. The rhythm of their voices wasn't such to suggest singing, more a recitation of some form.

Holmes took the lead, scurrying over the wall, stooping close to the ground to avoid detection, and moving closer up the little rise. The rest of us followed in his wake. As we came closer, the figures became more distinct, as did the invocation from the leader.

"Not to go on all-fours; that is the Law. Are we not men?" said the standing figure, immediately greeted with a mix of garbled voices repeating the line. "Not to suck up drink; that is the Law. Are we not men?" Again, repeated, then followed with, "Not to eat fish or flesh; that is the Law. Are we not men? Not to claw the bark of trees; that is the Law. Are we not men? Not to chase or harm other men; that is the Law. Are we not men?"

The standing figure stopped for a moment, as a general murmur ran through the group, followed by several strange animalistic noises and shushing sounds.

"One of us has broken the laws. One of us has brought us all shame. One of us must pay." Looking to the other side of the flames, the Law Sayer, pointed and spoke. "Brother Hannibal, join me."

My eyes grew wide as a huge figure stood and towered above the flames. I almost gasped in horror at his visage. His eyes were large and round, almost filled with iris and pupil. His nose was wide and flat, with huge nostrils. His chin and jowls sported a light covering of red hair. I couldn't tell in the firelight, but I swear he had horns atop his head. Below that head, sat a massive barrel-like chest, covered in the same course hair. Then I saw his hands. Misshapen, with no visible fingers, just a pair of strange clubs, like the hooves of a cow.

Oh, you poor man.

The man, I use the term as I had no other to ascribe him, approached the Law Sayer. A look of hopelessness seemed to envelop his being, and a murmur ran through the group.

"Brother Hannibal," said the Law Sayer, "You broke the law. There are some that say you killed. Another man no less."

"Accident," the large shape said in a deep bellowing tone. "It was accident."

Another murmur rose from the group.

"What does the law say?"

After a moment's hesitation, the accused replied, "Not to chase or harm other men."

"Again?"

"Not to chase or harm other men." Pausing for a moment, he added, "It was accident."

"We must see the Master. He will know what to do."

The large red-haired figure reacted, pulling away from the fire in horror. "No. Not the Master. There will be a return. I do not want to return."

"I think we have our man," Holmes said in my ear.

Overhearing, Holmes' words, Roberts chose that moment to stand up, the light of the fire spilling across his face. "Hold it right there, boyos. I am Senior Constable Roberts. This man is wanted by the police."

The group reacted as one, rising to their feet they turned to face us and broke out in a series of screeches and squeals, all the time backing away from us to the other side of the fire. Their noises were unlike any group of men I had ever encountered, but it was when I stepped forward and saw them in the full light of the flames that my voice almost joined theirs, such was the horror.

Each man, and I use the term loosely, bore severe disfigurements like their larger companion. One group was no more than three feet in height but displayed no kinship with either midget or dwarf. Their eyes were alighted with fire, centred with oval-shaped pupils. Their noses were but small buttons in the centre of their face, their ears pointed and positioned towards the top of their head. Like their larger counterpart, their hands were malformed into tiny clumps of flesh, with small fingers that extended only out one knuckle and sported long nails that upon examination disappeared somehow into the flesh itself.

Another member of the group was similar in that his height was barely four feet. He sported a long face, dominated by the sloping nose, sitting above a wide mouth with protruding teeth from a severe overbite. His ears were large, and lacking cartilage which caused them to fold over.

Two others had long faces with dull eyes. Their hair a closely curled white, that flowed down from their heads as if they wore judges' wigs.

It was when my eyes finally fell onto the features of the Law Sayer that I felt my very sanity depleting. He stood five feet tall, sporting the similar white curled hair as the last two, and the long ovoid face, but the feature I had mistakenly attributed to hair, were, in fact, two curled horns sitting on either side of his face.

As the visual atrocity assaulted my senses, the audible cataclysm began to make sense. The screeches and squeals began to reform into recognisable sounds. Bleats, barks, mews, and the frantic lowing of a cow. As I realised what I was looking at, I made my realisation known. "They're animals."

"Incredible, isn't it?" said Holmes, standing by my side.

"What in the devil is this?" cried Roberts, his face a mask of terror.

A call began to rise from the group. "Master. Master. Master."

Holmes stepped forward, approaching the Law Sayer with hands held before him. "We mean you no harm, but yes, this Master, please take us to him."

A voice rose from the gloom. "There'll be no need for that Lucius, I am already here."

All turned towards the owner of the voice. He stood some ten yards away, highlighted by the orange glow of the fire. He appeared to be a man well into his sixties, with a creased face showing both concern and genteelness, and leaning on a cane for support.

"Gentlemen, I think you should follow me back to the house. Lucius, Hannibal, you should come too."

***

Following behind the limping figure, I looked around at the dour and confused faces of my colleagues, then at Lucius the Law Sayer, and Hannibal, who I started to refer, in my mind, as the bull-man. The clatter of our carriage floated through the still of the night. Smith had taken the opportunity and headed off to collect and bring it to the house's forecourt.

The door was opened by a tall, dark-skinned man, with a long face and large nostrils. It was when he bade us entry, by holding up a hand, that was just a hoof with a small hook tied to it, that I realised this was another of the animal men. A horse no less.

"Thank you, Ned," said our host.

I remembered that name from the pub. One of the farmer's had mentioned, Neddy, his horse. Another piece of evidence that meant our host had indeed absconded with the animals. Why? Part of that was becoming clear, the actual purpose not so much.

Ushering us into a large drawing-room, warmed by a small fire, our host motioned towards a sideboard where sat a flask of brandy and several glasses. "Help yourselves, gentlemen. It is a chilly night."

I made my way across and poured one for each of us, and another for the host. As I took it to him, he used the opportunity to introduce himself. "As you may know from the senior constable here, I am Dr. Edward Prendrick."

Holmes introduced himself, then me. Roberts simply nodded. It seemed he had met the man before.

"Can I ask why you have come to my farm at such an hour, senior constable?"

"Mr. Holmes and Dr. Watson, here, have come from London to solve several crimes."

"Oh, yes, and what were they?" asked Prendrick, taking a sip of his brandy before gently sitting in a chair by the fire.

Holmes, spoke up as he moved across the room and picked up a small red bound volume from the table next to the very chair Prendrick occupied. "I think you know perfectly well, what they were, sir." Holding the book, Holmes opened it and read the first page. "Several volumes of notes from a certain, Dr. Moreau, were stolen from a display case and the reading room in the British Museum. Those volumes recounted the science behind, and experimentation on animal subjects, the purpose of which was to create human-like beings." Turning towards Hannibal and Lucius, Holmes added, "Much like those that we see before us here."

"A fantastic accusation, Mr. Holmes," said Roberts, "Surely, these men were simply born with unfortunate deformities and disabilities. What you suggest is beyond comprehension."

"I would have hoped until I laid eyes on these men. But what evidence we have gathered points directly to my conclusion. It is my assertion that Dr. Prendrick here, sent three of his creations into the heart of London to retrieve the works of Dr. Moreau. A scientist of a like mind as his own. Two of those we have seen. One of the cat-men, and our Hannibal here. The other, a sheep, is locked away in Scotland Yard. What say you, Dr. Prendrick?"

The older man smiled for a moment. "I find humans to be such a violent and self-centred species, and ever since I returned from abroad, have long shunned their company."

"Abroad? The Pacific perhaps?"

"Yes. I was shipwrecked upon the island of Moreau. I observed his horrifying experiments and unwittingly played a hand in his demise. Once returned to England, I found, however, that I had lived among Moreau's beast-men for so long that I could not adapt to life with other humans. I shut myself away here for a decade before the loneliness became too much for me to bear. My research in chemistry gave way to further investigations into biology. There is an entire field awaiting investigation, but mine allowed me to develop a reagent that can change and re-configure the brain chemistry of an animal, allowing fuller development and intelligence."

"Incredible," I cried, looking once again at Lucius and Hannibal.

"As it is, yes. My successes have been few, my failures far more."

"But your process is not perfected yet, is it?" asked Holmes.

"No, no it is not. If the subject does not receive sufficient injections of the reagent, they regress back to their animalistic nature and form."

"The sheep?" I asked, "It was locked up overnight."

Nodding, Prendrick said, "Unfortunately for Bessie, yes, she returned to her true form. I can help her, if only she were returned to me."

"Moreau's notes? You hoped to find something in them?"

"Yes. I thought them burnt in the house. I never investigated the House of Pain, as the beast-men called it, the place where Moreau undertook his horrible surgeries. I read in the paper that the notebooks had been donated to the Museum, so I sent three of my friends to retrieve them for me."

"A cat, a bull, and a sheep."

"Yes. My comrades still retain much of their animal skills. They were perfectly adapted for the task."

"But one disobeyed your laws."

"Moreau's laws actually, but which one?"

"To not kill. A guard was killed."

Prendrick cried out in shock and stood up. "What? That was never part of my plan?" He looked towards Lucius, then Hannibal. "Is that what this is about? Hannibal, how could you?"

I read in the paper that the notebooks had been donated to the Museum, so I sent three of my friends to retrieve them for me.

"It was accident, Master. He surprised me. I did not mean to strike him. Then he fell and laid still. I am so sorry."

Shaking his head, remorse lit large upon his face, tears formed at the corner of Prendrick's eyes. "We cannot allow this, Hannibal. You know the laws. You broke them. Now you must pay. All must obey."

"No, Master, no." The bull-man's eyes grew wide, his expression one of stark terror. "No, I do not want to return. I am a man. I walk on two legs."

Prendrick stepped towards the frightened bull-man, placing a hand on his shoulder. "I'm afraid I can't allow that. Any man breaking the law can no longer be a man. You can no longer be a man."

Hannibal threw his hoofs forward, pushing the old man away from him. "No." Prendrick stumbled backwards, tripping over the edge of the fireplace, and crashing back against the stone surrounds. His head striking the lintel let out a sharp crack and left a smear of blood on the soot-streaked stone. He fell to the floor with a dull thud and lay still.

The bull-man took one look at his fallen master and let out a loud low of fear. "Master?" Taking one step forward, Hannibal stopped when Lucius spoke up.

"He has broken the law. Again."

The horse-man, Ned, stepped in behind Lucius and pointed a hoof towards the bull-man. "There must be punishment. He has broken the Law."

Glancing from the Law Sayer to the manservant with those huge dark eyes, Hannibal's face flashed an expression of abject horror before he pushed past both and bolted from the room. His hoofed feet leaving loud clopping sounds in their wake before the front door crashed open as he exited.

I ran to the fallen scientist and searched for signs of life. "Damn," I cried when none were to be found.

"Master?" said Lucius, joined by a worried appeal from the horse-man Ned.

As I turned, I saw Roberts run from the room but noticed Holmes standing stock still and glancing down at me. "Holmes, he's dead. We need to stop that beast."

"No. Roberts may catch up with him, but the source of his humanity is gone. You heard Prendrick say it, in a day or two all these men will be nothing more than beasts of the field."

"If Master is gone, who will be our Master?"

Staring up at their looks of confused innocence, I shook my head.

"We are alone," Lucius said, before turning and stepping from the room, with Ned close behind. The softer sound of their hooves on the wooded floor, echoed back as they stepped out into the night.

"The poor devils," I said, "To have tasted humanity only to lose it in such a way."

"They will be fine. I presume they will not remember once they regress. All that will be left is for Roberts to return them to their owners."

"What about the bull?"

"Honestly? The bull killed a man. If he were human, he would be hanged. I can only think he will end up at the butcher's within a week."

Staring down at the body, I added, "There is so much to learn here that is now lost. Is it that animals are so close to humans that a simple chemical compound can bridge the gap?"

"I have always found the opposite, so many humans are close to the animals, but crossing that void rarely even requires outside assistance."

The Man from Moscow

The story of Colonel Lysander Stark from The
Adventure of the Engineer's Thumb.

Metz, France, 1870

The crack of gunfire echoed through the silent night. Stark's head spun in the direction of the sound. He stopped rowing and listened for several moments before expelling his breath in a sigh of relief. The dark, still night belied the distance from the shooter.

Idiots. There's no point shooting at the enemy. We'll have them starved out in six weeks or less. After tonight, nobody is escaping from Metz.

Pushing the oar through the dark waters of the Moselle, Stark propelled his little boat towards the starboard bank. Several dark silhouettes stood well away from the shoreline. Their windows shuttered; lights extinguished. To the uninitiated, the town of Moulins was all but abandoned.

Stepping ashore, Stark pulled the little boat onto the muddy bank, stowing the paddle and pulling out his map and orders.

By the light of the waning moon, he oriented himself and determined the likely direction of his quarry. The hand-drawn map of the area, copied from the intelligence maps used by the high command, bore an X indicating a house on the outskirts of the little town. A single name, Teulet, was written near the house.

Stark's mind raced with images and memories of his recent briefing from Oberst Kruger.

"Leutnant Stark," the older man's creased faced stared deep into the younger officer's eyes, "Bismark wants Metz. Bismark wants the Army of the Rhine decimated." Stark stood stock still at attention, no movement, no expression. Continuing, Kruger said, "This little man, Teulet, thinks it is funny to enter Metz and smuggle the officers out. We have no idea how. We have no idea where. These French must have a network of tunnels or some such, I don't know, it seems fanciful, but our best intelligence officers agree."

Moving around his desk, Kruger spat at the thought of the intelligence officers, "I don't care what these idiots agree to. I want action." Stopping before Stark, he stared straight into the younger man's eyes, "Your commanding officers speak highly of you. They say you are a man of action. Will you eliminate this threat? This Teulet? Is that something you will do for me?"

"Yes, Oberst, certainly," Stark answered, knowing full well that one would never question a superior officer's request. "This French dog is as good as dead."

"Excellent. You will go alone. If you are captured, you know what to do."

Stark's eyes grew wide, but he nodded in agreement. "I will not be captured," he said, a sign of defiance at the thought, but with the dual meaning that his death would quickly follow any seizure by enemy troops.

"Good," said Kruger, placing a hand on Stark's shoulder. "Do this successfully, and you could end this war months earlier. Fail, and you will not have to worry."

Stark unconsciously nodded at the memory, before snapping himself back to the present and setting off after his goal.

The long trudge up from the shore, through the sodden dirt and grass, left his boots and coat streaked with mud and soaked with water. Stark's sense of duty tossed aside any thoughts of his appearance, his focus was on the mission, and the rewards its success promised.

The crunching of gravel under the thick iron and leather heels of Stark's boots was the only sound accompanying him on the short trek to the outskirts of the darkened town. A light breeze carried the report of another gunshot from the far side of Metz. Stark froze for a moment until the echo of the shot died down. He listened for any other sounds before hurrying onto the row of dark houses.

Sidling up to the third house along, Stark edged up to the shuttered window of the rear room and listened. Silence. It was almost midnight, the last German patrol for the night would be coming through soon.

The entire city of Metz was surrounded. The Army of the Rhine had retreated into the Metz fortress, whilst the German forces had surrounded the area. They intended to starve the army into surrender. To maintain order in the surrounding towns, patrols had been established and sent out on a regular basis. But Teulet and his group had successfully begun an operation under the noses of the German commanders, no doubt with the help of other locals. All intelligence pointed to Teulet's group moving the officers in the hours before dawn.

He must still be here.

Stepping up to the back door, Stark grasped the door handle and thumbed the door latch. Pushing it open, a loud squeal erupted from the rusted hinges and the door base grated across the slate floor. Jumping back in shock, Stark moved away and pressed himself flat against the stone wall.

Within a minute, a shaft of moonlight fell on the nervous face of a man of about forty. He appeared almost comical, standing on the threshold in his long nightshirt and holding a long-barrelled rifle.

"Put the gun down, Monsieur Teulet," said Stark, using imperfect French.

The man's face snapped towards the voice. His eyes grew wide as they spied the gun in Stark's hand. Teulet's hands twitched, the rifle swinging slightly.

"Another move and I'll shoot."

Freezing where he stood, beads of sweat formed on Teulet's forehead. "What do you want? I'm just a poor grocer. I have no money."

"If that were true, I would not be here."

"What do you mean?" Teulet deflated. "Your accent. German?" A curse floated out under his breath.

"Yes, and you know exactly why I'm here. I want to know how you keep smuggling the French officers out of Metz."

Teulet sneered. "Never. I will never tell you. You Germans will never win." The rifle rose and swung round, but the barrel never had a chance to spit death.

A single shot rang out through the silent night, followed by the clatter of a rifle against stone steps and the thud of Teulet's body collapsing to the ground. "Fine," said Stark, taking one look at the fallen man, before stepping into the house.

On a side table near the door sat a candle in a brass holder. A small brass platter held several matches. Striking one against the rough surface of the table, Stark had enough light to see by within moments.

The area was small, consisting of a combined kitchen and sitting area, with a passageway leading to the front of the house. A quick search of the room revealed nothing more than cooking utensils, dishes, and a few items of food.

Bedroom?

Holstering his pistol, Stark made his way down the hallway and into the lone bedroom at the front of the house. A bed lay in one corner, with a small table just inside the door.

Excellent.

Passing the candle over the table, the light revealed several maps of the Metz area and a collection of papers. Leaning in, Stark read a list of names and dates. Those in the past had lines ruled through them. A small grin came to Stark's face at the information before him, especially the map of the Metz fortress with a circle marked on it. From his knowledge of the area, it was a spot near the fortress wall where the sewers let out into the Moselle river.

A perfect spot for those French dogs to escape.

A small sound broke from the darkness in the corner of the bedroom. Stark spun, his hand dropping to his pistol. He brought the candle up before him, throwing light across the dark area. A small movement was accompanied by another sound. The tiny cry of a baby. Stepping forward, Stark glanced down at the cherubic face gazing up at him. Although he'd probably killed the poor child's father only moments before, his heart leapt at the sight of the baby.

Memories of his own daughter flooded his mind. Her innocent beauty. The love that filled his world on the day she was born. The happiness he shared with his wife during those first few months. Then the darkness. The dire tragedy of her slide towards sickness and eventually death. The last memory of his wife's despair lingered in his mind.

Reaching out a hand, he pointed a finger towards the child. Its eyes followed the finger and reached up with its own. A smile broke out on Stark's face as their digits touched.

His eyes flicked up to the small name carved into the head of the crib.

Elise.

***

Berlin, Germany, 1885

"Oberstleutnant Stark, come in, sit down," said the large swarthy man, his girth threatening to dislodge the arms of his chair. "I have heard a lot about you Stark."

Surprised at the remark, Stark's eyes darted around the sparsely furnished office before he took the proffered seat. "And what have you heard of me, Oberst Bremmer?"

"All good, all good," the large man chuckled, "Do not worry. You are highly regarded amongst my colleagues. That is why you are here."

"That was to be my next question. Why am I here?" Stark asked, his question dripping with suspicion.

Bremmer slid a small cardboard file across his desk and opened it. Whilst reading the front page, he said, "Oberstleutnant Lysander Stark, also known as Fritz. Middle name I presume?" Stark nodded. "Married, oh, I'm sorry. Widowed." Bremmer glanced across the file at Stark's stern expression. "Four years ago?"

The younger, leaner man nodded. "Yes, Oberst, my darling wife contracted a fever. The doctors said it was typhoid. She never recovered."

"Oh, I am sorry, not a nice way to die."

"No, it was not, I thank you for your thoughts."

Turning back to the file, he said, "Ah, you have a daughter. Something to remember your wife by then?"

"No, Oberst, I'm afraid not. The child was a foundling of the war. We had lost a baby many years before. Elise, for that, is her name, brought my wife many happy years."

Bremmer watched for any hint of joy in Stark's face. "Not you it seems?"

"No. She is a wilful child. One I must pay constant attention to."

Chuckling, Bremmer said, "Yes, I have children of a similar age. It is the younger generation. They have never known hardships like we did. Perhaps we need another war?"

"Perhaps."

Pausing for a moment, Bremmer read more of Stark's file, refamiliarizing himself with the contents. "Ah, yes, you were promoted after your little covert undertaking in Metz." Smiling, Bremmer nodded at Stark. "Good work that. Cut the length of the war by several months." The younger officer nodded in appreciation. "Then a little fieldwork, mostly desk work. Diligent. Two promotions from Leutnant to Major to Oberstleutnant since the war. Good, good." Bremmer closed the file and looked up. "You have been described to me as having a particular way about you. One that may fit well within the organisation that I head up."

"What organisation is that?"

"Well, you may have heard rumours that Field Marshal Moltke wishes to set up a new arm of the military. He has coined the name Abteilung, sort of a revised version of the old intelligence unit used during the war. Our neighbours to the east have been rattling sabres across the edges of Asia and even down towards Africa. The Field Marshall believes it is time to keep a closer eye on them, and perhaps, begin efforts to undermine their endeavours."

"How do I fit into this then?"

"Ah, well, the Field Marshall needs good men. Men who have no fear. Men who do not back away from getting their hands dirty when required. After Metz, and some of your other activities, you have been singled out as one who would fit that mould."

"Intelligence?" Stark stared at the Oberst for a moment. "Do you mean assassinations?"

"Only if necessary. More, information gathering. Exploitation of foreign nationals, that sort of thing." Seeing Stark deflate slightly, the Oberst smiled and said, "Oh, don't worry. The particular mission that we have for you should allow a man of your talents to express himself adequately."

"Alright, now you have my interest. What does this mission involve?"

***

Two days later, Stark found himself sitting in a tiny room, devoid of any light source except for the shafts streaming through the two circular openings in the wall before him. On the other side of the wall hung a very intricate still life painting by renowned German artist Georg Flegal. The small holes hidden amongst flowers and fruit allowed for unobserved viewing of the room beyond.

Leaning forward, Stark placed his nose against the wall and stared through the eyeholes as the door opened and a group of men entered the room. The first was Herr Weissman, a short, rat-like little man, that Stark had met the day before, his job was to run the foreign currency section of the Treasury.

Weissman stood aside, holding the door open as three more men entered. The first was Stark's target. Bremmer had called him The Man from Moscow as if that were meant to lend him any more presence than his physical countenance demanded. Stark simply saw a tall, well-built man, handsome in a severe way, with close-cropped fair hair. His name was Piotr Mazepin, and he held a similar position to Weissman, but from the Russian perspective. Joining Mazepin were two taller, and broader men, dressed in plain, dark suits. Stark could immediately tell they were Russian military, simply from the way they took up positions behind Mazepin as he sat and stood with their hands folded together in front and their legs splayed slightly apart, both sported bulges on their right hip, hidden by their jackets.

Mazepin took a seat at the long table, with Weissman sitting opposite. Both opened their small satchels and took out thick ledgers, placing them down and opening them, as if this were a prelude move to some form of strategic game.

Reading from his ledger, Mazepin spoke first, "By our accounts your treasury holds a million rubles."

"Give or take a hundred thousand. Our current estimates have the total as nearer one and a half million."

"Do you know what denominations you hold?"

Running his finger down a list of figures, Weissman answered, "Five hundred thousand in notes, nine hundred thousand in coins, with the rest made up from various denominations of kopeks."

"That is a lot of ruble coins, I wasn't aware that Germany held such a large amount in coins." Mazepin flipped through his ledger, mumbling to himself as he added up several figures in his head. Finally, he nodded, "Yes, we have brought enough with us, but it will mean our immediate return to Moskva once the exchange is made."

Stark's mind wandered as the two accountants checked their figures and journals. The details didn't matter to him. His role in this affair was to keep a close eye on Mazepin and ensure that he didn't get in the way of the end game.

It was the end game that was interesting.

Bremmer wasn't fully aware of the motives behind the scheme but had explained it as simply as he could. For their own reasons, possibly to save money, the Russians were changing the base metals that constituted the physical ruble coins from gold to silver. To do that, all existing ruble coins were to be taken out of circulation across Russia and Europe and replaced with the new silver standard.

Germany held a large reserve of ruble coins, to enable easier trade between the two countries. The paper notes were well known for their fragility, many in storage had degraded quickly from mould and damp, making them worthless, so that made the coins more attractive.

German intelligence had come up with a plan to perform a double exchange of the Russian rubles. The boffins in the science division had built a coin press, and an agent assigned to Moscow had infiltrated the Bank of Russia and absconded with a set of the original coin stamps. A million rubles worth of coins had been minted using the press and stamps by substituting a lower-cost mix of nickel and copper to form the metal.

Mazepin's presence here was to enable the exchange of the coins. Stark's presence was to ensure that the man from Moscow was none the wiser that his Nation's coins had been replaced.

To ensure that, Stark had other plans in train.

By the end of the tawdry drawn out meeting, Weissman and Mazepin had agreed on the exact exchange figure and set a time to meet on the following day. Stark discovered that the Russians had brought a large, secure horse-drawn wagon with them, containing dozens of crates of coins. It sat inside the grounds of the Russian Embassy and was under continuous guard by the embassy staff, the exchange would occur at the Berlin Treasury building, under the eyes of German army soldiers.

From Stark's observations, Mazepin did not exhibit any suspicion over the terms of the exchange. Handling millions in currency seemed a natural act to him, which made Stark more comfortable that they would be able to effect the switch with no problems but leaving it all to chance was not in his operating parameters. It was when the meeting began to break up and he overheard Weissman invite Mazepin and his two companions out for dinner, that Stark left to prepare.

***

Sitting at one of the larger tables in the bier Halle, Stark glanced around at his companions, four strikingly beautiful women. To the casual envious observer, much too beautiful to be sitting with someone as gaunt and skinny as Stark. He smiled at the fleeting glances aimed towards his group by the other male denizens of the hall. His pleasure was even more enjoyable when he pictured the looks on their faces if they became aware of the origins of the beauties. Each one was a German military officer, handpicked by Stark for this assignment. Bremmer had given him free rein to run the operation as he saw fit and had asked no questions. Results were all that mattered.

Purposely facing towards the rear of the hall, Stark became alert when, Anna, the blonde woman on his left, leaned across and whispered into his ear. "It looks like they are here." Lina and Freya, sitting across from Stark, raised their champagne and sipped, their eyes scanning the faces of the group, picking their assigned targets. Brigit, sitting on Stark's right, sat still, waiting for the group to pass as they were shown to a table nearby.

For the next hour, Stark's group maintained their observances of Weissman and the Russians. He and his four companions kept their alcohol intake to a minimum, while the other table saw a stream of beer mugs arrive, helped by the deep pockets of Herr Weissman.

It was when the group appeared to be quite inebriated that Stark whispered in Brigit's ear. Smiling, she nodded and rose from the table, turning back towards her group and laughing loudly at an untold joke. All eyes from Weissman's table turned towards the tall striking woman. Stark was pleased to see Mazepin gaze longingly towards Brigit. As the woman surreptitiously turned her sight towards the Russians, she noticed it too.

Turning to face the group, she stood with her hands on hips and a pout on her lips, deliberately making and holding eye contact with Mazepin for several seconds before sashaying across to the other table.

"Hello boys," she said, "It seems a shame that four lovely gentlemen like yourselves are sitting here all on your own." She nodded over her shoulder, and added, "Why don't you join me and my friends?" The men glanced across towards Stark and the other women. Smiles crossed the faces of each Russian.

"I think I would like to take you up on that offer," said Mazepin.

As the others joined him and picked up their stools, Weissman left his alone, and said, "I think it is time I bid you do svidanya. I must return to Frau Weissman, plus I am far too old for engaging in such frivolities. I will see you tomorrow at the Treasury building." Waving he strode past Stark's table, nodding to the military officer before striding from the bier Halle.

At Stark's table, Lina and Freya moved their stools apart, allowing Mazepin's aides to place theirs in the gaps. As they sat, both men introduced themselves to the others at the table. Brigit strolled over with Mazepin on her arm. Pointing to her vacant chair, she said, "I am sitting here, please join me, Piotr."

Smiling, Mazepin dropped his stool in the vacant space between Brigit's and Stark. As the two sat, Stark held out a hand and said, "I am Fritz, glad to make your acquaintance, Piotr. Please join us, my companions are very pleasant, but I yearn for some male company."

"I thank you, Fritz," Mazepin said, his voice holding a noticeable slur.

"A round of drinks should welcome you nicely," said Stark, turning and catching the eye of the comely dirn standing near the bar, whilst holding up eight fingers to indicate the number of beers required. The woman nodded and passed on the order to the barman. Within moments the same dirn plonked eight frothy mugs of beer on the table, receiving a chorus of thanks in return. Raising his, Stark said, "To new friends." The toast was echoed back, with each taking a long pull from their mug.

As the beers flowed, thanks to Stark's insistent ordering, the talk became louder. Brigit and Mazepin were deep in conversation, verging on intimacy, while the other Russians engaged in animated conversation with their companions.

Forgetting himself for a moment, Stark sipped his beer and glanced at each of his companions in turn, admiring the beauty of the women and the way they easily fell into conversation with their male partners as if they were lifelong friends. A nagging thought broke through his musings, a thought about his adopted daughter sitting at home. Ever since the death of his wife, the conversations between himself and Elise had drifted more into iciness, lacking any warmth or familial closeness. It was something he needed to address he told himself, but for now he had other business to attend to.

As the next round of drinks arrived, Stark spoke into Anna's ear. "Distract our friend for a moment." Nodding, she rose and stepped around Stark, putting her head into the middle of Brigit and Mazepin, and speaking quietly to them. Glancing around the table to ensure that all of the men were focused on their assigned beauties, Stark withdrew a small vial with a straw attached. He quietly slid the straw into the froth atop Mazepin's mug, before tilting it vertically. A fine white powder slid from the vial, down the straw and into the clear amber liquid below. Within seconds it dissolved. After stirring it, Stark quickly removed the vial and straw, slipping it away inside his jacket pocket, and pushed Mazepin's beer across the table until it clinked against the Russian's empty mug.

As Anna stood and moved away from the pair, Brigit picked up her mug and held it before Mazepin's face. "A toast. This looks like it is turning into a very good night, but it has only just begun," she said, a sly smile on her face, and a come hither look in her eye. Mazepin's eyes grew wide as he realised what she meant. He picked up his beer and clinked glasses with the blonde. "I think when you finish that beer, we might find somewhere a little more private."

To Stark's delight, Mazepin's beer disappeared within a matter of a moment. Brigit's smile turned to surprise. "Okay then," she said, taking a short pull from her mug before placing it down and standing. "I made a promise, I will have to follow through," she added, smiling that devious grin once more.

Taking Mazepin by the arm, she bid goodnight to the rest of the table. Mazepin spoke in Russian, telling the other two not to wait for him. He would join them at the Embassy in the morning, well before their appointment at the Treasury building. They both chuckled and nodded, bidding him a good night.

Stark watched Brigit and Mazepin leave the bier Halle before leaning in towards Anna and whispering in her ear. "We will give them five minutes, then follow. Everything is set, but by the time we arrive, Brigit should have him where we want him." She nodded and took a short drink.

***

The room reminded Stark of the similar set-up at the Treasury building. The difference being that instead of a painting with holes in it for eyeballs, a dark rectangular box sat on a metal frame. One end was pressed close to the wall, a brass cylinder poking through the hole cut into the canvas of a painting hanging on the other side of the wall.

Another smaller hole was cut into the painting near to the camera's lens. Stark bent and peered through into the room beyond. A

81

smile came to his face as he spied the unconscious form of Piotr Mazepin lying on the large bed that dominated the room beyond.

As Stark watched, Brigit and Anna entered the room, they had removed their heavy dresses and wore simple undergarments. They quickly set about removing Mazepin's clothes. Stark moved to the rear of the camera and lifting the dark fabric hood, ducked beneath it.

His first photograph was a little overexposed but gave him a good idea of how much light was trickling in from the bedroom. Pulling the slate out and quickly replacing it, he adjusted the camera and proceeded to capture several key moments. The photographs that followed were all highly staged, but to the uninitiated, and especially to the unconscious man concerned, they were sure to shock and cause immediate consternation.

After almost half an hour, the two girls pulled the bedclothes back over Mazepin before stepping away. He would awaken in a few hours in a strange room, with a head full of agony and fog, and no clue as to what had occurred.

As the girls left, Stark pulled the camera away from the wall and slid the hole cover back into place. He took one last look through the peephole, reassuring himself that Mazepin was fast asleep, and the girls were gone, before collecting up the plates and depositing them in the lightproof satchel.

He had one a short trip to Intelligence headquarters to drop the photographic plates off for processing before he could return home. His part of the adventure had only just begun.

**

The large, covered wagon ground its way across the cobbled street and entered the gates of the Treasury's rear courtyard. The heavy hooves of the four drays crunched on the gravel and bit into the loose stones for purchase. A fine sheen of sweat glistened on their coats. They each let out a short snort as Nicolai pulled on the reins to draw them to a halt.

Watching from the shade of the rear portico, Stark smiled at the idea that these three Russians had been tasked with carting so much currency across the continent in a horse-drawn wagon. Weissman said they had scoffed at using trains for the simple reason that their control would be lessened, and they'd have to organise wagons from the station to the Treasury buildings, adding time and inconvenience.

Stark noticed that Mazepin's eyes were downcast, his head hanging low beneath his hat. He smiled to himself, lightly slapping the satchel hanging by his side. Its presence itself another form of insurance.

Weissman stepped out through the open doors of the rear entrance and threw his arms wide. "Gentlemen, welcome, I hope your evening was enjoyable." All three Russians glanced at the German and mumbled in return.

Sergei dropped to the ground, his shiny, black boots, scraping the small stones. Turning to Mazepin, he held out a hand to help his superior from the wagon's seat. "Gospodin Mazepin is a little beneath the weather this morning." Mazepin swatted Sergei's hands away in annoyance, before dropping down to the gravel driveway.

Even from his position, Start could see the Russian's eyes were glazed almost to the point where he could succumb quickly to sleep once more.

"Let's get on with this, shall we?" Mazepin snapped, reaching into the rear of the wagon, and pulling out his notebook. Reading his entry, he turned to Weissman, "Eight hundred thousand rubles?" Weissman nodded. Speaking to his men, he said, "That will be thirty crates. Your vault is inside?"

"Yes, I'll have my men help."

Nodding, Mazepin said, "Good. Otherwise, this will take all day."

Weissman hurried up the steps, nodding to Stark as he went by. Within a moment, he was joined by four swarthy men, dressed ready for hard work, simply in shirts, pants, and boots. "In the vault, at the rear," Weissman said to the men, turning to Mazepin he added, "Would you like to inspect the exchange?"

"Certainly," Mazepin answered, following Weissman into the Treasury building. Waiting for a moment, Stark turned and joined them inside. As they made their way to the vault room deep in the building, Mazepin's ears pricked.

He stopped and spun to face the source of the footsteps behind him. "Do I know you?"

"Why yes, yes you do, Mister Mazepin, or should I say, Piotr, as that is the name you introduced yourself with last night," said Stark, "You would know me as Fritz, as that is a name I go by."

Realisation dawned on Mazepin's face, both of recognition of Stark, and of what happened the previous night. Pointing at Stark's chest, he said, "You were the man with those lovely ladies." His hand went to his head as a wave of pain ran through it. "Oh, Lord, it was you that kept buying the beer."

"I was feeling generous, yes," said Stark, "I only wanted to welcome you to our fine city and enjoy some other company for an hour or two."

"Some welcome," said Mazepin, his hand falling to his heaving stomach. Once he was himself again, he asked, "Why are you here? This seems untoward."

"Ah, yes," interjected Weissman, "Let me formally introduce you, this is Oberstleutnant Lysander Stark. A member of our military. We thought it might make things simpler if you had an escort to ease things at the border or at least dissuade any potential villains on the way."

"I do not understand the need," said Mazepin, "Nicolai and Sergei are both well-trained soldiers, and well-armed. We travelled here from Austria without molestation."

"And that is good, but my Government's concern is that we wish to see no harm come to you or your men within our borders."

"More that you wish to have no possibility of a diplomatic incident."

"There is that as well. Please as your host let Oberstleutnant Stark accompany you to the border," Weissman held out his hands to placate the Russian, "The other advantage for you, is that Stark here has access to the Government's funds. It is a good day's journey to the border, and you will need accommodation and refreshments overnight. So, consider it an act of goodwill on our part."

His weary face showing signs of concern, Mazepin nodded in agreement. "Fine. You will need your own horse, there is only room for three on the wagon."

"That shall present no problem, Sir, I will need transport back to Berlin anyway, and I have prepared my own ride."

Down a flight of stairs, they continued along a dimly lit corridor, to a wide-open area with two large steel doors folded back to reveal the contents of the massive room beyond. Wooden crates were stacked against two of the walls, long rows of shelves, stacked with bound wads of paper bills, lined the third. As they reached the vault, the first attendant arrived holding a heavy chest of coins. Weissman nodded towards the far wall, "Place them over there by the wall." Pointing at the crates lying near the entrance, he added, "In a moment you can begin to take these out to the wagon. Just don't get them confused." Smiling at Mazepin, Weissman added, "Would you like to inspect the contents, Sir?"

Nodding, Mazepin dropped down to one knee, and prized the lid off the nearest crate, revealing a mess of shiny and dull gold coins. Scooping up a handful, he held one to the light, examining the stamped seal on one side and the writing on the other. Weissman's eyes grew wide as he watched Mazepin handle the counterfeit coins. Stark's hand moved to his holster. It was a last resort, but he wanted to be prepared for any eventuality.

"We have sorted them into denominations of one, three and five rubles, to make things easier for you. There is also a mix of grades. Some were taken from circulation by our staff; most you will find are relatively new."

Dropping the coins back into the crate and sliding the lid back into place, Mazepin grunted as he rose back to his feet, and drew out his notebook. He quickly counted the crates and wrote down the number. "What is the mix of denominations?"

"Ten of five rubles, eight of three and twelve of ones," answered Weissman.

"Good, good, the sooner we get this over with, the sooner we can be on our way." When Mazepin withdrew a kerchief and mopped his brow, Stark took his hand away from his hip. A smile played on his lips as he realised this may go smoother than he first thought.

***

As the four draft horses snorted and strained against the weight of the fully loaded wagon, Stark trotted from the small stables at the rear of the Treasury property on his black stallion. He drew level with Weissman, just as the Russian wagon reached the gates and exited. Stopping briefly, he spoke to the Government official. "They don't seem to have any suspicions, which is excellent for us. If they manage ten miles an hour then we shall reach Fürstenwalde near nightfall. I have sent two agents ahead to inform the constabulary and prepare rooms in one of the local inns there."

"I don't think you will have any real trouble. If you supply them enough with beer once more, then all should be fine."

"Though I think they would be a little warier of drinking too heavily tonight. They will simply be very weary and should fall asleep early enough without my added involvement."

"Then away with you. I will await news on your return." Nodding, Stark kicked his heels into the stallion's rump and sprang away after the wagon.

***

The horses did a sterling job, once they were up to speed they settled into a comfortable rate and arrived at Fürstenwalde just as the sky was reddening with the approach of dusk.

Stark, having stayed well behind the wagon, preferring his own company than attempting to converse with the Russians as they were jostled about by the wagon's ride over the often-rough country roads, picked up speed and drew level with the others. "I recommend we stop here in Fürstenwalde. There is a very reputable inn, which has good beer and food."

Nicolai and Sergei nodded in agreement. Mazepin's eyes flickered open as he returned from slumber. "What? What's that you say?" The other two filled him in. Nodding he spoke to Stark, "Very good, lead on. Is there accommodation for the horses and wagon?"

"Yes. There is a stable nearby. It should be large enough. I will also inform the constabulary to lend us a policeman or two to look over the wagon during the night."

"That won't be necessary, we will protect the wagon, but food would be good," said Mazepin, his eyelids closing once more, "Tell me when we arrive." The other two groaned at Mazepin's insistence that they would be in charge of securing the wagon.

Glancing up at the line of houses in the near distance, Stark said, "Well it won't be long till we are there" Looking at the other two, he smiled, "I'll head off and arrange things. There is only one main street, so you should easily find both the inn and stables. Some cold beer would be most welcome, don't you think." The two Russians nodded. With that, Stark trotted off towards the little town.

By the time the large wagon arrived, Stark stood at the entrance of the stables with a short, stocky man dressed in the dark blue uniform of the Polizei, and another dressed in a simple shirt and dark trousers. The simply dressed man pointed to the vacant area before the stable doors, and Nicolai guided the large wagon to the spot.

As the three Russians dismounted from the wagon, the policeman strolled up and bowed. "I am Polizeihauptmeister Mueller. Your wagon will be safe in my care. I have several polizeimeisters who can watch over it during the night."

"That is all well and good, but we would prefer to see to its security ourselves," said Mazepin, much to the continued distaste of his compatriots.

Mueller clicked his heels together and bowed once more. "As you wish, the offer is there." He bid a good evening to the three Russians and Stark, before adding, "Hans here will see to your horses. I understand that rooms have been prepared in the inn for you as well."

As the policeman left, Nicolai spoke to Mazepin," Are you sure you don't want the constabulary to assist us? It has been a long day and a good night's sleep would be most welcome."

Casting a sideways glance at Stark, "I am appreciative of the offer, but the wagon and its contents belong to Mother Russia and has been entrusted to us, I cannot in good faith delegate such a responsibility to foreigners. We will do our duty to the best of our abilities." Patting Nicolai on the shoulder, "You shall take the first watch, we will secure our rooms and return with food and drink."

Stark simply shrugged and said, "The offer is there in good faith. This will be your last night in Germany, I simply thought you would like to relax before returning to your homeland."

"And I thank you, Herr Stark, but we shall handle things ourselves," returned Mazepin, a tinge of anger, or tiredness, in his words, Stark wasn't quite sure.

***

With the approval of the stable master, the three Russians built a small circle of stones and gathered wood from the field next door. Within an hour they had a roaring fire going to take the chill of the night away. They planned to stay together until later in the night, then one would stay on watch while the others slept. Each taking turns for two to three hours at a time.

Several townsfolk gave them disapproving looks as they strode along the street and entered the Inn. Even Polizeihauptmeister Mueller stopped for a moment to examine their temporary campsite and once again offer his assistance. Mazepin thanked him again but declined help. By that time, they each had tankards of frothy beer and were more than set for the evening.

As night fell, Stark appeared in the firelight with the inn's waitress in tow. They each held trays of food, enough for four people, which they set on the crates that the men had brought out from the wagon to use as seats and tables for their beer. A small grin crossed Stark's face as he glanced at how the crates were being used, but it disappeared when he realised they probably contained the counterfeit coins. He asked the waitress to bring more beers, then sat down and joined the Russians as they enjoyed the local fare of bread, sausage, cheese, and pickles, but couldn't take his eyes away from the crates, visions of the coins heating up and possibly melting if the boxes grew too hot.

After a few more tankards of beer, the Russians relaxed and took on the same level of joviality that Stark encountered the evening before. Mazepin was more reserved, still nursing the effects of the chloral hydrate Stark had slipped him. Mindful of the accountant's more alert demeanour, Stark joined in the conversation, swapping stories of his life in the military, with Sergei and Nicolai who shared a history of serving their country.

Nothing untoward occurred throughout their evening until the conversation relaxed and Nicolai stood up to feed more wood to the fire. After throwing a couple more logs into the belly of the blaze, he bent to drag the crate of coins away from the heat of the flames as they started to lick at the new wood. Stark breathed a sigh of relief and took another draw from his beer.

"One thing has concerned me today," Nicolai said.

"What?" asked Sergei.

Turning to Stark, Nicolai asked, "Herr Stark, how far is it from Berlin to this little town?"

Lifting one quizzical eyebrow, Stark answered, "About fifty miles, why?"

Turning to his countrymen, Nicolai asked, "What speed did we average before we arrived in Berlin?"

The other two glanced at each other for a moment before shrugging. Sergei replied, "I have no idea. What do you think?"

"Our trip from Prague to Berlin was about two hundred and twenty miles, yes?" The other two nodded. "And it took how long?" Both shook their heads, with Sergei shrugging. "Well, I think it took us about twenty-eight hours all up, across four days," continued Nicolai.

"Okay, good, we've been travelling for a few weeks," said Sergi, "I for one am thankful that the Germans held so much currency, we have to return to get more, cutting our trip short."

"Yes, what is your point, Nicolai?" asked Mazepin, a hint of annoyance at the conversation.

"Well, the question I have is, that the journey here was fifty miles, it took us just over four and a half hours to cover that distance." The others nodded, with Mazepin cocking his head at the notion. Nicolai swept an arm out towards the horses in the stables. "I don't think our horses have grown more muscles overnight, plus," he said, holding up a finger whilst standing and pulling the cover off the crate, "The horses should be slower with the heavier load. After all, these coins should weigh more than the coins we had in the wagon before we entered Berlin. Isn't that the whole purpose of our trip, to exchange the older heavier rubles made with gold, with the new rubles made with silver?" Adding, "The coins that the Germans gave us should be heavier than the new ones," as he raised a handful of the coins to the flickering firelight.

"I've known you a long time, Nicolai, and have never seen such an intelligent position come from your mouth, but there is something in what you say," said Mazepin, stepping across and scooping out a handful of coins before striding into the stable. The other two followed after him.

Concerned, Stark rose and peered through the gloom after the three Russians.

From inside the stable, a match flamed, a moment before a small gas lamp was lit, throwing a glow across the area. Stark noted that Mazepin had found a bench built into the side wall. He held a coin up to the light, studying it carefully, and turning it over and examining both sides and the edge.

Stepping closer, Stark heard their conversation, his hand quickly slipped to the leather pouch at his right hip and unclipped the fastener.

In the stable, Nicolai's hand dropped to his pocket, he fished inside and brought out a gold coin. "I've had this one on me since we left Moskva, it's an original ruble, I plan to change it over when we return." Mazepin took the offered coin and felt its weight. He picked up one of the coins from the workbench and compared it to Nicolai's. "These should be the same weight."

Giving them to Sergei, Mazepin asked, "What do you think?"

After a moment of holding both in each hand in turn, and comparing their weights, Sergei answered, "They seem to be different." He placed Nicolai's coin down and retrieved one of the German coins. Comparing the two exchanged coins to each other, he finally said, "These are the same weight." Repeating the process with Nicolai's coin, after a moment, he said, "Both of these German coins are lighter than Nicolai's coin."

Nodding, Mazepin said, "I agree."

My Lord, you are right. These are lighter.

Snatching up the German coins and his own, Nicolai repeated Sergei's assessment. His eyes grew wide, and he said, "My Lord, you are right. These are lighter."

All three turned as one towards Stark, who now stood on the threshold of the stable, silhouetted by the firelight behind him.

Mazepin took a step forward, "What is the meaning of this Stark? Is our assessment correct? Are these coins that your Government has exchanged for Russian currency real, or fake?"

"I can only say that my Government would never knowingly deceive another country's officials. You must be mistaken."

"We must return to Berlin. These coins do not seem to be genuine. We must retrieve our currency, and when you can prove the authenticity of these coins, we will undertake the exchange once more," said Mazepin, a hint of authority creeping into his voice.

Stark's hand moved quickly, the Russians' eyes growing wide as they saw the object in his hand. "I think not," Stark said, pointing the pistol at each man in turn.

"You will not get away with this," said Nicolai, his hand grasping for the pistol sitting in its holster on his right hip and raising it towards Stark.

The loud retort of the gunshot echoed across the large room. The horses whinnied in fear, stamped their feet, and tried to pull themselves free. The men ignored them, staring at the bloom of red spreading across Nicolai's shirt. He gaped at his chest, then at Stark, mouthing an obscenity before falling forward into the dirty straw strewn across the floor.

"No, Nicolai," shouted Sergei, ducking sideways and snatching his pistol out. As he raised the gun towards Stark, another shot shattered the still night. Sergei was flung backwards, sprawling in the straw, and lying still.

Mazepin's terrified face turned from his stricken countryman back towards the German. He raised his hands in surrender, he was not armed. "Will you kill me now?" he said, his mouth trembling in fear.

"No. I need you alive. You will make sure that this currency enters Russia and circulates amongst your countrymen."

"I would never do such a thing. Never."

A broad smile grew across Stark's face, he holstered his gun and drew his satchel from behind his back. Snapping the clasp open, he withdrew the cardboard folder within. Grinning malevolently at Mazepin, he said, "Oh, I think you will. Especially after you see what I have here."

***

"Congratulations, Oberst Stark, as you can imagine by your immediate promotion, my superiors in the intelligence division are highly impressed with your performance on this assignment."

"Thank you, Oberst Bremmer, I am honoured and look forward to serving in my new role."

"Yes, yes, we will get to that in a moment. Now," Bremmer said, leaning forward and placing his chin on his steepled hands, "I have read your report, but want to know everything from the horse's mouth, as they say."

"What details would you like?"

"The accountant, this Mazepin, he was the last survivor, but how did you convince him to cooperate."

"Ah," said Stark, a grin crossing his face, "The man from Moscow. Such a sad fellow, and so timid, for such a tall, handsome man." Nodding towards the folder beneath Bremmer's elbows, Stark continued, "I deduced that I needed to prepare in the eventuality that the Russians found out about the counterfeit coins. To that end, if you inspect the photographs in the folder on your desk, you will see what I had to work with."

Bremmer opened the file, his eyes growing wide as he viewed the first photograph, leafing through the others his mouth dropped open at the debauchery portrayed within. "My word," he said, glancing up at Stark.

"Yes, that was Mazepin's reaction when he viewed them as well. He became extremely compliant with my demands when I mentioned that copies of those are held by German agents in Moscow. He almost fainted when I said that any deviation from my demands would see them sent to his wife, and to his superiors within the Treasury." Smiling, Stark waited for Bremmer to finish and close the file once more. "From that moment on, I received no further complaints or whimpers from him for the entire journey to the border the next morning."

"What happened then?"

"Using the papers of the dead Russians, the two agents I sent ahead to Fürstenwalde took on their identities and travelled with Mazepin. Their orders were to ensure that there was no trouble. Once they were at the Polish border, and had crossed into Russian territory, I left them."

"You didn't stay with Mazepin?"

Shaking his head, Stark said, "No need. We have an agent in the Russian border forces. He confirmed our agents' identities, and as I watched him from my horse, I was pleased to see our agent wave them on without another word."

"The dead Russians?"

"Mueller came out of inn not long after my gunshots. Mazepin pleaded with the man that I had killed them in cold blood. Mueller is a good German and simply agreed that it was self-defence. It was then that Mazepin knew all hope was gone. Mueller simply had the bodies buried in the town cemetery."

"Excellent. You have done a magnificent job. We have also pressed more rubles and sent them to our agents in Moscow, if the time comes we will use them to undermine the populace's trust in their currency by unveiling the fakes."

"Thank you, Oberst. What is my next assignment?"

"Ah, now this will be an interesting one for you. How much do you know about England?"

"Nothing really, why?"

"Well, if you take the assignment, you will be there for quite a while. I suggest you take that young daughter of yours. You have said she is spirited. The English countryside might be good for her."

"How long is quite a while?"

"Well let me put it this way. This little exercise of counterfeiting Russian currency was a simple precursor. We wish you to undermine the English economy, slowly but surely, with counterfeit British coins."

"We? Are you talking about the Intelligence division? The German government?"

"Partly. On behalf of the Government, my division has developed a partnership with a private individual."

"That seems peculiar. Who?"

"Well since you would be working with this individual for a while, it is only fair you should meet. He is here in the building."

Standing and moving to the door, Bremmer looked out and motioned to someone in the next room. Returning to his seat, Bremmer said, "He will be here soon."

Within a few moments, a knock on the door was followed by the entry of an extremely tall man. Stark gazed at the thin figure, with his pale clean-shaven face, in confusion.

"This is he?"

"Yes," said Bremmer, "May I introduced Herr Moriarty."

The tall man smiled and extended a hand towards Stark, "That's James, Professor James Moriarty, at your service." Stark could not overcome the uncanniness of Moriarty's resemblance to him. It was almost like looking into the reflection of an older version of himself, if not slightly thinner and more gaunt in the face. He felt Moriarty's recognition of the same, the older man looking Stark up and down, with a wry grin growing on his face.

"I do believe," Moriarty said, "that I could not be more comfortable working with someone who looks the way you do. I think our future endeavours will be most profitable, to both of us."

The Adventure of the Tesla Coil

Staring out across London from the top floor of the manor, my mind drifted back to a simpler time. A time before the new machines. A time before the rise of the steam engines. A time when my good friends were still alive.

Outside, the heat of the summer's day had given way to a cooler evening, the cloudless night allowing the city to be seen in all its glory. Large airships nestled next to the tall buildings of the central district, the chosen transport of the city's busy business leaders. Their happenings played out in towers far removed from the average people who spent their lives in a constant buzz of survival down at street level.

Gouts of orange flame burst from pipes in the sides of many buildings, releasing the excess gas and heat from the steam engines beneath, and reflecting off myriad plates of brass decorating the edifices, a gaudy show of wealth to those same denizens whose sweat and toil built the towers in the first place.

My eyes fell on the newest addition to the skyline. A looming structure, newly constructed and nearing completion, all but dark as if still lying in its womb awaiting entry to the world. I had read in the papers of the mysterious owner and purpose of the building, but the details hadn't concerned me at the time and the facts were quickly forgotten. I assumed that my young ward would have heard of him and could recite the man's history to the letter.

Watching the self-propelled carriages moving their way through the byways of London, and the smaller dirigibles floating above and weaving their way between the buildings, I couldn't help think, what an age of wonder we lived in. Modern man's harnessing of the power of steam had opened avenues to all, negating the reliance on horses for transport and muscle, and bringing about a new era of self-reliance and prosperity.

Though, as history dictates, any increase in wealth amongst the populace brings with it an increase in criminal activity taking advantage of that fortune.

Glancing across London towards the Houses of Parliament, I imagined I could see the busy offices of New Scotland Yard and especially, Commissioner Lestrade, close contact and confidant of my housemate.

As if on cue, a noise echoed out from the bowels of the great house.

Hurrying inside, I stepped into the master's study, devoid of his attendance, but filled with his presence. Upon his large oak desk sat a device that only he and one other possessed. It had been designed by an acquaintance of mine

but brought to reality by that man's grandson, my ward, Sherlock Holmes.

Grasping the earpiece in one hand, and the speaking tube in the other, I addressed the caller. "Hello, Commissioner, how may I help you?"

"Ah, good evening, Watson. Is Holmes in?" Commissioner Lestrade's voice sounded hollow, an effect of the transformation of the electronic signal speeding down the telegraph lines that Master Sherlock had installed for this very purpose.

"The master is preoccupied and asked not to be disturbed, but I can relay your message to him. I'm sure he would quickly rearrange his priorities."

"Good, good," said Lestrade, "Please have him meet me in the vault of the Bank of England."

"Very good Sir. I shall convey your wishes directly."

Lestrade said a quick goodbye and within seconds I was greeted with the hollow sound of silence as if I was listening to the void of space. Hanging the two small devices back on their hooks, I turned and hurried to the bookcase in the far corner of the room.

On the third shelf, an ancient leather volume of Shakespeare's works was connected to a hidden spring system. Pulling the book forward, a loud click greeted me, followed by the slight creak of the bookcase sliding forward and opening to reveal a narrow staircase leading down into the stygian darkness.

As I stepped forward, hidden sensors recognised my approach, igniting light bulbs on either side to illuminate my way forward. Within a minute of climbing down, the staircase opened into an incredibly large cave, hidden deep inside the hill, and well beneath the manor.

This was my master's true den. Of late, it was where he spent most of his waking, and a lot of his sleeping, hours.

Though the cave's current use was not the sole agency of Master Sherlock, that had been the responsibility of his grandfather, Nikola. An incredibly intelligent and inventive man, whom I had the pleasure of knowing for many years before his sudden death. This had been his laboratory, home to all manner of inventions, the most ingenious still stood in the middle of the cave. A large circular coil sat upon three angled legs. It looked like an oversized children's stool, except for the large bolts of lightning that erupted from time to time and arced across the roof of the cave.

The coil was fed by a steam-powered generator, that huffed and puffed in the far corner of the cave, but it was the coil that provided amplified and transmitted power to all the devices spread across the cave, and the house itself.

Chief amongst those machines was the carriage that Master Sherlock used as his personal transport. A sleek, low-slung, black contraption, that belied the bulky inefficient designs of other carriages running off steam engines. Sitting inside the front section was an electric motor, that ran virtually silent unlike the noisy steam vehicles with their coal-burning power plants. The engine was another of his grandfather's inventions that had only found reality when Master Sherlock applied his ingenuity to it.

The electricity provided by the large coil found its way into the storage batteries onboard the carriage. Lying in wait until needed, where it was fed to all four wheels immediately, unlike its steam compatriots which required a build-up of pressure before unleashing their power.

Looking across to the workbench and laboratory area, I was surprised to find it empty. When I'd earlier brought the Master his supper, he had been hard at work examining items and information obtained at the site of a recent death. I was about to call out when I heard thumping noises and several grunts echoing out from deeper in the cave.

Stepping further into the cavern, I turned and spied Master Sherlock engaged in physical training; punching, and kicking a large thick leather sack, filled with sand, and hung from a metal hook embedded in the ceiling of a cave where it sloped down markedly. The Master wore padded leather gloves and performed a series of strikes, punches, and kicks at the bag. Standing there, I marvelled, as I had at many times in the past, at Master Sherlock's skills in both boxing and an oriental martial art he learnt during his travels in the far east.

I stopped near the entrance of the gymnasium area and stood next to a set of hand weights, pondering what Master Sherlock would need while I waited for him to notice me or stop his training.

"What is it, Watson?" he said, without breaking from his regime.

"Commissioner Lestrade contacted you on the communication machine. He wishes to see you at the Bank of England. He didn't say why."

Finishing his exercising with a flurry of short sharp punches to the bag, followed by a winding kick with the back of his heel, he said, "Well, that would be obvious, wouldn't it? There's been a robbery."

Concern crossed my face, as I imagined all the nefarious villains that roamed London, pondering who could be involved. "You don't think it was Miss Adler, do you?"

Glancing across at me with a slight look of derision on his face, Master Sherlock said, "Why would you say that?"

"You have shown a marked interest towards her activities of late."

"She has turned her attention to stealing jewellery of increasing value. The victims of her crimes can absorb the financial impacts but are prone to seek vengeance through their own means. I'm merely looking to find and apprehend her before she becomes a victim herself."

Nodding, I added, "An honourable stance, Sir. Do you wish me to draw you a bath?"

Frowning, he said, "Now, why would I take a bath, that would waste far too much time." Grabbing a small towel from atop a nearby bench, he wiped the sweat from his brow and face before adding, "I assume there's fresh attire for my nighttime persona to don?"

"Yes, Sir, I always make sure all is ready for your nocturnal pursuits," I answered.

As he walked past me towards the nearby dressing room, he dropped the damp towel across my shoulder, smiled, and said, "Thank you, Watson, I really would be lost without you."

Moments later, the *clomp* of thick leather boots on the rocky floor of the cave, announced Master Sherlock stepping out from the dressing room. He was covered from head to toe in the garb of the deepest black, the uniform of the ninjitsu warriors of the far east, the design brought back from his years spent abroad. He had made several modifications, adding a thin layer of strong steel armour plates beneath, and changing the headwear, to expose his mouth, while covering most of the top half of his head, except for eye holes and his nostrils.

Many months ago, when I had asked about that aspect of the design, Master Sherlock stated that he wished to be heard and that he didn't wish to obscure his senses of smell, taste, or sight.

Moving across to a nearby display rack, he took down a wide leather belt, adorned with various pockets and devices, and quickly fastened it around his waist. Whilst he had dressed, I'd ensured that all items were restocked just in case they were needed.

Stepping up to the dark carriage, he bent and pressed a hidden button. The high-pitched whine of several small motors echoed out, and the door slid up to allow him entry.

"This could be virtually nothing, Watson, or again it may lead onto something of possible interest. I am hoping for the latter, but who knows. Regardless, I have other interests on my mind at the moment, so please prepare a hearty breakfast for the morning."

"Shall I turn down your bed upstairs?"

A grin crossed his face, "Do you actually think I'll use it?"

"No, Sir, but one has hope," I said, "I shall refresh the cot down here then, shall I?"

"Good man, Watson, good man."

With that, the door slid back into place, and a higher-pitched whine emanated from the front of the vehicle. It jolted forward and sped from the cave, only the whine producing any noise, and when gone, the silence descended once more.

I had taken it upon myself to chronicle Master Sherlock's adventures, but sadly, always from afar. My life was in this great house, and in my heart, I knew all too well that my days of adventure were long gone. To ensure any story was properly captured, I relied on Master Sherlock's memories, and the answers he gave to my barrage of questions. At other times, I would seek out any others that had provided assistance, such as Commissioner Lestrade, the most senior policeman in Scotland Yard.

***

Given the scale of the matter at hand, Commissioner Lestrade had involved himself directly in the solution. He had faith in the aptitude of his people but would quickly involve the man he knew simply as Holmes, and whose face he had never seen, if he felt that things may be beyond them.

When the small device on his wrist began to flash, Lestrade knew help was close by. He brought about the quick closure of the investigation and sent his people home for the night. After spending several hours at the scene, Lestrade believed there was nothing more they could glean from the evidence at hand, and he was loathe to have the area despoiled any further.

As Lestrade stood waiting in the great vault of the Bank of England, he examined the damage and devastation that had occurred. At the far end, a solidly built two-foot-thick wall of bricks, mortar, and concrete, now sported a massive, almost perfectly round hole, large enough for several men to quickly enter and make off with much of the contents of the vault itself.

Well, that's how it seemed to have been used.

According to the night guard, tasked with performing routine inspections of the vault every couple of hours, he had found the room in this state on his eight o'clock rounds. Two hours previously the vault had been full. Now only a handful of crates and boxes lay scattered across the room.

"These were no common thugs, this took some planning," came a familiar, low, rasping voice, from behind Lestrade.

"They were well-coordinated and thorough," he replied, not needing to turn to identify the voice's owner.

"Time?"

"Guard found it this way at eight o'clock."

"Previous rounds?"

"Six."

"Fast work." The dark garbed figure stepped past Lestrade and began to inspect the room. Experience told the commissioner to keep quiet while Holmes undertook his examination. He simply watched as the man pored over almost every square inch of the room, pulling out a magnifying glass to focus on some minutiae or detail. Lestrade hoped that he could bring some of Holmes's techniques into the training of his men, but the shadowy figure was very cautious about revealing his methods. Lestrade was unsure if it was to protect Holmes's identity further or simply protect his position of trust with the police.

Sidling up to the hole, Holmes peered through into the darkened tunnel beyond. Reaching for a small black cylinder clipped to his belt, he brought it up and pointed it into the darkness. With a *click*, a small beam of piercing white light cut through the gloom. Holmes played it around the area for a moment before speaking. "This is part of the underground system. A service tunnel perhaps." Shining the light on the ground, he added, "Tracks. They loaded everything onto carts and headed off into the bowels of the system."

"Yes. We followed the tracks. They reach one of the underground train lines, so I assume they loaded their booty onto a carriage and exited that way."

"Doesn't sound like common criminals then?"

"No. They were well prepared."

Playing the light across the edge of the hole, Holmes murmured to himself, before leaning in closer with his glass. "This was drilled out, not made by explosives. If they had a steam-powered cutter, the noise would have been horrendous."

"The guards said they heard nothing."

"Intriguing." Running a finger along the edge of the cut, he added, "This was prepared over several attempts as if the perpetrators had been drilling for days in short bursts. Possibly how they kept the sound down." Turning to face Lestrade, Holmes returned the light to his belt before asking, "What was stolen?"

The commissioner pointed to several empty racks, "These held boxes of gold bullion and sterling. I've had the head of accounts here. The poor man was in tears, even though none of the money was his. He said it was near five hundred thousand pounds worth of gold."

"No wonder the gentleman cried, but it's nothing compared to what the head of security will be feeling when he receives word of this." Dropping to his knees for a moment, Holmes examined the spaces where the bullion crates had been. Shaking his head, he said, "Footprints. Overtrodden by your men. I can't draw anything from them." Standing, he moved across to the wall adjacent to the hole. The entire area was covered with small metal plates all with keyholes. "Safe deposit boxes?"

Nodding, Lestrade said, "Too difficult to break into, it seems. They were completely left alone."

"Not completely," said Holmes pointing to one box in particular and pulling the door up to reveal a vacant space behind.

"What?" coughed Lestrade, his eyes wide at the sight. "Why didn't those fools see that?"

"Because only three have been disturbed," Holmes added, indicating the other two. "Can you find out who these belonged to? There is damage on the bottom of each. They were presumably forced open, but to do so in such a random manner gives me pause to think that these were targeted."

Pulling out the small notepad he kept on him as a legacy of his days on the beat, Lestrade copied down the box numbers. "I'll check with the Bank in the morning."

"Good," said Holmes moving back towards the hole in the rear wall. Retrieving his light from its belt clip, he shone the beam into the darkness, and said, "I'll investigate the tunnel and see if I can't find our lawbreakers' destination. Please send me those names in the morning, I'll keep you informed of my progress."

Lestrade nodded before Holmes disappeared into the obsidian gloom.

***

Early the next morning, I found Master Sherlock standing at his workbench. An array of electric lights, mounted among a rack above the bench, threw a bright aura across the object of his interest. As I drew closer, I noticed he had installed a strong magnifier and was meticulously examining the article.

Placing the breakfast tray down on the nearby side table, I joined Master Sherlock at the workbench. It was looking down at the item on the bench that memories I had long since buried came rushing back into my mind.

"Is that?" I asked.

"It appears to be," said Master Sherlock, "I found it in the tunnels leading away from the rear wall of the main vault. After drilling a hole through the wall, and robbing the vault, the miscreants had taken their haul to one of the side tracks and loaded it onto a waiting train."

"How do you know that?"

"There were cart tracks dug into the ground leading away, plus fresh scratches in the metal of the rails. Rails that should not have seen a train in months as the service tunnel was unused. Sadly, I could not tell where they went after joining the mainline, but then I found this tossed casually aside along the tunnel."

We both stared down at the green woollen balaclava. On its own, it would be nothing more than a winter garment to be worn to protect against the bitter cold. But the style of garment and the colour meant so much to the history of the Holmes family and sent me back to a time over twenty years previously, to an event to which I sadly had firsthand experience.

I had been in the service of Sir Mycroft Holmes for many years, enjoying his company and building a strong friendship to complement my position. That time had seen his romance and eventual marriage to Mathilde Tesla, with her father Nikola soon after joining us in the Holmes family manor to pursue his research.

Sir Thomas showed no animosity to the old man. I truly believe he thought him novel and eccentric. I certainly found his inventions fascinating, up until the moment they killed him.

Admittedly, Lady Mathilde's sorrow was short-lived when it was discovered she was with babe. The cavern beneath the manor was locked up, and Nikola's inventions and discoveries were forgotten until a young Sherlock found them years later.

During the early years of Sherlock's life, the manor brimmed with love and humour. The young boy was bright, intelligent, and inquisitive. Something that Sir Thomas attributed to Mathilde's side of the family. The Holmes's were diligent and hardworking, but none had ever shown the level of inventiveness or a thirst for science that young Sherlock indulged in.

It was however that fateful day of young Sherlock's tenth birthday that everything changed for him.

The family was to attend a matinee performance of Alice in Wonderland at the Prince's Theatre in Piccadilly. In a private conversation with young master Sherlock, I found that he didn't want to go, but was doing it to make his parents happy. He stated he would rather attend the exhibition of variations of Watt's and Stephenson's steam engines that were being held at the Crystal Palace. I agreed and promised to ask permission to take him to the exhibit later in the week, which brought a wide smile to his face.

Sir Thomas expressly asked us to leave an hour earlier than the performance starting time, as he had to attend to some business at the Clydesdale Bank in nearby Plough Court. Sherlock and I waited in the carriage, while Sir Thomas and Lady Mathilde went inside. As master Sherlock and I talked about many things, he pointed to a dark carriage that approached and stopped directly outside of the bank.

I almost failed to even notice it until the young master pointed to the driver who wore a dark green balaclava over his face. When the four other men sprang from the cab, each wearing a similar face covering and carrying an unholstered pistol, I shouted in fear.

Glancing around for any sign of a policeman, I failed to notice the young master climb down from the buckboard and race across to the bank building.

Without a second thought, I jumped down, for I was lither in those days, and sprinted after him. I caught the boy just as the first shots rang out within. Holding him in my arms, I dragged him away from the entrance, moments before the doors sprang open and the first of the hooded men burst out and bolted towards the waiting carriage.

The other three followed each man carrying cloth sacks filled most probably with money. As the last man exited, I noticed two horrid details, he held in one hand, both a sack of money, and a long strand of pearls, and his shirt was sprayed with crimson though he did not look injured. He turned once and saw the two of us, our eyes wide in terror.

He brought his right hand up and aimed the pistol towards us. A thin line of smoke rose from the barrel, punctuating his immediate past deed. A cruel smile issued from the mouth hole of the balaclava, as the man thumbed the hammer closed on the pistol and said, "See you later kid," before he turned and joined his companions in crime.

Moments later the first whistles echoed across the area and men in dark blue uniforms appeared before racing towards the Bank. Still shaking in fear, young Sherlock stared up into my eyes and asked, "Mummy? Father?"

Taking him by the hand, for he had regressed to the little boy he was, we walked up the stairs and through the dark doors. I immediately regretted my actions and wish I could retrace those steps to this day. The image of Sir Thomas and Lady Mathilde lying on the floor, in a spreading pool of their blood, haunts me to this day.

In less than ten minutes, not only had I lost a pair of good friends, but the boy that would be entrusted into my care lost his parents and found his life forever changed.

Finally, after my memory finished, I gasped, "The Robin Hood gang?"

"Only if they've found the fountain of youth. They'd all be well into their sixties by now," said Master Sherlock, "Except of course the member I tracked down. He found his fate at the end of a rope."

That had been one of the first moments in Master Sherlock's life of fighting crime. Using his freshly honed skills to track down his parents' killer and bring him to justice. Something that the newly appointed Commissioner Lestrade was quite thankful for.

"Could it be someone using their old modus operandi?" I asked.

"Perhaps," he mumbled, turning, and grasping a small pair of tweezers before concentrating on the balaclava. Within seconds he withdrew a long slender filament of metal and placed it next to three others, and a single grain of what appeared to be black dirt.

"What have you got there, Master Sherlock?"

"At this stage I'm unsure," he said, "The black granule appears to be pure carbon, possibly coal. The other four pieces are threads of metal. These may have been picked up by the balaclava's owner either at their hideout or along the way. I'm hoping they will lead to a pathway back to the gang's location." Staring at the young master's face I didn't think he believed what he was saying at all.

"Did you get any sleep last night, Sir?"

"An hour or so," he shrugged, "I have much to do. I'll sleep later."

"You do remember what tonight is don't you?"

A confused look crossed his face, "No?"

"A charity event at the Iceberg lounge in Soho."

Master Sherlock's face screwed up in disgust. "I assume it's hosted by that horrible little man."

"Yes, Charles Augustus Milverton. Contrary to popular belief, he is supposedly a fine upstanding citizen."

"Not in my experience," scoffed Sherlock.

"Regardless, Sir, in your role as an equally fine upstanding citizen and one of London's leading businessmen, it would be well within your interest to attend, if only to be seen."

"Do you know who any of the other invitees are?"

"I did delve into the gossip pages of the paper to undertake my investigations. Nobody knows who is sponsoring the event, but it does appear that many of your contemporaries will be there plus members of academia from London University. My take on it has been that the benefactor wishes to facilitate investment in the University itself, by introducing some of the staff to these businessmen."

A grin appeared on the young master's face, "You may be onto something there, Watson, well done." Thinking for a moment, he then added, "Yes, I will attend. Make sure to have my suit ready, you just never know what will happen where Milverton is involved." I took that to mean more than just a gentleman's formal attire and went about my duties.

***

A *whooshing* sound, followed by a pall of steam loosed from the turbine at the front of the town car, announced our arrival before the Iceberg lounge. A red carpet, flanked by two long lines of braided gold rope, ran from the entrance of the building to the gutter where each steam carriage drew up and deposited its occupants.

As I exited and moved around to let Master Sherlock alight, I noticed a large group of less elegantly dressed people pressed together on the opposite sides of each rope chain. They were either there to catch a glimpse of any person of note or in the hopes of some titbit of currency being flung their way. Their encroachment onto the carpet was impeded by the bulk of two hefty, but well-dressed men. These were obviously two of Milverton's guards, simply standing there, with arms crossed and their backs to the crowds, forming a small but formidable guard of honour for the arriving guests.

Master Sherlock presented just as impressive a figure as his tall, athletic form stepped from the carriage. Murmured questions and gasps of recognition, with whispers of the name *Holmes*, issued from the crowd. Sherlock Holmes was, by virtue of his inheritance, the owner of one of the largest enterprises in London, but rarely entered into the public domain. The business affairs were managed by a long-time family friend and close confidant of Master Sherlock's father, leaving my ward time for himself and his own pursuits.

Stepping back into the car, I watched Master Sherlock ascend the stairs to the front entrance. I had urged him to bring a guest, but he had fobbed me off with his usual mutterings of wishing to remain unencumbered in case he needed to leave at a moment's notice. Having heard his protestations before, I reconciled myself with thoughts that he hoped to encounter Miss Adler, for I knew well that he harboured feelings for the woman, even though she dallied on quite the opposite side of the law as Master Sherlock walked.

At the top of the stairs, Master Sherlock was approached by a heavy-set man, who although short in stature and rotund in appearance, was dressed in an exquisitely tailored tuxedo, with a full white-tie accompaniment, finished off with a satin top hat. He wore a monocle over his right eye, which leant him a permanent sneer on one side of his face, but I noticed he had a long-stemmed cigarette holder clamped between his teeth to disguise the fact.

Charles Augustus Milverton, the owner of the Iceberg lounge, and host for the evening thrust one hand out to Master Sherlock who shook it amiably. I could only imagine the reaction of Milverton, were he to find out about Master Sherlock's other life. For it was via his nighttime activities, that a younger Holmes, just starting his crime-fighting career, had uncovered Milverton's secrets. The evidence gathered and presented to Commissioner Lestrade had relocated Milverton to Wandsworth Prison for a good two years and broken the back of a burgeoning crime syndicate. Supposedly, Milverton had used the last few years to re-establish himself and he now stayed on the right side of the legal system.

A loud, harsh honking from behind, broke me from my musings. Another carriage wished to set down its passengers. Engaging the gearing system and with one last look towards Master Sherlock, I lurched away with a belch of steam and coal smoke and headed for the allotted parking area nearby.

**

Irene Adler's eyes turned away from the elderly gentleman she'd engaged in conversation and settled on the figure at the entrance to the Iceberg Lounge. A smile crossed her lips as she studied the tall, handsome man, a direct contrast to the squat, rotund figure of Milverton at his side.

Sherlock.

Watching with amusement as Sherlock Holmes's piercing gaze scanned across every face within his vicinity and knowing too well that he would be scrutinizing and cataloguing details of each attendee in turn, Irene waited for him to pick her out of the crowd.

It wouldn't be too difficult, she believed, for Irene Adler had eschewed the frumpy look of her female counterparts, with their layers of fabric, and embraced the

fashions of the day, consisting of body-hugging leather and satin. To her, the skin-tight outfit was both a statement and complimentary to her line of work. To the many men in the room, it was a beacon, again proving useful to Irene's occupation, and made for a much easier source of introductions.

A rare smile broke out on Holmes's face as his eyes locked with Irene's. Turning to Milverton he bade the club owner farewell and crossed the floor, the guests parting in his wake, and was soon before Irene.

Standing to his full height, he bowed slightly, taking Irene's hand, and kissing it lightly. "Miss Adler, it has been some time."

Nodding, Irene replied with a grin, "In a public setting, yes it has." The memory of their previous encounter on the ramparts of the Tower of London, where Holmes had interfered in her attempts to secure the Hope diamond for a continental buyer with both physical force and intelligent reason, concluding in a mutual agreement to desist. Her client's outrage and communication to all and sundry within his circle had dented her reputation, but an anonymous deposit into her bank account the next day, matching the client's fee, had been most welcome.

"You are looking most resplendent this evening," Holmes added.

"And you do make a dashing figure," pausing slightly to punctuate her statement, "When appropriately dressed."

Before Holmes could respond with a suitable quip, the figure beside Irene cleared his throat, dragging their attention to him. Irene's eyes grew wide when she remembered the fellow she had been conversing with. "Oh, I'm dreadfully sorry. Professor Coram, this is Mr. Sherlock Holmes."

Holding his hand out, the gaunt man turned his dark piercing eyes up towards Holmes, and said, "I have heard much of you, Mr. Holmes. The bad news about your parents all those years ago."

Holmes was taken aback, mentions of his parents were few and far between given the time that had passed. "I thank you, Sir." Shaking the man's hand, he added, "Professor? Do I take it that you are resident at London University, or have you travelled from Oxford?"

"Pah, Oxford," the man sputtered, "London, for well over forty years at last count. I am the Dean of the Engineering Faculty." Waving a hand around the room, indicating the expanses of gaslights, clockwork engines, and steam lines running the length of the room, he dropped his head before adding, "All these gizmos and gadgets that have come from Watt's engines can be traced back to our work at the University." He sighed, "But, in our innocence, we allowed the designs to freely flow into the industrial complex. Damn stupid that." Looking up into Holmes's eyes once more, his gaze appeared sad, the intensity lost, "And that brings us here, with cap in hand to request monies from the likes of you." Holding up a hand to stop Holmes's immediate response. "I like it less than you would think, but we are at the mercy of industry and have lost many a good academic to employment within these new businesses. Even great minds need to feed their bodies."

"And as one who owes his existence to academia, I can concur with your thoughts."

Coram cocked his head slightly, "I don't follow."

"My grandfather. You may know him or have even worked with him. He was an esteemed academic at London University before he was mysteriously castigated for some affront and banished from the place."

"Who was he? I don't remember." Coram trailed off as a memory came to the fore.

"Tesla. Nikola Tesla. Grandfather on my mother's side."

His eyes opening wide, Coram stuttered, "My word. I never made that connection before. You are the grandson of Nikola Tesla?"

Before Holmes could answer, Coram glanced around, before bidding them adieu and making a hasty retreat.

"What was that all about?" asked Irene, "I hope you haven't scared off a potential client."

"Client? Or mark?"

Irene thought for a moment, "Considering that conversation, neither."

"He may be of no interest to you, but to me, he is a potential lead."

"Why?"

"As part of my private interests, I have been helping Scotland Yard."

"As always."

"Yes. You may have heard of two recent shooting deaths."

Irene's eyes grew wide. "My word, those Oxford professors?"

Nodding, Holmes added, "Yes, but both were originally from London University. The other aspect is that I was called to a break-in at the Bank of England. You wouldn't know anything about that would you?" Holmes studied Irene's expression for a moment.

Maintaining an innocence that belied her profession, Irene answered, "No details, just rumours."

"Rumours?"

"Yes," she said, taking a short sip from her champagne, "There's a new player in town. No idea who it is, but he wants to make an impression, shall we say, on the criminal world. What has Professor Coram to do with this? He's not even a businessman, just a simple academic."

"You were interested in him?"

"Yes, in a professional sense. A client is interested in something he possesses."

"Then we may have similar interests. Coram owned a security deposit box that disappeared in the robbery. His and two others."

"The two Oxford professors?"

Nodding, Holmes smiled, "Yes, well done. They belonged to Doctor Grimesby Roylott and Doctor Leslie Armstrong, both of the engineering faculty."

"You think they are linked?"

"Given they were the only boxes stolen, it seems likely." Looking around the room, Holmes said, "Now where has Coram gone? I feel the need to speak with him once more."

Stepping forward, level with Holmes, Irene nodded past him. "Seems to have found someone else to talk to."

Coram was visible through a pair of open doors in the far wall. He stood just outside on a small patio, talking animatedly with another man.

"Do you know his companion?" asked Holmes.

"No," said Irene, staring at the short, rotund man, "Another academic, by the looks of him."

As they both studied the two men, the sharp retort of gunfire shattered the scene. The tall figure of Professor Coram fell forward, knocking over his companion, and crashing to the paving stones, a fine spray of crimson splattering the stonework. Screams, shouts, and cries erupted from around the room. In their panic, people ran away from the open doorway, pushing and shoving others out of their way, regardless of their identity.

Dropping to the floor at the sound of the gunshot, Irene slowly composed herself and stood up. Glancing around, she found herself alone. Sherlock Holmes had disappeared, the only evidence he was ever there was his jacket, shirt, and tie lying discarded nearby. Her eyes moved to the open doorway, and the corpse lying on the ground outside.

***

At the moment the sound of the gunshot reached Holmes's ears, he took in as much of the details of the assassination as possible. In his mind, time slowed down as his eyes flicked across the scene. Measuring the angle of Professor Coram's head as it snapped back from the impact and projecting the path of the bullet as it flew towards its victim.

Within seconds, his jacket, shirt, and tie were falling to the floor as Holmes sprinted towards the open doorway. Stopping for a moment, he glanced in the perceived direction of the shot.

Across the road sat a three-story building. Holmes spied movement in the darkness on the rooftop. Pulling his mask from a hidden pocket in his dark-coloured outfit, he quickly pulled it on, covering his identity, before sprinting across the street. Angling his trajectory to match the path of his target, he quickly closed in on the corner of the building.

As he ran, Holmes pulled one of his many devices from his belt and aimed it towards the roofline. A sharp *snap* was followed by a small piton dart streaking out, trailing a thin, but immensely strong, line of metal strengthened rope. A second later, the dart buried itself deep into the brickwork of the upper story, followed by the line rewinding, pulling Holmes up the building as he ran. A casual observer would have witnessed the incredible sight of a dark-clad man sprinting up the side of a building with giant strides.

Holmes leapt the last stride, vaulting onto the roof and landing with his feet against the sloping slate tiled roof. He let go of the device, letting it clatter against the wall, its purpose fulfilled.

The man in Holmes's sights had reached the corner of the building and was tossing a rope, fastened to a chimney stack, over the edge.

"Stop."

He turned at the sound of Holmes's gravelly voice, a wide grin crossing his face. "Ah, the great detective," he said, slowly raising his hands to reveal he still held the rifle used to cut short Professor Coram's life only moments before.

From the lean, athletic figure, and broad handlebar moustache, Holmes was quick to realise who he was dealing with. "Colonel Sebastian Moran, if I'm not mistaken. World-renowned hunter, a former member of Her Majesty's Army, and as of late, an assassin for hire."

Chuckling, Moran answered, "You have me at a disservice, Sir. You know my name, but I cannot tell yours."

"We'll leave it at that for the moment," said Holmes, "I cannot contemplate any connection between you and Professor Coram, so can only deduce that you are on contract." The clanging of bells echoed up to them, followed by the squeal of brakes as several steam carriages, containing London's finest, slid to a stop in the streets below. "If you tell me who your client is, I'm sure I can arrange it with the Yard to alleviate your sentence somewhat."

Moran took a glance at the gathering beneath them before turning back to Holmes. The smirking grin grew on his face as he stepped up onto the low brick parapet. "My sentence," Moran chuckled, "If the Yard captures me, I'll be swinging in the breeze within a matter of hours. Besides, I may not know your identity, Sir, but are you not the world's greatest detective. He says you are anyway."

"Who is he?" asked Holmes, a hint of frustration leaking into his tone.

Moran laughed out loud. "I think he may be wrong. If you haven't deduced it already. Or at least determined where to find him."

"How could I do that?"

"You were at the Bank of England, were you not?" Moran took Holmes's silence as an affirmative. "Well then, you have everything you need to reckon where to find him."

Filled with confusion, Holmes failed to notice Moran glance up once, then down, before shifting backward. Holmes darted forward, just as the assassin stepped back and dropped out of sight.

"No!" Holmes shouted, reaching the now vacant spot.

The loud drone of several large engines burst from above. Holmes glanced to the heavens to see a large, black airship hovering high above the roof and slowly ascending away. A long, black, rope ladder trailed out from the belly of the behemoth. Within a few seconds, the smiling figure of Colonel Sebastian Moran, clinging to the rope ladder, rose above the roofline of the building, passing within a few yards of Holmes.

"Sometimes it is convenient to have friends in high places, Detective." Waving his free hand at Holmes, he added, "Until we meet again, which I do hope won't be too soon."

With a roar of propellers, the airship lurched, pointing upwards and rising quickly away. Within moments, it had disappeared from view, leaving only the softening whirring sound of its engines in its wake.

As Holmes watched the dark object slowly fade from view, his mind kept replaying the last moments of his conversation with Moran.

I should already know his location.

"But how?" he spat into the night.

With a roar of propellers, the airship lurched, pointing upwards and rising quickly away.

***

The drive back to the manor was rather silent, with Master Sherlock brooding in the rear of the car for the entire journey. I attempted to prompt him for more information about the evening, especially the appearance of the gigantic, black airship, that stole away with the prime suspect. With his continued silence, even under my barrage of questions, I finally gave up and drove the rest of the way in quiet myself.

Before I had even finished the shutdown sequence for the car, dropping the steam pressure slowly to avoid stress on the engine, and bringing the boiler temperature back down to compensate, Master Sherlock had exited and disappeared from the garage. It was times like this that I wished we could develop another of the electric motors that Master Sherlock had fitted to his night carriage so that we could avoid the tedious routines required to start and stop our town car.

After setting Master Sherlock's jacket, shirt, and tie, in the laundry room for later cleaning, thankfully rescued by Miss Adler, I prepared a light snack and some coffee. I had seen these moods before and knew that my ward would set his mind to a deduction for hours without ceasing. I felt he would need nourishment, as I didn't believe he'd had time to partake at the soiree.

As I placed the tray on a small table near Master Sherlock's workbench, I found him hunched over his powerful magnifying glass, staring at the green hood, and the tiny fragments he had discovered.

"I have brought you a light supper, Sir, and some coffee. I thought some nourishment might stimulate your thought processes." I received a simple grunt in return. "Is there anything that I can help with, Sir?"

"What?" said Holmes, finally recognising that I was standing there. He peered up from the glass, first at me, then at the food, then back to me. "Sorry, Watson, that Moran fellow has me confused. He knew about the Bank. He knew that I had been there. That leads me to believe that it was all orchestrated in advance, just to force my attendance. If so, then this," he indicated the hood, "Is the vital clue. But how? There is some sort of riddle here, but I can't put my finger on it."

I noticed something written on the chalkboard nearby and gazed past the young master to see that five sets of letters had been written on it; Sn, Sb, Zn, Mg, and C. I determined that they were connected to the four filaments and black grain that he had discovered on the hood. Even from my rudimentary knowledge of the sciences, I recognised them as chemical symbols. Tin, Zinc, Magnesium, and Carbon. I had no idea of the fifth.

Turning away from the board, my eyes lifted to the large copy of Mendeleev's table of elements affixed to a board on the wall nearby. I found the symbol Sb and realised it was antimony, a nugget of information that may never prove useful again but would stay with me. Each chemical symbol had a number written below it, above them, Master Sherlock had added his number, giving the set of symbols a regular progression and order.

"Master Sherlock, do the numbers have any meaning? I mean in the context of your riddle?"

Sherlock's gaze joined mine. I chanced to glance back at him and saw his eyes widen. He jumped from his seat, and picking up some chalk, redrafted the series of symbols with the smaller numbers sitting above, and the larger numbers below, before stepping away to examine the chalkboard. Pointing at the sets of numbers, Sherlock said, "This series that I have added is a new system currently being determined by a young scientist called Mosely. They are being called the atomic number. The other series are the atomic weights."

"I still don't know what the significance is."

"Moran said, I would already know where to find him."

"Do you know what he meant?"

"No, but..." Stepping up to the board again, the chalk sang, the five atomic numbers, fifty, fifty-one, six, thirty, and twelve; separated and written near the top. Moving away again, Sherlock stared at the numbers for several moments, before speaking. "It's the where. Where to find him." Finally, a broad grin broke out on Sherlock's face. "Do you know the latitude and longitude of London?"

Shaking my head, I answered, "No."

Moving to a large bookcase nestled against the rock wall, Sherlock returned with a leather-bound volume and placed it on a table. Opening it to a map of London, he pointed at the lines running across and down the page. "Zero longitudes. The Greenwich meridian. Latitude fifty-one." Glancing at the numbers, he calculated in his mind, then pointed at a spot on the banks of the Thames near Wapping. Fifty-one degrees, fifty minutes, and thirty seconds north, zero degrees, six minutes and twelve seconds west."

"Isn't that the location of that monstrous new building?"

A broad smile crossed Sherlock's face. "Yes, yes, it is. The Reichenbach tower. Well done Watson, I believe that's where I'll find this mysterious villain."

***

The almost silent night carriage whirred through the streets of London, slipping past surprised onlookers, whose stark, wide-eyed looks suggested their memories of the craft would stay with them for years to come.

Sherlock Holmes slowed down as he reached the building site of the Reichenbach Tower, parking the carriage in the darkness of a side alley out of reach of the waning moonlight, and exited. Standing in the near-black shadows, he blended almost seamlessly with the gloom, only his mouth and chin visible.

Staring up at the building, he formulated a plan.

The Reichenbach Tower was a marvel amongst the newly assembled marvels of the modern age of London. Harnessing the power of steam had leant the last vestiges of the Industrial Revolution a renewed vigour, producing machines of immense complexity, and buildings taller than ever before. No longer was St. Paul's Cathedral the loftiest structure of the city, that honour now stood with this newest of skyscrapers.

It stood fifteen stories high, constructed of dark, black brick, and rimmed with brass and steel plating. The very top consisted of a circular, disc-shaped penthouse, comprised of curved windows running around the entire floor, purportedly giving the lone occupant a full view of the city below. The strangest part of the top floor was the way the penthouse's wall extended well beyond the supporting structure below it. It leant the building the appearance of an enormous candle holder as if the penthouse was waiting for any wax dripping from a towering flame above. It was the huge black airship hovering a hundred yards from the circular room that convinced Holmes the villain was here.

He wants me here. To kill me? No. Moran could have killed me easily. There's something else.

Scanning the shear side of the building, Holmes concluded that climbing the outside was a fool's errand. He'd need to scale the lower floors, then enter and ascend via the internal stairways.

Noticing a small balcony running around a part of the second floor, he brought out his scaling device and pointed it towards the building. With a sharp *snap*, the piton fired out, trailing a fine black line. Holding the device, Holmes vaulted quickly up the side of the building and onto the balcony.

To his surprise a pair of glass and metal doors stood wide open, begging for him to enter. Unhooking and replacing the piton device on his belt, he stepped cautiously in through the doors.

The entire floor was empty, ready for whatever business would eventually be undertaken there. The wall adjacent to the balcony was dominated by a pair of open-cage style elevators, and an entranceway into the stairwell. A single electric light glowed above the stairway; the only light on the entire floor.

Electricity? Not gas. This becomes more intriguing.

Holmes approached, scanning from side to side for any obvious, or indeed hidden, traps. Convinced that his host had no intention of harming him, he entered the staircase and began to climb.

At each exit doorway, Holmes stopped and scanned the floor beyond. For several floors, the area was dark and empty, sending him upwards. He continued to climb until the staircase stopped, presenting him with a closed door and no further route up.

Slowly pulling the door open, he found a darkened room beyond. Stepping inside, the door slammed shut as soon as he let it go, the inside had no handle, and pushing against it only assured him that he was locked inside the room.

Suddenly, several lights illuminated, casting a bright glow around the room.

Holmes's eyes were immediately drawn to the loud clicking of a clock above a door at the other end of the room. The clock was set to two minutes to midnight. In his mind, the time was significant and represented a countdown of some sort. The pipe sitting below the clock proved it. The sound of gas escaping came to Holmes's ears. Sniffing, his eyes grew wide.

Almonds? Cyanide.

Launching towards the door, he soon realised it was stuck fast, and any amount of strength would not dislodge it before the countdown ran out.

Looking down, he saw a small table sitting by the door. It held a single long knife.

Is that it? Death by my hand? Or by poison?

Scanning the room, he noticed other objects. A settee lay along one wall. A single-throw cushion at one end. Against the other wall sat another small table. It held a chessboard with several chess pieces arranged along one side. Above the chessboard was written the words: *None shall take another.*

Holmes stepped over to the chessboard. There were seven queens arranged along one side, with a vacant square in the middle.

One's missing?

Studying the board for a moment, his head snapped around to the settee, and then the knife. Snatching the knife up, he moved quickly to the settee and slashed at the cushion, pulled the stuffing out, and found a small, but hard object inside. Another Queen.

Racing back to the board, he placed the chess piece down and studied the board.

None shall take another. Queens can take other pieces in any direction, except…

Moving the first piece forward two squares, he realised the concept. Each queen needed to sit on a square where they could not take another queen. Glancing at the clock, which was closing in on one minute to midnight, Holmes turned back to the board. Moving several pieces, he scanned the board once more. The fifth and seventh queens were in line.

Damn.

Resetting the pieces, he tried again, redistributing the pieces in an almost circular pattern around the board. A feeling of accomplishment filled him until he saw two on the same diagonal.

Frustration grew in his mind, a glance at the clock only caused more, twenty seconds left. Taking ten seconds to study the board and bring his breathing under control, Holmes reset the pieces, bringing the fourth queen towards the centre of the board, and shifting the sixth further away. Five seconds left; a hissing sound penetrated the silence. The cyanide was building. A quick movement of the first and seventh, then the eighth piece, and Holmes was sure it was done. Two seconds.

No.

Dragging the third piece to the seventh row, just as a clock chimed midnight.

I did it. Why is it chiming?

As the third stroke sounded, another loud click emanated from the door as it sprang open revealing another room beyond. Relief swept across Holmes as he stepped up to the doorway and entered the room. A loud hiss followed him as the gas streamed from the pipe, forcing him to slam the door shut, cutting off any escape back into the chess room.

Staring around the darkened room, Holmes found a feeling of disorientation filling his mind. Light flooded one side of the room as electric globes flared along the adjacent wall, drawing his attention. A door sat in the middle of the wall, the only other visible exit from the room. Noticing writing on the door, Holmes moved across to read it.

There were seven three-digit numbers written in three rows and columns. With three questions marks in the bottom, right corner.

813	274	596
672		384
549	836	???

As he read them, a cacophony of *squeals* and *groans* erupted from behind. Turning towards the sound, his eyes grew wide as he spied a room-wide steel grid-shaped frame grinding its way across the floor towards him. Each vertex of the grid sported a long metal spike, pointed directly at the opposite wall. Holmes judged he had two minutes until the spikes were on him.

Reading the door again, he noticed the set of numbered buttons situated a foot below the puzzle. A frantic minute passed in which Holmes calculated sums and differences, then performed several permutations and computations. Nothing made sense.

The squealing began to play on Holmes's mind, filling him with annoyance, something alien to his mindset. His preferred method of contemplation was calm, in a quiet location, with ample time to dwell on the problem at hand.

Cursing himself, he closed his eyes for a moment, took a deep breath, and stared at the numbers again. A pattern formed. The top row and left column contained every digit, once. Quickly, he pressed the one, two, and seven, corresponding to the missing numbers in both the bottom row and the right column.

A loud *clack* broke through the squealing noise, and the door snapped open. Holmes pushed through into the next room, just as the metal spikes ground into the brickwork on the other side of the wall.

Closing the door, Holmes readied himself for the next trial. As the lock clicked into place, lights flared all around the room, revealing it empty save for an ornate brass caged elevator in the middle of the room. Scanning the floor for any obvious traps, Holmes moved to the elevator and examined it. Nothing seemed untoward, and the elevator presented the only visible exit from the room.

Stepping into the cage, Holmes braced himself for the next phase of this adventure. Immediately, the door swung shut and the grinding of gears echoed out from the walls as the cage ascended through the floor into the room above.

Within a minute, the cage door opened onto the floor of the large circular penthouse. The line of windows looking out across the London skyline was mostly dark given the time and the height of the tower. At one point the windows gave way to a pair of doors, thrown open to the night. A small platform led out, suspended above the drop below. Through the doors, Holmes could see the shape of the large airship, waiting to be called into service. He understood it was common practice to leave airships tethered when not in use but seeing this one floating free left him with a feeling it was being kept ready for immediate use or escape.

He discerned movement off to the right and suddenly several lights flared around the room, throwing brightness across a tall, gaunt figure as he stood up from his desk and moved forward. "Ah, Mr. Holmes, welcome. I'm so glad you could join me."

Still feeling slightly annoyed, Holmes interjected, "A welcome doesn't seem to have been your intent. Not after those two death trap rooms."

"Oh, pish, a man of your intelligence and wit would never have fallen foul of those simple riddles. I merely use them as a form of insurance to stop would-be thieves making their way to this chamber. I never for a moment believed you would succumb." With a flick of a hand towards Holmes, "I think you can dispense with the mask. I discerned your identity a while ago, and you confirmed my deductions yourself when you appeared at the Iceberg lounge and conversed with that Adler woman. "You really should be more careful of your associations. Modern technology is a wonderful thing. I had listening tubes installed all around that room before I organised that little shindig last night."

"Who are you?" Holmes cut the man off. The face, gaunt and skeletal, with a simple whisp of thinning grey hair, was in no way familiar. "And how did you come by the technology to generate electricity?"

"Ah, yes, I apologise. I am Professor James Moriarty."

"Professor?"

"Yes, London University. Mathematics. Though I left there over twenty years ago. Haven't taught or undertaken research since."

"Were you there when Professor Coram attended?" Moriarty nodded. "Roylott and Steinmetz?"

"Well of course, and before you ask, your grandfather also. I knew Nikola Tesla quite well. In fact, I helped in the development of that coil device of his. He charged me with determining a lot of the mathematical equations surrounding the transference of electricity through the air. Though we never completed the project. It was

124

Tesla's designs that helped me build my own version of the electricity generator, and of course these wonders," he waved a hand at the lights embedded in the ceiling.

Holmes spun, scanning the room. Apart from the light bulbs, the ceiling held a vast network of cables, running in concentric circles, with several thick knots of cable crossing from the edge to the centre and dropping into the midst of a complex series of box-like machines.

"Ah, good," said Moriarty, "You've guessed. Quicker than I thought."

"This entire room is a larger version of Nikola's coil." It was a statement rather than a question.

"Yes, it is."

Studying the array of dark boxes, Holmes added, "It doesn't work." Turning back towards Moriarty, he noticed a grin cross the old man's face.

"Not yet, no. That is why you are here."

Before Holmes could react, two burly men stepped from the darkened gloom at the other end of the room and grasped each of his arms, pinning him between them, he struggled, but rather than enter a physical battle calmed himself. There were more important facts to glean. "Me?"

Pulling a key attached to a gold chain from his vest pocket, Moriarty stepped towards the machine console, inserted the key, and turned it. Immediately, lights sprang awake across the face of each box-like device. "Why yes. You have a working model of this coil. You brought it back to life after your grandfather was killed." Waving his hands around the room, he raised his voice and said, "This. This has been my dream since those days at the University. I, Nikola, and those three buffoons put this design together two decades ago. We saw the coming of the steam age but knew that there was untapped potential in electricity. The inventions that your grandfather designed and built. Engines that could harness the power of the electron. And this, this coil, designed to transmit that energy through the air."

Moriarty stepped up toe to toe with Holmes and stared straight into his eyes. "I have spent the last twenty years building an empire."

"A criminal empire, including the green hood gang. You were responsible for killing my parents."

Faltering at the accusation, Moriarty stepped back. "Not directly, I assure you. Yes, I financed them and took my cut. I used their signature to gain your attention, but what does that matter. The purpose of my enterprises was to accrue money, to build this. Your grandfather dreamed of building a coil of this size, to transmit electricity freely to all of London."

"But you have other plans."

"Well, of course, dear boy. I'm a businessman. Once society realises the potential of electricity, they will toss these steam machines aside." Bringing his hand up level with Holmes's eyes, he closed it into a fist. "Once they have a taste, they will become addicted to it. They will need more, and there will only be one source."

"You?"

"Me."

"But it doesn't work."

"Yet." Pointing a finger at Holmes's chest, "That is why you are here, Mr. Holmes. You fixed your grandfather's prototype. You run this," he waved a hand at Holmes's costume, "This second life on the electricity generated and dispersed through your grandfather's coil. You have already embraced the technology, but you hide it in that cave of yours."

Holmes's eyes grew wide. "How do you know so much about me?"

A nonchalant wave of a hand. "Oh, come on Sir, once I realised who you were, it was a simple matter to send spies into the bowels of your manor house once you left, like on the previous two nights. They returned with explicit details, which matched the knowledge I already had of your grandfather's toils, and your extension of his ideas and dreams. Tonight, you will do that for me."

"Why? Why would I do anything for you?"

"Oh, you won't be doing it for me. You'll be doing it for yourself, and of course the citizens of London."

"That's very magnanimous of you, but I thought the aim was to enslave the populace to your production and delivery of electricity."

Moriarty let out a small chuckle, "Oh, you misunderstood me it seems. When I meant you would be doing for the citizens, I didn't mean providing a means to gain electricity, I meant to stop this enormous bomb from wiping out the entire east end of London."

"What?"

"Did they never tell you how your grandfather actually died?" Moriarty waited, studying Holmes's confused expression. "It was when he tested his coil. The power grew so rapidly it sent an out-of-control pulse through that underground cavern beneath your house, killing him instantly. Whatever you did had solved that problem." Moving back to the console, Moriarty flicked several more switches. Lights flashed up and down several of the rows. "The same will happen with this version. Unless," stepping back, he grinned into Holmes's face, "You repeat what you did and you save all those people, plus you will help engender a new age. The age of electricity."

"I refuse."

"Then you will die along with thousands," Moriarty shrugged, "I will simply invade your manor house and retrieve your design. I'm sure my engineers will have no problems emulating it." Without another word, Moriarty turned away and walked slowly towards the airship platform.

Holmes watched the old man move away. The man that had caused his parents' death. The man that hired an assassin to kill seemingly innocent university professors. The man who would kill thousands to coerce someone into helping him against their will.

"Moriarty," Holmes yelled.

The Professor stopped, slowly turning back towards the detective. "You wish to help willingly."

"No, I just want to know. Why have you had your old friends killed?"

"Oh, simply revenge. They mocked me and caused my dismissal. I thought they could be useful, I presumed they had Tesla's missing designs, but no. Plus, they are the only other people that know about this coil. Eliminating them was simply logical." Looking past Holmes towards the console, Moriarty smiled and pointed, "You might want to turn your attention to that. It won't be long now. And you can't turn it off, this is the only key." Showing the activation key, before putting it back in his pocket, the old man turned and stepped out onto the platform. Reaching into a pocket, he brought a small gun and fired a flare towards the black airship. As the orange flash burst across the sky, the loud whir of engines echoed back.

Can't let him leave. Must bring him to justice.

Holmes pushed left, raising his right foot, and lashed out, kicking down with the flat of his boot into the knee of the man on his right. *Crack.* The man howled with pain as his knee shattered and let go of Holmes's arm, falling to the floor.

Spinning, Holmes blocked a punch from the left-hand man, then drove his right fist into his throat. The man gagged, clutching at his neck with both hands. A kick followed, striking him in the chest and sending him sprawling. The drone of engines filled the area, as the airship arrived to collect Moriarty.

Holmes looked towards the exit doors, Moriarty was stepping towards the gondola of the airship, within a moment he would be away and out of reach. Sprinting towards the open doorway, Holmes pulled a device from his belt and held it out before him.

As he reached the platform, the engines roared, turning the craft around and moving it slowly away from the building. Moriarty stood in the gondola's doorway and shouted, "You don't have much time Mr. Holmes." His smiling face turned first to surprise, then fear, as Holmes raced towards the end of the platform, pointed the device towards the ship, and pulled the trigger.

The piton raced across the gap, piercing the skin of the airship just above the head of the stunned Moriarty. Leaping into the air, Holmes retracted the line and landed deftly next to the professor.

"I didn't see this eventuality," said a shocked Moriarty.

Snatching at the gold chain, Holmes tore the key from Moriarty's pocket. "Firstly, I need this. Secondly, you must face justice." Throwing an arm around Moriarty's waist, Holmes lifted the lighter man and jumped from the airship's gondola. The device fired once more, sending its piton towards the Reichenbach building as both men plummeted towards the streets of London.

Lodging in the metal skin of the coil, the device retracted dragging Holmes and Moriarty quickly through the open space and dumping them onto the wooden platform. The key and chain were knocked from Holmes's hand and skittered into the darker room beyond.

Both men picked themselves up, Moriarty turning to stare at the great airship as it gently veered away. Suddenly, the massive stern engines roared into life, blasting all with a high-powered vortex of wind. Moriarty was driven towards the edge of the platform, his arms windmilling as he lost balance and fell. Holmes dived forward, grabbing Moriarty's hand as he disappeared from view.

"I've got you," said Holmes, straining to bring the older man back to the safety of the platform.

"To take me to justice? I think not," said Moriarty, a smile creeping onto his lips. "Dying at the end of a rope was never part of the plan." With a cackling laugh, the glove Holmes held emptied, and Moriarty's form quickly disappeared from view as it plummeted towards the streets far below.

"Damn," said Holmes, losing sight of the old man within seconds.

***

"But the authorities found no corpse?"

Nodding, Master Sherlock said, "No. When I'd finished stabilising the coil, I made my way back down and could find no sign of him either."

"Very strange."

"Indeed."

"But what of the coil and the building?"

"I have undertaken to purchase the building as part of my company. A team of engineers will examine the coil, using the design of my oscillation dampener that stopped the explosive pulse, as a basis. I truly believe I can complete Moriarty's work, or should I say, my grandfather's work, and create a source of energy that can be shared with millions."

"Nikola would be proud of that."

A smile grew on Master Sherlock's face, "Yes, Watson, I believe he would. And I will rename the tower."

"To what?"

"My grandfather's notes and designs had a single name assigned to his proposed transmission tower, and I think it would be fitting to use the same name."

"And that is?"

"Wardenclyffe."

The Strange Case of the Unicursal Hexagram

"It... it wasn't there yesterday," said a distraught Lady Marjorie, as Holmes leaned in to examine the strange design on the basement door. "I became fed up. We have a dinner party at the French Embassy tonight. Sheldon locked himself in there four days ago, and I hadn't heard a peep out of him since."

"Does he do that often?" I asked.

"Oh, yes, silly man. Normally he will at least accept trays of food and answer when I call, but this time nothing for the last three days. Wilson, our butler, said that the food goes untouched. Such a waste."

"And this symbol. You stated that it appeared this morning," asked Holmes.

"Oh, yes, as I said, I'd become fed up. Normally, I'm happy for Sheldon to go off on these little hermit holidays of his, but we needed to prepare for this evening. I asked Wilson to bring the keys and unlock the door. To both our astonishment, as soon as the key entered the lock, that horrid symbol appeared."

"What does he do down there?" I asked.

"Oh," Lady Marjorie's shoulders deflated, in an expression of resignation, "He's found religion."

Glancing back at the symbol, I couldn't place what religion it belonged to. The design was a hexagram of sorts, in the shape of two overlapping and interconnected triangles, not unlike a Star of David, but with the top and bottom points extending well beyond the rest. In the middle was a flower, or a sort of five-leafed clover.

"Have you ever seen anything like this before, Holmes?"

"I can't actually place it, at this stage," he said, "If it is religious, I would say it belongs to one of these strange new esoteric cults."

I nodded in agreement. I'd read of many new religions springing up. It seemed that any person with half a mind could hang a shingle and call himself a priest or prophet of his own religious order. "Something like those Swedenborgians or that Eliphas Levi fellow?"

It... it wasn't there yesterday.

"Exactly," said Holmes, turning the key still set in the keyhole. It wouldn't budge. Pulling it from the lock, he examined it closely, then leaned in and studied the lock itself. Nodding, he turned back to Lady Marjorie, "Have you had your man check for other keys, just in case this is the wrong one?"

A voice piped up from nearby, "Yes, sir, I did." It was then I noticed the butler standing at a polite distance and just out of sight.

"It's a Beddows lock, put in there by Sir Sheldon himself. He kept one key for himself and gave the other to me, for just such an occasion."

"Intriguing, then, that it doesn't work now."

"Yes, sir, it was annoying. I did offer to bring in a locksmith or even break the lock, but Lady Marjorie preferred a less destructive approach—and was also worried about the master's extended absence. That's why she requested help from Scotland Yard."

It had been an unlikely caller to 221B Baker Street that prompted this entire episode. Holmes and I had been ensconced in the morning papers, enjoying our mid-morning repast, when we heard the bell downstairs. Within moments, Mrs. Hudson had shown the tall, but stout, figure of Inspector Bradstreet into our parlour.

Dropping his paper on a side table, Holmes had risen and met the policeman with some enthusiasm, possibly hoping for another intriguing quest. "Ah, Bradstreet, to what do I owe this pleasure? I do hope something hasn't befallen young Hatherley again?"

"No, Mr. Holmes, nothing like that," Inspector Bradstreet replied, though his demeanour showed a touch of embarrassment at approaching Holmes for assistance. "I've been assigned to a queer case in Kensington, at the residence of Sir Sheldon Tallinger."

"Tallinger?" replied Holmes, shaking his head, "I can't place him."

"Nor I," I piped in. Searching my mind, I failed to find any notable information about the man in my memories from reading the society pages.

"No, quiet family, keep to themselves. Retired from military service, went into some sort of manufacturing business. Retired from that now, as well. It seems to be his normality that's the key."

"Why do you think that?" Holmes asked.

"You'll see when we get to his house."

Within half an hour, we found ourselves standing in the Tallinger house, looking at the strange design on a stubbornly locked door.

"I had one of my best men here," said Bradstreet. "Tried everything, even pulled the faceplate off, but the locking mechanism is stuck fast. I suggested to Lady Marjorie that we may need to break through the door, but she insisted we do everything we can to avoid that. I know that it's probably a simple mechanical problem, but given that symbol, plus the fact that the lock is not that old and seems completely undamaged, I thought you may have some insight."

"Hmm, I will admit that I'm not as intrigued as I thought," said Holmes, his patience a little strained as such a seemingly simple problem. Shrugging, he drew out his lock-picks and set to work. After several moments, and several murmurs and harrumphs, Holmes packed them away and stood staring at the lock.

"Anything, Holmes?" I asked.

"I reverse my previous comment. This is intriguing. None of my picks went even close to opening this one." He looked at the key once more and shook his head slightly. "Yes, from the arrangement of the tumblers within, this is indeed the key to that lock." Inserting it again, he jiggled it several times, before withdrawing it once more. Shaking his head, he said, "This is extraordinary. The key fits. The lock is in good condition. There is no mechanical reason for it not to work." Grasping the doorknob, he turned it and pulled. The door didn't move even slightly. Letting go, he said, "The only way to get through this door is to remove the lock altogether, but I'm not even sure that will work. We may have to break the door apart."

"Even if you tear the wall down, you will never enter that room." The voice that spoke had a deep, resonant tone, one that suggested compliance without any tinge of force.

All three of us spun to face the speaker. I would have placed him in his mid-thirties. With a plain, smooth face, and shock of dark hair, but it was those eyes that held me. There was an intensity in his virtually unblinking stare that drew my gaze to his and held me there until I forced my sight away.

It was Bradstreet who broke the spell. "Who are you, sir? How did you arrive here?"

"And more to the point, what did you mean by saying we will never enter this room?" asked Holmes, his tone less forceful than Bradstreet's.

"To answer the Inspector's questions first. I am Simon Iff. I was invited here by Sir Sheldon."

"When?" interjected Bradstreet, "And where is Sir Sheldon?"

"It was only this morning. And if the message was clear, Sir Sheldon resides within that room."

"What?" sputtered the Inspector, "How could he have messaged you? If he's in this room, he hasn't left for days."

Iff replied, with a calm, but assertive voice, "That is true. His spirit visited me and asked me to assist. We are associates."

"His spirit?" cried Bradstreet, "What twaddle. Are you some sort of spiritualist? Come here to prey on Lady Marjorie and Sir Sheldon, or something?"

Holding his hands before him palms up, Iff shook his head and said, "I assure you, Inspector, I am neither a spiritualist nor a charlatan. I do, however, know what that symbol is. It is a unicursal hexagram. We use this particular version as a potent locking mechanism, but only in extreme circumstances. Even with all your intelligence and experience, I doubt you would even be able to break its spell."

"Spell?" Bradstreet's voice had risen in pitch to the point where he might lose all control if left unchecked. Thankfully Holmes stepped in at that moment.

"Inspector," he said, snapping Bradstreet's attention to himself, "You know me as a man of logic and science. I would have no truck with any self-proclaimed spiritualist or magician, but on the odd occasion I am happy to let someone of that ilk have their time in the sun, if it proves useful."

"What are you suggesting?"

"Let Mr. Iff here break this so-called spell and allow us entry into the room beyond. If he fails, then we send him on his way; if he succeeds, then we have gained. He has asked for no money." Turning to Iff, he asked, "I assume you would not ask for recompense?" When Iff shook his head, he added, "Then what is there to lose?"

"Fine."

Smiling, Iff stepped up to the door, examining almost every inch in the same way that Holmes had only moments before. After a minute or two, he dropped one hand into his pocket and brought out a small metal rod, with a crystal attached to one end. Placing the device in the centre of the flower, he closed his eyes and bent his head forward. A deep murmur arose from Iff, as he spoke in a strange language for several minutes, occasionally moving the device to the six points of the hexagram, then back to the centre.

It was on the third rotation of the metal wand around the hexagram, that a sharp, metallic *click* echoed out from the door. Grasping the doorknob, he turned it and pulled the door open. A breath of stale, foetid air blew up from the dark basement below.

"Candles," Bradstreet yelled at the surprised butler, who rushed off and quickly returned with two fully lit candelabras. Snatching one for himself, Bradstreet hurried to the head of the staircase and began the descent.

I offered to take the second, leaving Wilson on the ground floor, rather than force him to follow us into the bowels of the house.

Trailing after Holmes, I stepped carefully down the steep staircase, and into the chamber below. Bradstreet found the nearest gas lamp and lit it, throwing light across the room.

"GoodLord," I gasped, at the sight of a man lying in the middle of the dusty floor.

"Watson, would you be so good as to test for life signs? Be careful not to disturb anything that may help my investigation, though," asked Holmes.

Handing him the candelabra, I dropped to my knee next to the body. Placing two fingers on his neck, I waited. Nothing. Leaning over I listened intently at his mouth. Again nothing. Foolishly I hadn't brought my bag, leaving it for several home visits I needed to undertake in the afternoon, so turned to Holmes and asked to use his glass. Holding it against the man's mouth, it remained clear for some time.

Shaking my head in sorrow, I gave the glass back to Holmes, before placing my hand on the man's forehead. It was still warmer than the room temperature. Finally, I stood, my head hanging slightly.

"I believe we are too late. This man has no pulse or breath, but he is still warm. I can only conclude that he died almost within the last hour or so."

"Damn," said Bradstreet, "That damn stupid door. We could have saved him. How will I break the news to Lady Marjorie?"

Holmes continued to gaze at the man, without a change in expression. As if staring at a curiosity rather than the corpse of a man who had breathed his last so recently. "Have you nothing to add, Holmes?"

"Not yet, Watson, not yet. You say that he was alive while we were still toying with that infernal door?"

"Possibly, he may have perished just before we arrived. Why?"

"Well, I think he's been lying here for quite some time, possibly ever since he entered the basement and locked that door."

"Why?"

"There are several candles scattered around that have burnt out, and there's a light covering of dust on his person."

I looked back and realised he was right. He had lain completely still for some time to accumulate such a covering. "If he'd been there for so long, why did he only just die?"

"Of that I am unsure." Pointing to the floor beneath the body, Holmes added, "And this design inscribed on the floor. It seems similar to the unicursal hexagram on the door. What do you make of it, Iff?" We both turned to look for the stranger but found no one else in the room.

"I could have sworn he followed us down here."

"I also," said Holmes, "How peculiar."

"I apologise, I was too concerned with the body to take any notice of that man," added Bradstreet.

Glancing around the room, I finally took in the full details around me. Behind us was a large bookcase filled with thick leather-bound texts, and an array of strange objects, some similar to the metal wand that Iff had used. Before the bookcase was a desk, covered with open texts and loose sheets. Moving closer I recognised a diagram of the unicursal hexagram. "Here, Holmes, these may help."

Stepping up next to me, Holmes scanned the open documents and said, "They may, except for the strange language they are written in. I would need to seek out one skilled in that script." Looking closer at the texts I realised what Holmes was on about. Beneath the various diagrams were blocks of text written in a strange form of lettering, which may have been another alphabet, or even some strange form of code.

***

While Bradstreet oversaw the arrival of the coroner's wagon, and the removal of the body of the poor unfortunate Sir Sheldon Tallinger, Holmes and I undertook interviews with the house-staff. As far as we could see, there was only Wilson and Charles, Sir Sheldon's valet, on duty in the house. The latter provided a spark of interest in Holmes's mind.

"Do you find it a little peculiar that there are only two house staff? And no cook? Especially in a house of this size, with an ageing matriarch such as Lady Marjorie."

"I feel that retirement has not found Sir Sheldon in the best of times, so to speak."

We found Charles downstairs in the laundry, shining SirSheldon's shoes, and pressing his shirt and suit. From my observations, Charles looked like a man who'd spent quite a deal of time, the previous evening, imbibing at one of the local pubs. His eyes were downcast and half-closed, his movements slow and stilted, as if to avoid any head shaking.

"If I were you, I'd find some time to yourself and have a good lie down. You could also try placing a wet cloth with a little vinegar sprinkled on it, across your forehead," I said."Should relieve a little of that pain you're feeling."

The valet slowly looked up from his duties, his eyes crossing both of us in a confused manner. "You're not police, are you? What have I done now?"

"Nothing, as far as we know, but what do you think you've done?" asked Holmes.

Dropping his head, the valet stared down at the clothes laid out before him and said, "I don't know what I'm even doing now." He pulled a stray piece of lint from the lapel of Sir Sheldon's morning coat, and added, "I'm preparing a dead man's suit for his funeral, but I feel like I'm preparing my dismissal from this house." Shrugging and turning towards us, his eyes slightly damp, as well as bloodshot, he added, "I'm sure I saw him last night. It could be the drink, but he was

138

outside the house, large as life. And then this morning Mr. Wilson says he's dead." Thumping the bench with his fist, he exclaimed, "What's to become of me now?"

Trying to calm the poor man, I said, "I'm sure that Lady Marjorie will ensure you are taken care of, at least in the short term. You were Sir Sheldon's valet, is that right? That leaves you in good stead for another position with a suitable gentleman."

"I'm also his driver. I also help out Mr. Wilson, as footman, and between the two of us, we take on the cooking duties. It's the only way we get fed."

"Ah, a man of many talents then," said Holmes, "Did Sir Sheldon step out on many occasions? Perhaps to his club, or some other societies?"

Thinking for a moment, Charles wiped his moist eyes on his sleeve, before answering. "He didn't frequent any clubs. Lady Marjorie put a stop to that a few years ago. I heard they couldn't afford the memberships. Of late, Sir Sheldon's only excursions were to the temple."

"Temple?"

Staring at the blank wall opposite for a moment, "The Herminatic Order of the Yellow Dawn, or something like that. Had me drop him off in a rundown building off the Clapham high street, Nelson's Road, or something. He'd be there for hours, a couple of times a week."

"Do you know what he did there?" I asked.

"No. I wouldn't stay around. He told me to be back at a certain time, so I'd go down the pub or come back here, there's always things to be done here. He never discussed anything. I suppose you could ask Lady Marjorie, but pretty sure she wouldn't know either."

I could see Holmes thinking for several moments and could only imagine the cogitations going on inside that brain before he asked another question. "You mentioned that you saw him last night, but surely you knew he was locked in his basement room."

Glancing up into Holmes's passive countenance, Charles paused for a moment, collecting his thoughts, before answering. "I... I know it was probably the drink, but I swear I saw Sir Sheldon outside in the yard. It was late and a dense fog had rolled in. I'll admit I'm lucky I managed to find my way back inside the house. I'd had a few at the Ladbroke, down in Notting Hill, and made my way down the back alley. Pitch black it was, but Mr. Wilson always leaves a light on in the kitchen, just in case. It was when I opened the rear gate that I saw him. He was moving around the yard. At first, I thought he was a burglar or something. I shouted at him, but he just ignored me." Taking a deep breath, he paused once more. "And he was glowing. That's the only way I knew it was Sir Sheldon. He turned around, and looked straight through me, but I could see his face as plain as day. He seemed lost. Looking at him filled me with sadness. Like I'd lost all hope. Then he just disappeared. Took a while for my eyes to adjust back to the darkness, but all I could hear was my heart thumping in my chest. I made my way inside as fast as I could, went to bed and hid under the blankets. By this morning I'd recovered, but I'll never forget that look on his face. And now I'll never see his face again."

When Charles hung his head once more, staring at the suit before him, Holmes and I mumbled our thanks and left him to his sorrow.

"What do you make of that, Holmes?"

"Intriguing Watson, intriguing. There's nothing to say that our victim wasn't playing a prank. You have estimated the time of death, so it would seem that Sir Sheldon was alive at the time Charles arrived home. That's if he even saw anything other than a vision formed of his alcohol intake." Glancing down the tight corridor, Holmes added, "I wish to return to Sir Sheldon's basement room. There's more to see in there, I think."

"I need to leave, as I have several errands to attend to and patients to visit this afternoon."

"Very good."

***

It wasn't until morning on the following day that I laid eyes on Holmes once more. His slow movements and red-rimmed eyes, with dark shadows beneath them, told me he'd had a very late, and sleepless night.

"Are you well, Holmes? You look as if you've patrolled the streets all night after some felon or other. I've warned you about these late nocturnal endeavours."

Sitting and waving away my protestations, Holmes fixed himself a cup of coffee, downing and refreshing it quickly before he finally found the focus to reply. "I spent all yesterday afternoon and evening at the Tallinger house, before taking to the streets in search of answers."

"Did you find any?"

"Yes and no. The questions that keep arising are the most troubling aspect."

"Fill me in then. What happened?"

"After you left, I waited with Bradstreet as the coroner arrived, made his assessment, then removed Sir Sheldon's body to the morgue. There was nothing more either of us could add, though the coroner did come to a similar conclusion as yourself."

"And that was?"

"The poor man died within hours of our arrival. A thermometer confirmed that his body temperature was still quite high, in light of the cool nature of the room. He applied similar techniques as you, listening with a stethoscope for any heartbeat or breath. There was no indication of life. The internal examination will be performed later today, so hopefully, a cause of death will be found."

"Damn shame we weren't quicker then."

"Perhaps." He drew another sip of coffee. "When all had left, I spent the next few hours poring over Sir Sheldon's papers and books."

"From my cursory inspection, he was dabbling in the black arts or some such."

Holmes chuckled. "Not quite. I tried not to take too Christian a view of the works in his possession, but rather a more disconnected look. The books and papers were not of some satanic nature, but of an obscure religious doctrine which is being discussed by some, apparently, under the suggested title of Thelema. Some texts that you saw were in a strange language, others were in English, German and French."

"Thelema? What nonsense is that?"

"It appears to be one of the more esoteric of the new wave of religions that have arisen over the last few decades. Thelema is not yet a full 'philosophy', but an undercurrent which draws on several ancient ideas, from the Egyptian, Greek, and Eastern yoga, and the more modern Qabalah. The ideals behind the movement are not that far removed from Christianity, Judaism or even Islamism. It's the practice that has changed."

"In what way?"

"The open texts on Sir Sheldon's desk point to several rituals whereby the practitioner can seek a higher plane of consciousness through meditation, incantations and the use of herbs, or medicines."

"Drugs?"

"Oh, yes. That may be the key that the coroner will need to seek out. There were many pots of burnt herbs scattered around and containers of powders and liquids on several shelves that would need examining. Probably only stimulants, but possibly poisonous in nature, which could account for Sir Sheldon's demise. I have sent a note to Bradstreet to have them examined."

"Have you drawn a solution?"

"Not as yet, but I feel that Sir Sheldon undertook a course of stimulants, then dropped into a meditative state in search of this higher plane of consciousness. During that experiment, his body gave up and he died, possibly after a few days of oblivion."

"Horrible."

"Yes, but even more disturbing, I'm not completely convinced that he is actually dead."

"What?" I blurted out, horrified at the suggestion.

"It was while I sat reading through those strange texts," Holmes began. "The room grew colder, even though Wilson had stoked a fire for my convenience. Looking up, my sight was drawn to a cloud of fog that had formed in one corner of the room. Perplexed, I studied the mist as it collected and coalesced into an almost human form. The figure floated gently across the space, coming to rest in the centre of that strange symbol. It did not become distinct enough for me to ascribe any identity to it but stayed for several moments before simply vanishing."

"A ghost? You're describing a ghost? Impossible."

Waving my protestation away, Holmes continued. "Highly improbable, I would say, but until we have proof that such cannot

142

exist, I would not call it impossible. As we know there are many strange occurrences in this world, many we have investigated ourselves. Most are a result of simple natural causes, but some have evaded explanation."

"But, you're saying that this spectre—Ghost? Vision?—is Sir Sheldon's spirit?"

"Not exactly in those words, but such is implied in my readings of the Thelema texts completed so far. The adherents of the religion practised a form of meditation that enabled their spirit to escape their physical form and wander the world." Holding his hands palms up before him, he added, "Now, I cannot imbue any credence in that philosophy without further data, so I feel I need to investigate until I can dismiss or prove its existence. In all probability, it was simply a parlour trick involving light and the thick clouds of dust in that room."

"Highly irregular," I said. "But why do you believe that Sir Sheldon is still alive?"

"Ah, that also lies in the texts. There is an explanation that the meditation process, coupled with herbs and other substances, will lower the respiratory system to that of complete hibernation. The effect is that the person will appear, in all regular circumstances, to be dead."

"Preposterous, I examined him myself. So did the coroner."

"Yes, but think back, for how long did you search for a pulse?"

"About thirty seconds. No need after that."

"And breath?"

"The same."

"Did you know that a hibernating bear will breathe once every minute? The heart follows the same pattern, beating only once the animal breaths. If we assume that Sir Sheldon had fallen into a hibernating state, then it is possible that his respiratory system is following the same pattern."

"But…I…that…"

"No need to be incensed, Watson, it is a reasonable suggestion and no smear on your professionalism. It would also account for Sir Sheldon's body temperature at the time." Downing the remainder of his coffee, he stood. "I have sent an urgent telegram to Scotland Yard, but have heard nothing. It is my imperative to seek out the coroner and stop Sir Sheldon's autopsy." Checking his watch, he added, "I just hope we are not too late."

***

At the Yard, we learned from Inspector Bradstreet that Sir Sheldon had been taken to the Royal Brompton Hospital in Chelsea—and that a warning not to begin the autopsy had indeed been despatched, as Holmes had requested. Bradstreet was a little concerned with our presence, and our questions, and chose to accompany us.

Sadly, the coroner was not present when we arrived, forcing us into an interminable wait seated nearby. Bradstreet attempted to hurry up the proceedings by plying the interns and nursing staff with questions, but none seemed to possess any knowledge of the workings within the morgue.

To pass the time, Holmes filled Bradstreet in on all that he had discovered. By the end, the Inspector's face was aghast in horror.

"What you are suggesting is preposterous," he said.

"Echoes of my words," I added.

"As I told Watson, I will not discount anything until I have proof. Much of what I read suggests that Sir Sheldon placed himself into a drug-induced hibernation. All other aspects should have logical solutions which can be established at a later date. For now, the unfortunate victim is our primary concern."

Just as Holmes finished, movement at the end of the corridor caught our attention. Thankfully, it was the same coroner from the previous day, followed by two burly interns who carried a stretcher between them. The bulging of the sheet over the stretcher indicated another unfortunate soul was on his way to the morgue.

As the coroner drew close to us, he stopped and said, "Inspector Bradstreet? Mr. Holmes?DoctorWatson? To what do I owe this pleasure?"

Holmes butted in before Bradstreet could begin. "Sir Sheldon? I have reason to believe he has not passed but is in a deep hibernating state." Pausing for a moment, he added, "I simply hope I'm not too late and that you haven't undertaken an autopsy as yet."

Strangely, the coroner's face broke into a wide grin. "Remarkable that you are here. I stayed late last night to catch up on my workload. Staring down at Sir Sheldon's reposing form, I held my knife above his chest ready to press it into his flesh, when his mouth opened, and he took one long deep breath. To be honest, I was flummoxed. Snatching up my stethoscope, I stood and listened for almost a minute before a single heartbeat echoed from his chest. I've never seen anything like it in my life."

Relief flooded all three of us.

"Where is he now?" asked Holmes.

"We've moved him to a private ward. A doctor has been assigned, with nurses keeping an eye on him around the clock."

"Any change in his condition?" I asked.

"Not as far as I know, but for now it is out of my hands. I was going to drop by later. He's in ward 2C."

After the coroner left, we followed Inspector Bradstreet to the ward. He found the attending doctor and plied him with questions while we stayed back and waited. Finally, Bradstreet joined us.

"I think every person in this hospital finds it remarkable that Sir Sheldon is still alive," he said. I noticed a wry smile on Holmes's lips.

"What are their plans for him?" he asked.

"Well, he is stable, if unresponsive. They feel that he has slipped into a stupor, from which he may or may not emerge. Until they can observe him for several more days, then they are not concerned." Shrugging, Bradstreet added, "My next course of action is to return to Kensington and inform Lady Marjorie." Glancing back at the bedridden man, he added, "Though, I am unsure if having her husband in this vegetative state for some time will be better or worse than having him simply die. I have known of others like this. They simply hang on to life for years, causing nothing but misery to their families with the unknowing."

"Yes, a sad state of affairs," said Holmes. "Though, I feel that we may be able to bring this to a conclusion in a much swifter manner. I need to return to Kensington myself. The answers lie in those arcane scripts of Sir Sheldon's."

"We can ride together, but I must make a short trip to Mayfair on the way. In fact, you may as well come with me."

"Why? Another case?" I asked, hoping that there may be more for Holmes to be occupied with.

"Yes. The sad passing of Sir Hubert Mumford, though from the report I received earlier today, there does not seem to be any foul play. The poor man simply had a heart attack overnight. I have heard he was old and rather portly."

***

"Who was he?" I asked Bradstreet, as we stood in Sir Hubert Mumford's study and watched the coroner's attendants remove the rather overweight figure from the room. Even though they were both well-built lads, they strained to lift the dead man's bulk onto the stretcher and carry it from the room.

"An industrialist. Owned and until recently ran Mumford's Gearing, an engineering business that had a large concern in the rail industry."

Holmes held up a hand to the attendants and asked, "Might I have a quick look at something?" They both groaned as they stopped, bending to place the corpse-laden stretcher once more on the ground.

"What in the devil are you doing?" asked Bradstreet.

"Won't take a moment," Holmes said, moving across to the stretcher and dropping to one knee. He drew the sheet down to reveal the final expression on Sir Hubert's face.

"Good Lord," I exclaimed. As the coroner had covered the body before we arrived, we hadn't been privileged to see the unfortunate man. The stark look of horror on his face was as disturbing as it was incredible.

"He looks like he was scared to death," said Bradstreet.

"That would account for the sudden heart attack, even with his obvious level of fitness."

"Why did you feel the need to look at his face, Holmes?" I asked.

Pointing to the far wall, Holmes said, "That certificate of business registration."

Stepping across I read the framed document, proudly displayed on Sir Hubert's wall. I gasped as I saw the name of the company. "*Tallinger and Mumford engineering*," I read out loud.

"Yes. I think with a little digging, we might find that Sir Hubert's business enterprise was once a partnership. Possibly one that changed recently to benefit him more than his previous associate."

"Sir Sheldon," said Bradstreet, "That's a little too much of a coincidence."

"Quite so," said Holmes, "I think now might be the appropriate time to speak with Lady Marjorie."

***

"He's alive? But, Doctor Watson," Lady Marjorie exclaimed, pointing towards me, "And the coroner. They both said my poor Sheldon was gone."

"Yes, it was only after a more detailed examination that life signs were found. He is being cared for at the hospital and I will keep you informed if there is any change in his condition," said Bradstreet.

Staring at the cups of tea, in light of the stunning news, I stood and suggested that Lady Marjorie may require something a little stronger. "Brandy?"

Glancing up towards me, a slight wetness in her eyes at the hope her husband would be well again, she nodded. Looking around I noticed Wilson was not in sight, probably off undertaking another of the myriad tasks he would need to fulfil given the lack of staff. Moving to a nearby sideboard, I was delighted to find a small set of glasses and bottles hidden away from sight.

Pouring a stiff drink for our hostess, I brought it back and was surprised to see it vanish in one gulp. "Thank you, Doctor, my heart is still fluttering," she said before holding up a hand, "But I think that should do me for now."

"I'm sad to say, though, Lady Marjorie, that our visit here is not all good news," began Bradstreet, "We have just come from the house of Sir Hubert Mumford."

"That cad," came a spiteful reply, seemingly out of character from the lady of the house.

"You know him then?" asked Holmes.

"Yes, I know him." She held the glass out towards me, "I think I will have another; my mood has altogether changed."

I rushed away to pour another glass, while Bradstreet continued. "Unfortunately, Sir Hubert is dead. Possibly a heart attack," he added.

"Good riddance to bad rubbish," said Lady Marjorie, accepting the glass from me and downing the brandy in another swift drink. Pausing for a moment, she placed the glass down and looked at each of our stunned faces in turn. "Oh, don't think of me as so callous. Sir Hubert is no saint. It is because of him that we find ourselves in this parlous situation. All that my husband built up over so many years was spirited away by that man, leaving us near destitute in our dotage."

Glancing around the room, she added, "This house will be next. It is all we have left."

"Can you tell us what occurred," asked Holmes.

"Yes, I have let the cat out of the bag, so I must finish. My husband and Hubert built up Tallinger and Mumford Engineering over many years as partners. My Sheldon was older and reached a point where he believed he had earned the right to retire." She hung her head before the next statement, shaking it sadly before adding, "But Hubert was always the legal man. He drafted a contract with Sheldon to procure our half of the business. Thinking all was in order, Sheldon, my trusting Sheldon, signed everything without reading it. It wasn't until our accountant called to examine the books, that we even realised what had happened. That scoundrel had deposited only one-tenth the value of the company into our account. A mere pittance, but so easily disguised by dropping a zero from a figure."

Pulling a small kerchief from her sleeve, she dabbed at the corners of her eyes. The memory was obviously still very raw and painful. "We spent five years with lawyers and judges trying to overturn the contract. But, Hubert," her face screwed up as she said the name, "had employed better lawyers. The contract was unbreakable. The payment stood, but it only covered the costs of the legal representation. We were almost destitute. A life of toil washed away with too much trust and the stroke of a pen."

"My word," I said.

"I know it hit my Sheldon quite hard, not that he would say anything, mind, but I could see it in his eyes and in his stance, especially on days that found him more despondent than normal. He did talk of fixing things at times, but I knew my Sheldon, and I thought that meant only that he would find the money somehow."

Leaving Lady Marjorie, we spoke briefly in the entry foyer before Bradstreet bade us goodbye and left. I thought about joining him but instead followed Holmes to the basement room.

As he stepped up to the bookcase, overflowing with tomes, many showing their age, with aged and cracked leather bindings, I glanced around the room once again. With the body of Sir Sheldon now removed, I could clearly make out the design painted on the floor. It was similar to the unicursal hexagram we had seen on the door upstairs, but instead of a five-leafed clover in the centre, it sported a cross where each side was the same length.

"It's a simple design change. The Thelema religion seems to thrive on the hexagram itself, with the central motif instilling the usage. The cross seems to be of Greek origin, but I think that is just a coincidence. It could be a plus sign for all I can determine."

"Have you discovered what this Thelema doctrine believes to be the symbol's purpose?"

"Oh, yes, it is used as a doorway into the astral plane."

"The what?"

"The astral plane. The world between worlds, where the spirits live out existence once they have been shod of their earthly bodies."

"Surely you don't believe that."

A fey grin crossed Holmes's face as he stood staring at me. I began to feel uncomfortable as my mind raced that perhaps Holmes was buying into all this crackpot spiritualist guff. Finally, he spoke. "No, of course not Watson. Don't be foolish. There is nothing I have seen, nothing in these books and diagrams, that provides me with enough evidence to believe that a man's spirit can leave his body and walk amongst us."

"Good, good," I said, very relieved, "You almost had me there."

A strangely familiar voice echoed out of the far side of the room. "You might need to rethink that position when I'm done."

We both turned as one to see the same mysterious man from the previous day. "Ah, Mr. Iff," said Holmes, "I do hope you've come to return those items you seem to have borrowed."

"Very good, Mr. Holmes," Iff said, sliding a worn, leather-bound volume from a satchel slung around his shoulder. The book was plain except for the Roman numerals, XXXVI, embossed on the front cover. "You may not know the name, but this is *The Star Sapphire*, volume thirty-six of the intended sacred Thelema texts. Or it will be when Crowley and others have finished."

"I can only assume it is the volume that contains the spell used to resuscitate our poor unfortunate Sir Sheldon."

"Supposedly. Intriguingly enough, I've never seen it used. Sir Sheldon is the first member of our order to actually attempt astral projection. I discussed it with the head of our order, and he was most infuriated, especially when I pointed out that Sir Sheldon had *borrowed* several volumes of the sacred texts." Reaching into his satchel, once more, Iff brought out a metal rod with a small cross affixed to the top. "This is Sir Sheldon's personal magick rood. We all have one; you probably saw mine yesterday when I broke the spell on the door outside."

"I assume your order believes that those can channel your power, or some such."

A slight grin broke on Iff's face. "Yes, you could say something like that. Though I would have to assume that non-followers, like yourselves, would place as much faith in that idea as an antelope would place in a lion."

Holmes nodded, a sly grin on his face. "A curious analogy, but with merit. Why did you choose to return at this precise moment?"

"Ah, now that is interesting. Up until these last two days, I had very little to do with Sir Sheldon. I'm relatively new to our order, and I'm not exactly well set within polite society, but our head priest has taken me under his wing, so to speak, and has tasked me with developing certain deductive skills. One of the associated tasks is to undertake information gathering about other members. Sir Sheldon was one such member."

"Oh, yes," said Holmes, "And to what ends was this information-gathering exercise directed?"

"Nothing illegal, or even immoral by your standards, just precautions. Ours is a very new religion, and therefore comes under greater scrutiny, especially from more established theological organisations."

"Such as the Protestant and Catholic churches?"

"Precisely, so we need to ensure all our members are protected from any salacious inquiries."

"And what did you find out about Sir Sheldon?"

"Ah, yes, our poor Sir Sheldon. I'm only young, so do not have the experience to understand the pain of losing everything that you have worked for during virtually your entire life, but I can imagine an immense sense of despair and animosity has lingered inside Sir Sheldon over the last few years as events have played out."

"I agree. I've seen that sense of hopelessness play out in the most dramatic of ways many times. What more do you know?"

"I know that a certain Sir Hubert Mumford has passed away unexpectedly."

"Good Lord," I said, "How would you know that?"

"I have my ways, Dr. Watson."

"But you had nothing to do with it, I assume?" asked Holmes, his grin had vanished, replaced with a stern countenance.

"And I assure you, that I did not. The poor man was in ill health, his heart simply waiting for any chance to give up. It may or may not have been due to a spectral visitation from the subject of our discussions."

"Sir Sheldon?"

"Yes. I think his resentment towards Sir Hubert overcame him, and he resorted to means that few should even conceive of, let alone enact. The order has tasked me with bringing him to trial before them."

"How do you envisage doing that?" I asked.

"With your help, and that of Inspector Bradstreet's," Iff said, matter-of-factly.

***

"This is all very distressing," said Lady Marjorie upon hearing Iff's request, "I mean, I don't even know who you are, Mr. Iff."

"And that is fair, Lady Marjorie, I can only ask you to trust me, as a member of your husband's religious order. I truly believe that I can reverse the process that your husband has used, thereby bringing him out of his self-induced stupor."

The woman studied the younger man's face for quite some time until Holmes intervened.

"If I may, Lady Marjorie, at some point, I'm sure that Sir Sheldon would need to be brought home from the hospital, if not for financial as well as health reasons. He is in no danger, and his convalescence would be more assured in his own home."

Nodding, she said, "I can see that point. Especially from the financial. Though I'm a little livid at Sheldon for his foolishness."

"I would be more than happy to lend my services to ensure that your husband is made comfortable and well-cared for here," I added.

Heaving a large sigh, Lady Marjorie added, "Fine, then. I shall have Wilson prepare the spare room. I only have one request though; I wish to be present at this *ceremony*."

***

The next few hours were a flurry of activity.

While Iff went into the basement to prepare, Holmes and I journeyed to Scotland Yard to discuss matters with Inspector Bradstreet.

"Spirit? Ghost? Have you gone mad, Holmes?" Like myself, Bradstreet was incredulous when presented with Iff's story.

Holmes, in his inimitably calm way, preceded to soothe Bradstreet's initial anger. "Understandably, Inspector, this is all very peculiar, and I can appreciate your concern. Regardless of what this Iff character says, the delivery of some curative through the casting of this so-called spell may be what is required to restore Sir Sheldon to full health." Pausing for a moment to let Bradstreet decipher his intent, Holmes added, "Besides, we have questions for Sir Sheldon. The strangely coincidental death of his long-time business partner, for one."

"But the coroner himself has signed that off as a mere heart attack."

"And I wouldn't question his findings, but I'm intrigued by any outside forces that may have triggered that heart attack." Holmes took a deep breath, and I could tell that something was troubling him. "I must admit that I have investigated this Simon Iff and he is an enigma. His history is minimal, and the links to this supposed religious sect are vague at best. I don't understand his interest or even his motives in this matter."

"Yes, the Yard has been keeping a close eye on the Hermetic Order of the Golden Dawn for several months, especially an up-and-coming fellow called Crowley, who seems to be making his mark in their circles. Apart from improprieties due to the hedonistic nature of their gatherings, there's nothing we can actually pin on them from a legal perspective." A stern look crossed Bradstreet's face. "Do you think this Iff fellow can restore Sir Sheldon?"

"We can only try. From my reading of the texts, regardless of the religious significance, Sir Sheldon imbibed a strange concoction of toxins that rendered him into a state of deep hibernation, one that modern medicine treats simply as a prolonged stupor. There may be some restorative benefits to the reverse *spell* that is worth trying."

"Fine with me. I'll accompany you to the hospital and we'll arrange transportation. I'm sure they'd be happy to free up the bed."

Two hours later, an ambulance transported Sir Sheldon to the Kensington house, with the two orderlies settling him into his new room. Even with Bradstreet in attendance, we were wary of attracting too much attention to the goings-on and decided to move Sir Sheldon once the ambulance had departed, at which point I assisted Charles in moving his master once more into the basement.

As we descended, I spied Lady Marjorie sitting in a comfortable chair off to one side. I felt a tinge of anxiety over her presence, nothing to do with the subject matter, just the nature of what may happen to her husband.

Engaged in setting several pots of pungent herbs on each of the hexagram's points, Iff noticed our arrival and motioned for us to place Sir Sheldon on the floor, his head and feet positioned to run along the longest axis of the design. Iff placed the magick rood, which he had retrieved during his last visit to this room, on Sir Sheldon's chest, and moved away.

Charles left the basement, taking the borrowed hospital stretcher with him. I quietly moved across to join Holmes and Bradstreet, our eyes all focused on Iff, intent on watching the *ceremony* play out.

The adept of Thelema struck a match and lit each of the small bundles in quick succession, filling the small space with the cloying but sweet scent of the burning herbs. He moved and stood near Sir Sheldon's head, before extending his arms and speaking in some strange, unknown tongue.

"Fahf adept mgep epgokafahf shuggog."

I held back a slight chuckle. The guttural tone of this strange language was almost comical in the way Iff uttered it. Holmes turned and gave me a slightly angered glance, before turning his eyes back towards Iff as he continued.

"Throdog ehye. Hafh fahf shuggoth back l' h' orr'enah ahna. H' uh'e h' gotha nogephaii. H' ymg' ah nyth'drn. H' ahor uh'eor ahnyth ph'nglui h' bthnk."

Pausing for a moment, Iff threw his head back, his eyes closed, beseeching whatever pantheon of Gods his religion venerated.

"Nogephaii h' hai!Nogephaii h' hai!" This last incitement shouted much louder than the rest.

I still swear that the lights dimmed somewhat as if a dark pall or cloud enveloped the room. Then a brightly glowing orb of blue light shone out from the far corner of the room. I know I gasped, and I could hear others inhale in astonishment.

The glowing sphere grew until it was the size of a football. It moved across the room, floating halfway between floor and ceiling, and headed towards the prostrate form of Sir Sheldon.

As it hung in the air above the body, Iff proclaimed another stream of unintelligible words. *"Vulgtmnah ulnah ahf' ymg' ah hai. Nogephaii h' l' c'."*

Slowly, the orb descended towards the body. Casting a dull blue glow across Sir Sheldon's pallid skin, before touching his chest and sending waves of blue light into his body. Dropping further, it seemed to enter his body, and within a moment, the globe disappeared completely, leaving only the strange blue glow on Sir Sheldon's skin.

"*Ymg'ah ehye ephaii,*" said Iff, his voice softer. He moved around and knelt near Sir Sheldon's chest, lightly tapping him on the cheek. "Sir Sheldon. Wake up. You are back in your body."

As shocking as the blue orb had been, what I witnessed next shocked me even more. The eyes of the man, who only yesterday I had pronounced dead, fluttered, and opened.

Their gaze flicked around the room, before finally settling on the face of the man above him.

"Iff?" Sir Sheldon croaked. "What in blazes are you doing here?"

"Welcome back, SirSheldon, now please take your time to gain your senses once more."

"Take my...?" said the older man, as realisation dawned on his face, "Oh, Lord, I did the Star Sapphire spell didn't I?" When Iff nodded, Sir Sheldon dropped his head and muttered, "Damn fool. What was I thinking?" Holding out an arm, he told Iff to help him to his feet. Standing unsteadily, he scanned across the faces in the room. "Who the devil are these fellows?"

Iff quickly introduced us, but Sir Sheldon only had eyes for his poor, unfortunate wife. Taking one step forward, he held out a hand towards Lady Marjorie. "Oh, Maggie, I'm so sorry, I've been such a fool. I believed I could change things, or at least find out how to get our money back." It was then his head snapped back towards the three of us, realisation dawned on his face. "Holmes? The Detective? Bradstreet? Scotland Yard?" His mouth dropped open. "Is he dead? I think he spied me. The last I saw of him, was his hands clutching at his chest. Then I was lost to the void once more." Grasping at Iff's shirt lapel, Sir Sheldon's eyes bulged as he asked once more, "Is he?" As Iff nodded slowly, Sir Sheldon gasped, "What have I done? Even he didn't deserve that." Suddenly, he let out a groan, his hands leaving Iff and grabbing at his chest, as his face screwedup in excruciating pain.

The old knight dropped to his knees with a sickening *crack* before toppling forward. I ran to my medical bag, which I'd made sure to bring this time, not wanting a repeat episode. Dashing back to the fallen man, I urged Holmes or Bradstreet to roll him onto his back. Listening for a much longer period, my head dropped when there was no evidence of a heartbeat.

"Damn," I mumbled under my breath, before reaching into my bag for a syringe. I'd read of small doses of nitro-glycerine being used for the treatment of heart attacks and kept a dose for just such an emergency. Even after the needle emptied into him, Sir Sheldon's body refused to comply. It was a miserable period of time during which I tried all manner of treatments to bring the man back to the land of the living, but this time my diagnosis was correct.

Finally, I turned towards his widow, shook my head slowly and said, "I'm so sorry, Lady Marjorie. There's nothing I can do for him this time."

Instead of an outburst of tears or wailing, she simply stood, looked down at the reposing form of her husband and said, "Damn idiot," before climbing the stairs and yelling back over her shoulder, "Wilson, it's dinner time."

To be honest, I was flummoxed. "Good Lord."

"I think she may have tired of Sir Sheldon's pursuit of Sir Hubert and had already grown comfortable with the fact he was dead or in a prolonged stupor before we brought him back to life, that is," said Holmes.

"Where's Iff?" asked Bradstreet.

Looking around the room, I was surprised to see that the young devotee of Thelema had disappeared. Holmes moved across to the large bookcase and indicated the now-vacant shelf.

"It's not just Iff that's disappeared," he said, "All the Thelema texts have joined him."

"He stole them?" asked Bradstreet.

"Well, according to Iff, Sir Sheldon had already procured them from the Temple, so technically Iff has simply reclaimed them."

Blowing out a lungful of breath in a long sigh, Bradstreet glanced around the area and said, "I have no idea what I'm going to write up about this little escapade. I can't even see an actual crime. Not one that my superiors would believe, anyway. That said, I can't believe what I saw here tonight. Blue lights. Spirits supposedly reinhabiting their bodies. Magic spells. None of it makes sense."

"Only if you look for the impossible," said Holmes. "At its simplest, we have a man who accidentally induced a stupor upon himself. One of his fellow compatriots knew the concoction of herbs that would bring him out of that stupor. The only problem was that the health of the subject was not great and he possibly suffered a heart attack because of it all and died."

"The lights?"

"I'm sure I could find evidence of some simple parlour tricks if you'd like me to investigate. They may have been set up by Iff when he was alone down here."

"Hmm. No matter; do so for your own interest's sake. What about Sir Sheldon's statement of causing Sir Hubert's heart attack?"

Shrugging, Holmes said, "In that, we have no physical evidence. There are no witnesses. Sir Sheldon believed he could leave his body to haunt Sir Hubert. Wishful thinking on his behalf, but pure coincidence is the more likely culprit."

"And Iff?"

"A charlatan, perhaps? But no reward was sought or given. The texts? Perhaps you could pursue him over those, but I feel that they probably do belong to the Golden Dawn. So, again, there does not seem to be any evidence of a crime. I doubt that Lady Marjorie would be willing to press any charges over the matter."

Bradstreet harrumphed, before saying, "I am embarrassed. I feel like a complete dolt. I brought you into this and simply wasted your time. I will think hard before doing such again."

"Don't worry yourself, Inspector. Though we haven't uncovered a crime, I have learnt so much about this strange esoteric religion and ideology that it has been worth my while. I may never use the knowledge, but am still richer for the experience."

"Good, then," said Bradstreet, though I did not feel that he was altogether satisfied. "I will give my condolences to Lady Marjorie before organising for the coroner to call again. "Good day, sirs, and I hope we meet on more favourable terms next time."

As we bid adieu to Bradstreet and listened to his footsteps climbing the stairs, I turned to Holmes and asked, "Do you believe anything you've just said?"

"Now, Watson, that's very cynical of you."

"I mean the blue lights. The whole spiritism thing. The magic spells. True or completely fake?"

"Now, you know me, Watson. I never discount anything until I have facts and evidence. I'm not even sure I will find evidence of chicanery, but I'm not even sure I want to. Perhaps leaving it at that will leave me hungry for more knowledge in future."

"The locked door?"

"That, I think, was a trick using magnets or some such. I'd need Iff's magick rood, to trigger off any hidden mechanisms within that door."

"And this Simon Iff character?"

"Ah, an intriguing man. Shows up at the most opportune times. Seems to possess information that he shouldn't. He's only young, but I think that he has an interesting future ahead. I certainly will be keeping an eye out for anything relating to him from this point on."

With that, we left. My last view of the basement was the unicursal hexagram with its even-sided cross drawn in the middle. A nagging feeling still clung to the outer reaches of my mind, that there was something lying just a little outside the knowledge of ordinary man in all this esoteric doctrine. Like Holmes, I wondered if we would ever again encounter Simon Iff, Thelema, or other members of the Hermetic Order of the Golden Dawn.

The Disappearance of Dr. Markey

It was in late July of 1887 that I found myself extremely occupied with quite a number of patients. Sherlock Holmes, however, found himself in quite the opposite situation. A dearth of interesting cases has plunged him into a drawn-out period of boredom, in which I caught sight of him, on many occasions, unclasping the catch of his neat Moroccan leather case containing the implements with which he partook of his horrid little habit.

Dismissing thoughts of Holmes and his addiction, I journeyed to the abode of Lady Marjorie Ingrum, a patient of mine. I had received a telegram earlier that morning that, even through the medium of the stilted printed word upon the sheet, instilled a feeling of desperation, a certain sense of urgency within me.

I was greeted by Townsend, Lady Marjorie's butler, and was quickly presented to the Lady in her sitting room. Even though she was almost twenty years my senior, her ragged appearance and drawn face made me think she was well into her seventies.

"Lady Marjorie," I exclaimed, moving across and dropping to one knee while taking her hands in mine. "Your telegram sounded frightfully urgent. What is the matter? Have you taken ill?"

A trail of tears scarred the heavy makeup she wore, lending a more sorrowful look to her appearance. A sad shake of her head. "No, Doctor, it isn't me that I've asked you here for." A glance upwards drew my stare in that direction. "It's my son."

As I helped Lady Marjorie ascend the stairs, she told me, "I haven't known what to do with him for many months now. Howard could keep the boy in train, but I've never been strong enough." I had never had the privilege of meeting Sir Howard Ingrum, as he passed well before Lady Marjorie became my patient, but his stern painted expression looked down from an assortment of vantage points around the house. "Wallace was always a willful child, and now in adulthood, is even more so. I know he's a layabout, and Lord knows I've asked

159

him time and again, but coupled with a lazy coterie of so-called friends, he prefers an almost Bohemian existence to seeking out any form of practical application of his skills and talents."

Nothing that Lady Marjorie said came as any surprise to me. I met Wallace Ingrum on a few occasions, mostly as he passed by in the corridors of the house. He always presented an air of indifference or, as it seemed, intoxication, and I think we'd barely exchanged more than a few sentences. Each time he was as Lady Marjorie depicted: Regularly dishevelled, with dull eyes sporting dark shadows beneath them, and a pallid complexion as one who never ventured into the daylight.

It was even less of a surprise when I was led into the young man's bedroom to find him lying fully clothed on top of his bedclothes. The powerful smell of vomit assaulted my nostrils as soon as I entered. I reeled back slightly, before recovering and moving closer to the bed. The source of the rank odour had spilt down the other side of the bed and covered the floor.

Lady Marjorie coughed at the smell and pulled a kerchief from her sleeve. "That wasn't there when I last checked on him." Turning to her butler, she said, "Townsend, have Mary see to that, please." The butler bowed slightly and hurried off.

"How long has he been like this?" I asked, moving to the bedside, and retrieving a stethoscope from my bag.

As I placed the cup on Wallace's chest, Lady Marjorie said, "He came in late last night. A lot of banging and thumping. I could hear him all the way down the hall, and simply presumed he'd returned after an evening with those friends. It was Townsend that found him like this. I asked him to give Wallace a mid-morning call to try and get him to at least rise before midday, but this morning he was unresponsive. I was only relieved that he was simply sleeping and not . . . ."

Her voice trailed off as she suppressed a sob. Turning to catch her expression, I grew concerned for her almost as much as my patient. "Is there something more?"

Nodding, she added, "Yes. I think it's the cocaine."

"He's a user then?" I asked, turning back, and reaching for the man's wrists. There were a substantial number of puncture wounds on the underside of his left forearm, a sure sign that he shared a similar habit with my compatriot at home. Scanning the area, I noticed a small glass syringe lying in the shadow of the bed. From its position, I surmised it had dropped to the floor then rolled out of sight.

I checked the man's chest and noticed a severely accelerated heartbeat, to the point that I was surprised I couldn't hear the thumping without the aid of my instrument. I placed my hand on his forehead. He was burning up. "Can you ask Townsend to fetch some cold water and some flannel cloths? We need to get Wallace's temperature down as far as possible." When Lady Marjorie left, I set about stripping the young man down to his undergarments. The room had a single window, so I drew the curtains, lifted the windowpane, and threw open the shutters. A slight breeze blew into the room. My hope was it could wash across the man's body and cool him. The only other course of action was to introduce water into his system, but with him unconscious, I could do nothing on that front until he awoke.

Thankfully, Townsend returned in a few minutes, with a young housemaid that I assumed was Mary. Averting her eyes from Wallace's half-naked form, she set about cleaning up the other side of the bed.

Retrieving the towels from Townsend and the bucket of water that he set down, I dampened and placed them on Wallace's forehead and chest. By the time Lady Marjorie joined us, it was a simple wait until Wallace regained consciousness. If he showed no signs of recovery in the next hour, I would send word to the nearest hospital and have the unfortunate man moved.

As Mary left with the dirty water, Lady Marjorie asked her to bring tea. I believe it was more to help pass the time than to alleviate any thirst. Townsend brought a pair of straight-backed chairs and a small side table and finished setting them up when Mary returned with a tray laden with a teapot, cups, and a small plate of biscuits.

After Mary and Townsend retreated to the bowels of the house, I watched Lady Marjorie for a moment and noticed her eyes barely leave her unconscious son. Taking it upon myself, I played mother and poured out the tea, establishing the need for sugar and milk as I did so.

"He will be all right, won't he?" Lady Marjorie asked.

"I'm sure he will be." Holding the plate of biscuits out to distract her attention for a moment, Lady Marjorie unconsciously picked one from the plate and bit into it.

After several minutes of silence, broken only by the sound of munching and the clink of china, Lady Marjorie seemed to calm down, possibly in anticipation of her son's recovery. "I have to confess, Doctor, that you weren't the first physician I approached to help."

Intrigued, I replied, "Really? I didn't realise you were seeing anyone else."

"Oh, I don't. It's just that I received a pamphlet from another local doctor who specialises in helping those who overindulge in the drugs."

I thought immediately of Holmes and became even more curious. "What would this physician's name be?"

"Dr. Dermid Markey. He has a practice just south of the River in Brixton."

"But he couldn't help you?"

"No. None of my telegrams were replied to. I stated just as much urgency and almost sent Townsend in person to seek out Dr. Markey's help, but then thought of you."

"I can only assume that Dr. Markey was simply detained elsewhere. It would seem peculiar that he didn't deem it appropriate to at least answer your telegrams."

"I was a little disappointed. From the word amongst my friends, he is very diligent, and quite against this whole epidemic of drug usage, especially amongst the younger generation. I had hoped he wouldn't just save my Wallace and help him recover, but could aid him in overcoming this compulsion to take these nefarious substances."

Thinking of my own version of Wallace sitting at home in Baker Street, I had to agree, and could only hope to find this physician and have him visit Holmes in the near future. I plied Lady Marjorie with more questions, with a view of learning more about this Dr. Markey, and to keep her mind occupied on other thoughts while we waited to see if her son recovered.

***

"Yes, I have heard of this Dr. Dermid Markey," said Holmes, seemingly in decent spirits following a splendid luncheon prepared by Mrs. Hudson. There were no obvious effects from any addictive substances in his system, which pleased me no end.

I had returned to Baker Street after staying with Lady Marjorie until young Wallace showed signs of recovery. Starting with a small series of groans, and a flickering of his eyes, I diagnosed that he was beginning to return to consciousness. Removal of the damp cloths brought out a series of goosebumps when the calming breeze from the windows wafted across his bare skin. His heightened temperature had indeed receded, boding well for him. Deciding there was little more I could do in any practical way, I covered him with his bedclothes and bid good day to Lady Marjorie.

"I think the worst has passed. He will need to sleep the rest of the effects off, but there is little more I can do for now. I'm happy to drop by in the early evening if you like to see how he progresses," I said.

"That would be most thoughtful," said Lady Marjorie, very effusive in her tone now that her son was on the way to full recovery. "You are a Godsend, Dr. Watson. A Godsend."

"I am a simple physician. Assisting the poorly is my duty." With that, I returned in the hope of a late luncheon before more attendances in the afternoon.

"But I neither see any need to meet with the fellow, nor how that could even be possible," said Holmes, a wry grin on his face hiding some snippet of information to which I wasn't privy.

"I simply feel that you may find some benefit from his views on the use of certain substances," I said, nodding towards the contents of Holmes's case on show in the corner. As I noticed his eyes drift in that direction, then back, the last part of his statement made itself known to my mind once more. Confused, I asked, "What did you mean by possible?"

163

"Ah, well," he said, moving across to a pile of newspapers and rifling through them, before turning back with the issue he sought. Placing the paper down, he opened to a page with a small article titled, "Local Doctor Missing".

I read and was dismayed to find that Dr. Dermid Markey had gone missing over a week before. The article stated that the last sight of him was just before attending a callout. A single witness described the hansom he hailed, but the driver was wrapped up for cold weather, a fact I felt strange given the wonderful weather of the past month. Not a word had been heard of him since.

"That explains why Lady Marjorie had no word from him then," I mumbled under my breath.

"Who?" asked Holmes.

"A patient of mine. I have just returned from helping her son overcome a cocaine overdose."

"Careless," said Holmes, matter-of-factly.

"Quite." Pointing at the article, I asked, "You didn't see fit to investigate this?"

"Not beyond a cursory examination of the facts. I have had no contact with anyone interested in instigating a formal investigation, so there has been no need."

Desperately trying to hide my annoyance at Holmes, I mumbled, "It wouldn't have anything to do with his stance on narcotics and stimulants?"

"Not at all. I will admit I don't like the man's intentions. He wishes to outlaw or bring in a higher level of Government regulation on the availability of perfectly legal drugs." Taking a deep breath to control his rising emotional state, Holmes exhaled slowly then added, "I know you wish for me to stop my usage, but it is all perfectly legal, and I only partake to maintain a level of stimulation in my mind. Besides, the product of the coca plant has proved a boon amongst your professional comrades, virtually replacing the use of ether as an anaesthetic and increasing the safety of many medical procedures."

Not wishing to look him in the eyes, I glanced down at the newsprint once more. A snatch of information buried in the middle of the short article caught my attention. "Did you pick up on this fact?"

"What would that be?"

"Dr. Markey ran for parliament in the last general election."

"Yes, I believe he ran as an independent on a strict platform of drug reform. I think the article mentions the winning Member."

Reading further, I replied, "Yes, Sir Benton McBrough, one of Gladstone's liberals, a backbencher. I haven't heard much about him."

"One can't keep abreast of all of these Parliamentarians. Why are you so interested in Dr. Markey?"

Finally glancing up into Holmes's face, I said, "He's a fellow physician, so there's a natural bond there. From what Lady Marjorie told me, he is a bit of a crusader – a do-gooder, I suppose you'd call him. That drags me closer to him as well. The fact that he is missing disturbs me, and draws me to wish to find him, or at least find out what happened to him."

"Very noble, Watson," Holmes answered, examining my expression for a time, and forming some opinion in that complex mind of his. Standing, he clapped his hands together and said, "In that case, I will seek out the whereabouts of this Dr. Markey. Consider it a favour to you, my old friend."

With that he disappeared into his rooms, leaving me slightly astonished at his change of heart.

***

Never one to dawdle when the scent of a case was in the air, Holmes returned within minutes, ready to depart. Where I had no idea, until he expounded that we were to start at the beginning: The rooms of Dr. Dermid Markey.

Holmes was quite effusive during our hansom journey across the Thames and into the south of London. To my ears, it was partly a relief to see a break in his sombre and distant mood, but also partly a concern that his disposition was due to something other than just the likelihood of an interesting mystery to solve.

As we turned down Kennington Road, Holmes quipped, "We don't come as a pair into this part of the city very often."

"Am I to assume that you travel here by yourself then?"

"Oh, yes," he said, a sly grin on his lips, "There is a definite undercurrent of the ways and wherefores of the criminal underbelly writing its way through the destitute backstreets of this area. I have spent many a night wandering and slinking my way around in search of information. I'm much happier to be entering the place in the fullness of the day, though. It can be a very rough area at night." He pondered for a moment, then added in a downcast voice, "Which sadly could account as a simple solution to our little mystery."

The cab turned into a small side street and pulled up before a modest two-story yellow brick terrace. A small wooden sign hung next to the front door, the names Dr. Markey and Dr. Carlton were inscribed upon it.

"He has a partner," I said.

"It would seem," replied Holmes. "This should be a good place to start then."

The front door led straight into the surgery's waiting room. It was filled with patients, together with the sound of coughing and the gentle murmurs of discomfort. The only light came from the front window and a sole gaslight affixed above the receptionist's desk.

Holmes strode across the short distance and stood before the young woman dressed in a simple nurse's uniform. I realised the practice was small enough to warrant the duties of nurse and receptionist to be undertaken by a single person. A simple nameplate sat on the desk, informing patients that the young girl's name was Nurse Jenny Calahan.

Within a moment, the lass looked up with a slight expression of surprise, possibly at our manner of dress or stature, and said, "We don't get such fine gentlemen around here too often. How can we help you?"

"Thank you, Nurse Calahan," replied Holmes. "We'd like to speak with Dr. Carlton if that's possible?"

"Is it a medical matter?"

"No. My name is Sherlock Holmes, consulting detective, I have undertaken to investigate the matter of Dr. Markey's disappearance."

"Oh, in that case, I'll see if I can catch him for you."

Just as she finished her statement, voices echoed from a nearby doorway. "Now, Mrs. Withers, please take one each day, and stay off

166

your feet as much as possible. The swelling should go down if you do."

"Oh, I'll try, Doctor," came the reply, "but my 'Arold's a useless fool around the 'ouse, so nuffin' will get done if'n I's just lazing around."

"Fine, but please do try."

As the old woman appeared in the doorway, followed by a young, handsome man in a doctor's coat and carrying a small card with him, an elderly man stood and shuffled across to take the old woman's arm. As they waddled towards the exit, Harold said, "Now, Diedre why's you go an' say that to the doctor?"

"Oh, don't worry 'Arold, 'e knows you well, so it comes as no surprise to 'im."

"Still," finished Harold.

I watched as they exited, then turned back towards the doctor, who eyed Holmes and myself suspiciously.

"And you gentlemen are?"

Jenny piped up, "Oh, this is Mr. Sherlock Holmes, Doctor. He's come to ask about Dr. Markey."

Carlton popped the medical card down on the desk near Jenny and reached for the top one on a small pile nearby. Reading the card he said to us, "Well, I'm sorry, but my waiting room is full. Jenny here can book you in, but it may be some time."

Smiling, Holmes bowed slightly and said, "No problems there, Doctor. I can see you are busy. It is a matter of some urgency, as it's about your partner, but I'm happy to fit in with your schedule."

Regarding Holmes for several seconds, Carlton finally turned away and called out the name of the next patient. "Mr. Gareth Jones?" The call was answered by a scruffily dressed man standing. His actions were immediately met with a short coughing fit, garnering disgusted looks from others nearby. Once composed, he trundled off into the rear rooms, followed by Carlton, who gave Holmes one last look before joining him.

Seeing that there were now two seats free, Holmes stepped across and sat down. I quickly joined him, a little frustrated that we were going to have to wait, but interested in seeing how this particular medical practice operated. My observations were a little short-lived, however.

Almost as soon as he sat, Holmes garnered the interest of the old man seated to his left. He looked well into his seventies, but could have been young as sixty. His face was lined with deep wrinkles, and his weathered and sun-burnt skin looked similar to the cracked leather of an ageing couch.

"Did me ears hear right?" asked the man. "You're Sherlock Holmes?"

Looking him up and down, Holmes gave the man a quick examination, before answering. "Yes. Yes, I am."

"The detective?" Holmes nodded. "Don't you work with the Yard to bring down criminals?"

Smiling, Holmes added, "Yes, I do work with members of Scotland Yard from time to time."

"So what are ye here for? Not here for Carlton are ye? I hope not. He's been me doctor for a while now. Good man. Never had a problem with him."

"No, nothing like that. I'm here to ask Dr. Carlton a few questions."

"About any of us?" asked the man, his expression changing to a look of shock. I noticed at that point, many heads turning our way.

"Well, really I can't say. That sort of thing is private to the case at hand, and nobody can be ruled out until the evidence says they are innocent. Take you for instance. Your accent reeks of Newcastle, but you've been in London for a number of years, or you came from London initially and spent time in Newcastle." Holmes pointed to the man's hands. "You worked the mines. Your hands still have a deep-seated hint of coal dust deep in their pores. That, plus the yellow stains on your fingers, tell me you are a heavy smoker. Both could be the possible cause of why you are here."

The man looked flabbergasted, a common sight following one of Holmes's dissections. He coughed loudly for a few moments, bringing out a kerchief to capture the effluent.

It was then I noticed another man on the other side of the room who had been staring at Holmes quite intently stand up and head for the door.

"Mr. Smythe? You're next." said Jenny, standing and moving around her desk. "Do you not want to see the doctor now?"

"Oi'll come back later," he said, turning slightly, but keeping his eyes on Holmes. "It's a little too busy roight now." As the door banged shut, the other patients turned from staring at Smythe to staring at Holmes.

Shaking her head, Jenny turned and disappeared down the short corridor.

After she had gone, a lady sitting near to me piped up and asked Holmes, "Did you just say that nobody was innocent?"

Holding his hands up, Holmes said, "No, no, I assure you. I merely suggested that until all the evidence is gathered, one cannot rule out the guilt of any person involved. I am only establishing the facts of the case in which I'm involved, but the same concept applies."

That one statement had a galvanising effect on the conscience of the gathered group. Almost as one they stood and headed for the door. Within a couple of minutes, Holmes and I found ourselves alone in the waiting room.

I turned to Holmes and asked, "Did you plan that?"

A wry grin crossed Holmes's face, "How could I have known that the power of a guilty mind could outweigh all logic and reason?"

Before I could answer, Jenny stepped back into the waiting room. A look of shock came to her face as she spied all the empty seats. "What happened?"

"I think they had more pressing engagements," said Holmes.

***

"Well, you have my attention now," said Dr. Carlton, looking very aggrieved that his entire waiting room was now empty, "I have no idea how I'm going to recover the lost earnings that just walked out of here. We barely manage to make ends meet at the best of times."

"I can sympathise with you Dr. Carlton," I said. "I have a number of patients myself that can barely afford to cover the costs of any medications I prescribe before they pay for my services as well. I almost wish that the Government would step in and bolster the medical industry as a whole – to somehow make it affordable for all."

Cutting me off, Holmes added, "Yes, Watson, but you also have patients that could buy you many times over. They afford you a level of fee that, I presume, Dr. Carlton could only dream of." Turning his attention to Carlton, he added, "Again, I can only apologise so many times, but our true quest here today is to ask about your missing colleague, Dr. Dermid Markey."

Carlton sat back, an expression of resignation on his face, which told me he'd been through this all before. "I've told the police everything I know, which is nothing. The last I saw of Dermid, he was heading out on a call, and he never came home. Devastating to his wife, and very damaging to the practice."

"You don't seem too affected emotionally?"

"Well, I've only known him professionally."

"For two or three years, I'd say?"

Carlton looked astonished. "How did you know that?"

"You look about twenty-four years old, give or take a year. Standard medical training should take four years. Unless you are a prodigy, you would have started in your eighteenth year. You have the look of someone from a public-school background. The clothes under your coat are neat and tailored, but starting to wear, meaning you like to appear well-dressed, but are struggling to manage of late. Could be a consequence of this practice's turnover."

The doctor merely gaped at Holmes. I took that to mean his assessment was spot on.

"You mentioned that the practice has been struggling." Carlton nodded in response. "Do you think that Dr. Markey would have taken on a loan to supplement the practice's finances?"

Carlton shook his head. "No. What I have found of Dermid was his pride and insistence on taking every burden upon his own shoulders. I would never believe he would borrow money under any circumstances. Sometimes I consider that a foolish stance, but one I had to admire. Why do you ask?"

Shrugging, Holmes answered, "Just gathering indications of any untoward attention from the more nefarious members of society. What about competitors, enemies, or any disgruntled patients?"

Again, the younger doctor slowly shook his head. "If you were to meet the man, you'd almost call him a saint. His patients all returned to him, time and again, even with another physician not far from here. I didn't know much of his private life, but he never gave me any cause to think he was hated." Stopping, he considered for a moment before continuing. "There was one incident during that d--n foolish foray into politics."

"Yes?"

"A stone was thrown through the surgery window. No note. No follow up of any kind. We didn't think much of it at the time – just youths being reckless."

"Why think of it now?"

"Because it occurred about a week before the vote. We'd never had any other incidents, but, just now, that one stuck out."

"Were there any other incidents during the campaign?"

"Just the idiotic stance taken by Dermid's opponent." He stood and moved to a small window that looked out upon the street. "McBrough stood for several hours on that street corner and handed out free samples of cocaine to any passers-by. I must admit that I watched him between patients. Couldn't believe his actions. An aged politician treating a dangerous drug as if it were sweeties."

"Intriguing. I've always taken the acts of politicians with a grain of salt. They tend to look after themselves first, then their constituents."

"Quite."

"One last question I would ask is about this final call that Dr. Markey went upon. Was it one of his addiction cases?"

A slight nod of the head was followed by a sigh and, "Yes. Damn fool. He would drop everything to go help another of these hopeless cases. They always turn out bad. The patient was either dead or so far gone that he would never recover. If it was a positive outcome, then any fee we recovered was chewed up by the costs of medicines and implements. Dermid would never ask for extra to cover them."

Carlton shook his head. "I warned him it would all go wrong one day."

"How many overdoses did Dr. Markey attend – per year say?"

"Too many. One a week, sometimes two or three. Especially in this area, and down towards Brixton. The loss of time and money on such a quixotic pursuit drove me to distraction."

"And with him gone, you're feeling trapped here? Am I reading that right?" Once again that astonished look crossed his face. "I – I – " He hung his head and shook it slightly, "I can't lie. Yes, I've been making enquiries. Looking for a place in a practice north of the river. Somewhere more salubrious." Looking up, his face took on a haggard, tired expression. "If I stay here much longer, I'll end up like my patients in the waiting room. Old before my time. One foot in the grave, the rest of my life spent just counting down the days."

***

As we stepped into the waiting room, I was a little pleased to see a few more patients had settled in for their wait. Holmes moved across to the nurse and asked, "Would you have the address to which Dr. Markey was last requested?"

Jenny said, "Oh, yes, I do." She flipped pages in a small diary and ran a finger down a column of addresses and notes. "Here. 23 Angel Road in Brixton."

"Hmm. Not a nice part of town," Holmes muttered.

"And the strangest part is, it isn't the first time we've had a call there either."

"No?"

Flipping back a few pages, Jenny pointed to another entry with the same address. I noticed the date on the page was two weeks earlier. "Dr. Markey was on another call, so Dr. Carlton went instead." Her face turned slightly dour, "He wasn't a happy chappy when he returned. He was muttering about a waste of time and something about addicts. I found out later that there was no one home, almost as if it had been a prank. I did mention that to Dr. Markey, but he dismissed it as a misunderstanding."

"Did you tell the police about this?"

"Oh, yes," she said, shrugging, "Not sure they cared or looked into it. Always too busy, the police."

"Quite so. Did you consult them when the stone was thrown through the surgery window?"

"Oh, yes. A young constable came around. Took one look, took some notes. Mumbled something about wild youths in the street, then we never heard from him again. Typical really."

Nodding, Holmes stood still for a moment, thinking on this latest information before asking, "Do you know if Mrs. Markey is in?"

"You might be in luck. She's been in a right state. I think she's looking to go off to her sister's in Windsor for a few days. I have the address if you miss her."

Nodding, Holmes said, "Thank you. I believe that the Markeys live next door, is that right?"

"Yes."

"We'll check there, but return if we need that address."

"That will be fine."

Holmes walked away, while I maintained eye contact with the lovely nurse for a moment before joining him.

***

"Oh Lord, have you found him?" said the distraught looking woman who opened the neighbouring door.

"No, I'm sorry we haven't," said Holmes, "I assume then that you are Mrs. Markey?"

A confused look grew on the woman's face. "Why yes. Who are you?"

"I am Sherlock Holmes, and this is my colleague, Dr. John Watson."

"Sherlock Holmes?" said Mrs. Markey, "The detective?"

"The one and the same. Your husband's disappearance was brought to my attention, and I would like to offer my services in finding him."

"I don't have any money to pay you," the woman said, accompanied by a pained expression of embarrassment.

"And like your husband, at times I do not charge. I believe that he has been offering quite a public service, and I wish to do the same."

Mrs. Markey poked her head out further, her eyes darting frantically to and fro as she scanned the street before stepping back and allowing us entrance. "Please, come in then."

We were ushered into a small sitting room near the front of the house and took the seats offered to us. It was a sparsely furnished and appointed room, a single gaslight providing a trifling amount of illumination. Looking around, I noticed a single framed photograph on the nearby mantel. From the looks of Mrs. Markey in the portrait compared to the woman sitting opposite me, the photo was several years old. It was presumptive, but I took the other two people in the picture to be Dr. Markey and probably their teenage son.

"Now we do apologise for the intrusion," said Holmes, "but I felt the need to speak with you prior to continuing my investigation."

"Thank you for even considering it, Mr. Holmes. The last week has been horrendous. I've never felt more alone. My family are all in Windsor. I'm tempted to visit, but the cost . . . ." She trailed off at that point. I made a mental note that money was high on Mrs. Markey's mind, almost akin to the loss of her husband.

"Firstly, and I'm a little loathe to ask, but is there any reason that Dr. Markey may have willingly gone missing?"

"What do you mean?"

"Again, I'm sorry to ask, but perhaps a lover?"

Affronted, Mrs. Markey sat upright, in a posture of defiance. "Certainly not. Dermid and I are firmly committed to each other." Thrusting out her left hand, I noticed a beautifully crafted engagement ring, with a less ornate but striking gold Claddagh ring. It took me a moment to realise that Markey must be of Irish heritage. "We both wear the same wedding ring, as a way of showing our connection to each other. Dermid rarely takes his off, even when seeing patients." Taking a deep breath, she forced herself to relax before adding, "Besides, he simply wouldn't have the time."

"Ah, that was my next line of questioning. The public service he has taken on, to assist those that have succumbed to addiction and overdose – I assume by your statement that this occupies much of his time."

"Yes. It's a double-edged sword. I can only admire his stance and his actions, but in the same breath, I find it takes him away for so many hours each week. Time he can ill-afford."

"Why is that?"

"It has affected the practice. His paying patients are made to wait while he goes off to help the next unfortunate. As it is, we're only scraping through with the surgery and the house to support."

"Therefore, I can assume that your husband took on no loans to assist with finances?"

"No. He is far too proud to rely on others. He'd rather sell off our furniture before asking for charity."

"I see. Good. I just wanted to ensure that there could be no involvement of nefarious elements looking for recompense."

"Does your son still live at home," I butted in, "or is he making his way in the world? Does he contribute or assist his father?"

With that statement, Mrs. Markey's face became a veil of sorrow. Immediately, I realised my misreading of the photograph. The boy was obviously gone from this world, hence why she had never felt so alone.

Through the onset of tears, Mrs. Markey answered, "No. Jason left us three years ago. Fell in with the wrong crowd. Took to drink and opium. He became Dermid's first overdose patient, and Dermid's first failure. It's what drives him so. He never wants another family to face the devastation that we have."

We were left in silence for a few moments while Mrs. Markey recovered herself, drawing a kerchief from her sleeve to mop the small flow of tears. Finally she looked across at the family photograph, took a deep breath, and slowly exhaled. "It's why Dermid chose to try his hand at politics." Turning she glanced first at me, then at Holmes, "He wanted to take a stand against the proliferation of drugs in the community. He has tried to spread the word through his patients and his work with addicts, but believed that he would finder a greater voice from the floor of Parliament. Sadly, that wasn't to be."

"Yes, he lost to Sir Benton McBrough, I believe," said Holmes, "a long-time Liberal. A very hard task for any man, especially one new to the cut-and-thrust of politics."

"That is true, but he did quite well, almost unseating Sir Benton in the last election. Dermid still aspires to Parliament, and holds out hope that there may be a repeat of the last two year's instability."

"He would be one of the few, other than those unseated by Gladstone's defeat. I don't generally dwell on matters of politics, but I do remember some details of the campaign. Sir Benton spent quite a large amount of effort in undermining your husband's platform."

I piped up as I recalled Dr. Carlton's comment. "Didn't Sir Benton make a bit of a fool of himself by promoting the use of cocaine, and indeed giving some away for free? I thought it very strange at the time."

A surprising smile came to Mrs. Markey's face. "Yes, the man became a little obsessed – or should I say fearful – of Dermid's commitment. I never really took much interest, but some of my friends brought that little incident to my attention. Dermid and I both found it amusing, if not a little disturbing."

"Politicians," said Holmes, a thoughtful look on his face. "Most will do anything to gain or retain power."

***

After bidding adieu to Mrs. Markey, Holmes vowed to keep in touch with any information he uncovered, and we made our way to the high street. Luckily we found a passing hansom and asked to be taken to the Brixton address. The cabbie was very hesitant at first, but a promise of a higher fee soon had us on our way.

The cab pulled up in front of a series of run-down terrace houses and, from the lack of movement within any of them, abandoned.

"Are you sure this is the right address?" I asked Holmes.

He nodded, showing me the piece of paper. "As far as we know."

"Can we at least ask the cabbie to wait? I can't believe we'll be long."

"Oh, come now, Watson – where's your sense of adventure?" Holmes vaulted from the cab and strode across to the reason for our presence.

I stepped out and paid the driver, stopping myself from asking him to stay before he drove away. Looking around, I noticed that the area was a reflection of our destination. The houses weren't quite derelict, but close to it. The street was strewn with rubbish, and there was a distinct lack of carts or wagons. The only bright spot in the street was the modest-looking church opposite. A small sign read "St. John the Evangelist". The doors were shut, and the grounds quiet and vacant – not surprising for the time of the week.

Stepping up to the house in question, I found Holmes standing a few feet from the front door and examining the steps. As I watched, he pulled out his glass and leaned down, peering closely at the area.

"What have you found?" I asked.

"Something strange indeed." He stood up, replaced the glass, and pointed at the area of his concern. "Can you see?"

I examined the spot for a moment before it started to become clear. "My word," I said, dropping down for a closer look. The dust and grime on the step and stoop were quite thick, and as there was no mat on which to wipe one's feet, one could clearly see where the dirt had been disturbed – but only from a single pair of boots that I could see. "What does it mean?"

"I can only presume that, of late, only one person has visited this door." Pointing to the few steps leading up, he added, "And that person only approached the premises and never left. Luckily for us, there hasn't been any rain for the last week or so."

"But if the person entered, then he or she must still be inside."

"Unless he or she left by a rear exit, which may be how the regular visitors gain access as well."

"Should we knock then?"

"We can, but I doubt if there is anyone inside."

The hollow sound of the knocker rang through the house, but there was no noise from within. I shrugged. "Well, I assumed you would be correct, but one must try these things."

Smiling, Holmes reached into his coat and brought out his lock picks. I glanced around to ensure we were undisturbed while he made quick work of the lock and swung the door open. I made to move inside, but Holmes placed a hand on my chest.

"Sorry, but I just want to view the scene before we enter." Intrigued, I followed Holmes's gaze and noticed that the floor within was filthy with dust and grime, much like the steps outside. However, three sets of footprints could be clearly seen in the dust. One set led to the door, with two sets leading away. "I assume you can see the sets of boot prints." I nodded and watched as Holmes stooped down once more, examining each set of prints in turn. Pointing to those leading in from outside, he said, "This pair has the look of boots worn by a city-based man, but this pair," he pointed to the other, "has a wider tread – something akin to a worker's boot."

"Strange."

"Quite," he said, entering the passageway and stepping lightly along the wall, preserving the trail of footprints as much as possible. I followed, shutting the door behind me, and keeping to his trail as closely as possible.

The line of footprints led down the long hallway and turned abruptly into a room at the end. Holmes stopped for a moment, studying the area before disappearing through the doorway.

My first view of the room brought a feeling of surprise. It was a combined kitchen and dining area, with two small windows overlooking a very overgrown rear yard. The state of the area confirmed my view that the house had been unused for some time. In the kitchen area, the small benches lay empty, devoid of cutlery, crockery, or items used for food preparation. The furniture in the dining area consisted of a small wooden table with four chairs, one of which lay upturned in the far corner. A thick layer of dust cloaked every item in the room, the floor especially.

Holmes squatted nearby, his eyeglass hovering above several impressions in the dust.

"More boot prints?"

"Yes. Two more sets in addition to those we have already seen. The scraping of heel marks and footprints through this dirt suggests that there was a scuffle of some kind." He pointed towards two parallel lines running from near the centre of the room towards the double doors that led out to the garden. "A quick summation would lead me to presume that the person entering this room was attacked, knocked unconscious – or worse – and then dragged towards the garden."

"Should we go out and check? He may still be there."

"In time. There are still many clews to uncover in this room." Then, peering closer to the floor, he cried, "Ah, yes!" Looking down, I saw him point to several dark spots on the dirty floor. "This may be blood, but I cannot tell fully in this light."

Noticing a gaslight nearby, I pulled out a small box of matches and endeavoured to light the flame, before giving up in exasperation. "There's no gas," I said, a little confused and surprised.

"That would corroborate with my assertion that this house has been unused for quite some time – at least for normal habitation, that is."

It was then I noticed a candle in a holder on the other side of the room. Deftly skirting around the periphery, I quickly lit it, shining a dull, yellow light across the scene.

"Thank you. Well done," said Holmes, snatching the candle from me and bringing it closer to the area of his attention.

Now that there was a little more light, I took the opportunity to glance around the room and noticed a glint of something metallic in the corner opposite. Pointing I asked, "What's that?" Holmes looked up as I skirted the centre of the room and retrieved the object. It was conical in shape, with circular openings at both ends. The brass had dulled slightly from age and use, but still retained enough shine to catch the light. "Intriguing," I said, "If I had to guess, I'd say this is the end of a stethoscope."

I passed the object into Holmes open palm. He quickly examined it under the glass and nodded in agreement. "I believe you're correct – different to the type you use, but common enough among your colleagues."

"Does that mean that Markey was here?"

"The idea gains credence," Holmes said.

While Holmes continued to investigate the room, my eyes kept wandering to the area outside of the rear doors. It was a singular mess and tangle of weeds and plants, though a pathway of broken cobblestones and tamped down grasses could be seen running through the brush towards the rear of the property. I almost jolted in shock when I felt rather than saw Holmes's presence at my shoulder.

"The owners of this property obviously don't entertain anyone in the rear yard," he quipped.

"I'm more worried about what they hide in there."

"Well then, let's find out, shall we?"

***

The first thing I saw as the door swung open was the definite line of muddied footprints leading up the garden path to the rear step. They had smudged slightly as boots walked back across them towards the rear gate once more.

"The mud only comes one way," I said.

"Yes. The owner obviously realised that his boots were filthy and cleaned them off there." Holmes pointed to a smear of dark, mud on the edge of the top step. Carefully stepping across to the dark patch, he bent down and tentatively poked his finger into the pile. I grimaced, my darkest imagination picturing where the mud came from and what it contained.

As Holmes rubbed the mud between two fingers, then raised it to his nose and sniffed. I said, "Be careful. That could be – "

"Excrement?" he asked before taking another sniff. "In fact, it is. Sheep or – " Sniffing the mud again. " – pig. There's definitely a hint of omnivore in it. Not strong enough for a carnivore. Possibly from a pig, and intriguingly still relatively fresh."

Holding back a sudden urge to gag, I said, "Where would someone find a pigsty around here?"

Wiping his fingers on his kerchief, Holmes said, "I doubt it was actually around here." He stepped to the side of the path and studied the footprints and crushed plants. After a few moments, he said, "Yes, there are actually three sets of prints. The mud-laden boots, plus two others. All came up the path in single file, then two of them moved side-by-side going back out. By the depth of the impressions in the grass, they were carrying something on their way out."

"Or someone?"

"Yes, it's starting to look likely that it was someone."

I followed Holmes as he slowly made his way down the garden path, stopping every once in a while to examine the footprints and crushed greenery. I noticed the privy set against the rear fence. It was unusable due to the build-up of weeds and grass around the door, almost hiding it from view.

The thicker weeds on both sides of the path appeared to have been completely undisturbed for weeks, if not months. Holmes confirmed this by ignoring them completely and making his way through the rear gate and into the service laneway behind. The road was a turgid mess of mud, I hoped it was mud. I knew well that the laneway was probably used mostly by the nightsoil men undertaking their nocturnal duties.

We both studied the wet trails of wagon wheels and horses' hooves, Holmes shaking his head at the state of the area. Any indications of a trap or cart behind our position had long been erased. It was then that Holmes's eyes fell on the rear door of the privy. As he carefully picked his way across to it, I gasped, "Surely you don't need to look in there?"

"Ah, but think on it. The night soil men would know by now that this house is unused, and to save themselves time and effort, would regularly skip this privy. But if you were to discard or hide something, what better place?"

As he slid the door up, I expected no less than a bucket of foul contents, but was greeted with a triumphant "A-ha!" Holmes pulled from the tiny room a brown, leather case. Even from where I stood, I could make out what it was.

Opening and peering inside, Holmes nodded and said, "A medical bag, as I'm sure you already determined. Unless there's a rush on disposing of medical professionals, I'm sure we can establish that this indeed belonged to Dr. Markey."

"The poor man. Where do you think he was taken?"

Peering down the laneway, Holmes gave a tiny shrug before adding, "To that, I have no idea as yet. I believe we need to involve the constabulary, as this case has deepened very quickly."

I was a little surprised that Holmes would look to bring in the police before having established all the facts of the case. It wasn't until we exited back into the street that it became clear.

As Holmes worked his magic and relocked the front door, I scanned the roadway for any witnesses or passers-by that might cause a ruckus, and noticed a young urchin hiding in the churchyard across the street. His attention was focused solely on us, which I thought strange, as I hadn't seen anyone on our way in, and from the looks of the boy, he knew we had entered and had been waiting all this time.

It was as Holmes turned and stepped down to the street level that the boy came out of his hiding spot and raced across towards us. I unconsciously stepped before Holmes as the boy approached.

"Mr. 'Olmes! Mr. 'Olmes!" he cried, alerting my colleague to his presence.

As Holmes stepped to one side, a smile came to his face. I realised immediately that he knew the boy.

"Jenkins, you look thoroughly flummoxed. What's the matter?"

"I'm sorry Mr. 'Olmes. One of our lads lives this way and sent word to Wiggins that you were here. He sent me in a hurry."

"Why? What can the matter be?"

"It's this 'ouse, sir. Do you know whose it is?"

"I have my theories, but obviously Wiggins was concerned about my presence, so enlighten me."

"What?" said the boy, a look of confusion on his face.

"Whose house is it?"

"Oh, yeah, it's Steelfist Wasser's."

"The criminal?" I blurted out.

"Ah, Derrick Wasser," said Holmes. "The scourge of South London,"

The little tyke nodded. "'E don't use it much, but I seen some men there last week. And a cart went off south. Big fella driving it."

A wide grin grew on Holmes's face. "The game is certainly afoot, Watson."

***

"Derrick Wasser," I said as the cab made its way back towards Baker Street. "I know a little about him, but mostly through reputation. Supposedly he runs a gang in South London, but the police have never been able to find evidence to actually incriminate him."

"That is true. I've kept an eye and ear open for any connection to the man, and his organisation, but until now there's been little. This could account for how self-assured he has grown."

"Yes, over-confidence leads to imprudence. I do know that the bulk of his activities are within legitimate businesses. Any mention in the tabloids have always brushed these aside as merely fronts to his other ventures."

Smiling, Holmes added, "Ah, well, I tend to read between the lines. The most important factor is that Wasser controls the importation and distribution of cocaine and opium throughout most of South London. A very large part of his business enterprises, I understand."

"That must be the motivation behind the disappearance of Dr. Markey."

"I think that's part of it, but the question I have is: Why would a man such as Wasser risk so much just to remove a minor player such as Dr. Markey?"

"If Markey's stance against these drugs were to take hold, they could severely limit Wasser's business. Would that be enough motivation?"

"I know only too well the legality of the drugs of which we speak. I'm more than happy for their prevalence in society to remain, while they are seen as legal. If their legal status were to change, then I would need to seriously rethink my own stance."

"To that, I would be most happy."

Slipping me a wry grin, Holmes added, "Quite, but I could only think that Wasser's business would be pushed underground, and frankly, become possibly more profitable per transaction, though much riskier."

"So?"

"I can't understand why Wasser would pursue Markey with such finality."

"Who else stands to gain from Dr. Markey's disappearance?"

"Who indeed? Who indeed? I think that I shall have to cogitate on that for a time."

Holmes slipped into silence for the rest of our journey back home. I was tied up with patient visits for the rest of the afternoon, and by the time I returned, he was nowhere to be found.

It wasn't until morning that Holmes appeared and joined me for a light breakfast. His face looked drawn from lack of sleep, but his eyes were bright with an inner eagerness. Sitting, he quickly downed two cups of coffee while I read the morning paper, seemingly composing himself before speaking.

"Watson, we must make a journey this morning. Are you free?"

"Why yes, I've nothing till later this afternoon. Where are we to go?"

"Dorking."

"What? Dorking? Why in blazes do you wish to go there?"

"We shall be visiting a piggery."

***

I sent notes to my afternoon patients to inform them that I wouldn't be able to attend until the morning and hailed a cab for the two of us. It soon had us at busy Waterloo Station. No sooner had we alighted than the lean form of Inspector Lestrade stepped out of the bustling crowd and greeted us.

"Ah, Inspector," said Holmes, "Glad you could join us. I thought you might send an underling in your stead."

"I'm intrigued, Mr. Holmes, plus anything that can pin an actual crime, especially one of this heinous nature, on Steelfist Wasser, is well worth following up. I'm still a little peeved at the local sergeant for not investigating that house in Brixton, but they rarely enter the area unless they have strong cause to. If this pans out, I'll be having strong words with him."

"Indeed. At this stage, I'm still a little wary of admitting success. It is a long bow that I draw, but after dwelling on the facts we know so far, and the other information I found from the voices in the street, I believe that we'll find what we're looking for."

I was still quite perplexed, but hoped that Holmes would divulge more in due time. I didn't have to wait long, as he wished for the three of us to be in solitude before speaking further.

The trip to Red Hill took all of an hour. Holmes had me purchase tickets for a compartment where we could speak undisturbed during that time. It was there that Holmes explained all he'd learned overnight.

"Inspector, this Wasser fellow: What is the word at the Yard about him?"

"He's as bent as a centuries-old willow tree," spat Lestrade, taking a breath for a moment to compose his next words, "Trouble is, we have nothing on him. Everything points to legitimate business interests, but he's got so many fingers in the wrong pies. We know it, but we can't prove anything."

"Well, hopefully, I can help you out."

"What have you got then? Why are we heading away from London?"

"One of Wasser's legitimate businesses is a pig farm on the outskirts of Dorking."

"Just another of his many."

"Yes, but he only owns the one farm. Speaking with quite a number of my contacts last night, I discovered that there have been several disappearances over the last few years. Many seem loosely associated with Wasser, in one way or another. Those facts, and the evidence of the cart, and excrement-caked boots, gives me pause to believe that this particular farm is used for very despicable purposes."

Holmes went silent at that point, leaving me to wonder further on his words. I could tell Lestrade was agitated, but I found him that way more often than not when Holmes was being cryptic.

We were met in Red Hill by a carriage with two constables aboard. Lestrade had telegraphed ahead, seeking support in case it was warranted. The bumpy ride on to Dorking was thankfully quick, and we found ourselves alighting outside of a rather run-down farmhouse and into the midst of the most God-awful smell, one that I was sure my sensibilities would take months to forget.

The farm was anything but, by my estimations. It consisted of a ramshackle house with a single large pen to one side that contained several overweight pigs. Two smaller outbuildings stood behind the pen – probably storage areas or, given the presence of the pigs, a butchery or similar.

Without a word, Holmes started towards the pigpen, leaving Lestrade, myself, and the two constables a little dumb-struck. A shout from the front door drew our attention.

"Oi? What the hell are you doing?" asked the husky man standing on the porch. "This is my property!" He thrust his stockinged feet into a pair of boots and shuffled off behind Holmes.

"Excuse me, sir," yelled Lestrade, stopping the man in his tracks, "Might I have a word?"

"No, you might not!" he yelled back, trailing after Holmes. "What's that blighter doing?"

"That is Mr. Sherlock Holmes, and I am Inspector Lestrade of Scotland Yard. You are?"

Stopping, the man looked Lestrade up and down before saying, "None of your business. I don't need to answer to the police, I've done nothing wrong."

"Well, if you would just let Mr. Holmes finish his inspection, we'll see if that's the case."

"What? What the hell do you mean by that?" Looking towards Holmes, the man added, "He's got no rights to be on my property or looking at my pigs."

By now all five of us were walking towards Holmes, who was entrenched in his examination of the pigpen. As we caught up with him, I grimaced in disgust, he was virtually kneeling in a pile of muck at the side of the enclosure. He had rolled his sleeve up and was pushing his hand deep into an unmentionable mess. It was then he exclaimed and pulled his hand out. "A-ha! Watson, come here – I think this will be of interest to you."

As I sidled up to him, Holmes held up several teeth. I immediately realised that they were human incisors and molars. "Good Lord."

With a grim smile on his face, Holmes pointed past Lestrade and said, "Inspector, I think we should detain that man." I turned to see the heavy-set man waddling as fast as he could away from us. Lestrade nodded and within seconds the two constables had nabbed and taken him to the wagon.

Turning to Holmes, I asked, "How?"

"It's a well-known fact that pigs can eat virtually anything, including almost every part of a human being. Flesh, organs, bone – but they struggle to digest teeth. They are also quite clean in that they will choose a specific spot in their habitat to defecate." Nodding towards the wagon, he added, "Our farmer has been helpful by pushing all the pigs excrement into one pile – probably how his boots became so caked in it."

It's a well-known fact that pigs can eat virtually anything, including almost every part of a human being.

"My word, Holmes. Good work!"

Without another thought, I followed the group to the cart, thinking Holmes would join us, but when I turned to find him he had disappeared. Assuming he had simply gone off to clean up or find more clues, I watched Lestrade interrogate the man as he was loaded into the back of the wagon. As the policeman plied the farmer with questions, I noticed his hands. On the little finger of his right hand, he wore a stunningly fashioned gold Claddagh ring, the twin of which I had only seen the day before.

Pointing at the ring, I almost shouted over Lestrade, "That ring – where did you get that ring?" The man's mouth dropped open in a gaping expression. "I take it from your reaction that it isn't yours. I don't wish to cast aspersions, but you don't look like the type of man to outlay so much money on jewellery."

"I . . . I found it. I liked it. So I wears it."

"Quite," I finished, placing as much cynicism on my single word as possible.

"Good observation, Watson," said Holmes at my shoulder, making me jump in surprise, "The existence of that ring, which I'm sure is the mate of Mrs. Markey's, plus what I just discovered, will certainly lead to a conviction."

"What did you find, Mr. Holmes?" asked Lestrade.

"It seems that the owner of those teeth isn't the only person to have found their final destination in the stomach of these pigs. There are multiple human teeth amongst a pile of older excrement at the rear of the property, plus in a small shed behind the house, I found clothes and other items that could only have come from elsewhere."

Turning to the farmer, Lestrade raised his voice, adding a hint of a growl to it, and said, "You're going down, my boy, but you can make things easier for yourself if you tell us who you're working for."

The look of fear on the man's face almost made me sympathetic to his plight, but as he told us everything, my anger rose.

***

The journey back to Red Hill was quiet. I believe it was Lestrade's way of surreptitiously sweating the farmer for information. Instead of an outright attack of questions, he let the man stew in silence until he was in the Red Hill Station, where the questioning could commence. There his reserve broke, and he wouldn't stop talking.

His name was Walter Bacon, at first an unlikely name and possibly false, until he confessed that his family had been pig farmers for generations. A chance encounter at the Spitalfields markets had seen him form a partnership with Derrick Wasser. The gangster threw money into the farm, keeping it afloat. The return agreement was for Bacon to use the pigs to eradicate the remains of anyone Wasser sent him. The pigs were the tool. Bacon eagerly, and almost proudly, told of how they could remove almost all traces of a body within a few hours. Some of the bones, especially the skull, could be troublesome, but he usually burnt those in the incinerator at the back of the property. Lestrade made a note to return for that evidence.

When asked about Markey, Bacon was nonplussed. He admitted that he never knew who the people were that the pigs devoured. He simply removed their clothes and prepared them. When he added that he used his butchering skills, learned over many years, I gagged slightly at the revolting thought of poor Dr. Markey's fate.

When pressed about the house in Brixton, Bacon admitted that he was regularly called up to London to claim the bodies and transport them away. That house was one of several that Wasser seemed to own.

By the end of the interrogation, I'd certainly had enough, and I hoped that Holmes was satisfied. Lestrade seemed to be ready to jump aboard a train and arrest Wasser, until Holmes said, "You still only have this man's word, which I'm sure won't stand up too well under courtroom scrutiny. We know how Markey was disposed of, but the reasons are still unclear. I believe our next step is to catch Wasser talking with the true villain of this piece."

***

An early breakfast greeted us the next day. Holmes had been resolute that we needed to be ready for a timely exit in the morning and asked Mrs. Hudson to prepare a substantial meal to set us properly for the day's adventures.

Upon arriving back at Baker Street the previous afternoon, Holmes had quickly disappeared, leaving me perplexed, but thankful as I was rather tired and looked forward to a hearty repast and a quiet night in. My colleague arrived back just prior to me making my way to bed and announced that the morrow would bring quite a few surprises.

Precisely at nine o'clock, the doorbell rang.

"Ah, that would be Lestrade," said Holmes, standing and donning his coat and hat. I followed suit and was just buttoning up when Lestrade's footsteps stopped outside our sitting room door.

As he let himself in, he looked a little weary from the previous day's journey and said, "All right, Mr. Holmes, what's this all about then? I would have had Wasser under arrest yesterday, but your words said otherwise."

"As I stated, Inspector, it is all well and good to arrest this so-called businessman, but in the case of Dr. Markey, we need the catalyst behind it all."

"As mysterious as always," said Lestrade, a wry grin on his normally dour face. "I wouldn't have it any other way."

Parked in the street outside was a covered wagon, with two bobbies sitting on the trap. "Expecting arrests then, Lestrade?" I quipped.

"Always when Mr. Holmes is on the case."

Sitting in the uncomfortable rear of the wagon, we drove through the streets for several minutes before pulling to a stop. We climbed out and looked around the area. It had the same aspect as any street in Brixton or Lambeth. "Where the devil are we?" I asked. "Back in Brixton?"

"Camberwell," Holmes said, nodding towards a building down the street. It was two storeys high, in the typical Georgian style, with a pub on the corner and what looked like residential houses behind. "That is Derrick Wasser's main office. It's where he can be found most days, and by sending telegrams to himself and one other first thing this morning, I've orchestrated a meeting between him and his client." He shrugged before adding, "Or I have wasted my money."

As Holmes spoke, a hansom drew up outside of the building. "Ah – the former it seems!"

A podgy looking man with a balding head stepped from the cab and across to the entrance. Even from our viewpoint, I could make out the insistent beating of his fist on the door. As it opened, an animated conversation began between the man and an unseen person inside.

As soon as the bald man entered, Holmes set off. Lestrade, myself, and the two constables followed in his wake. Lestrade instructed one of the uniformed policemen to remain outside, while Holmes tried the doorknob. It turned easily. The tenant was too preoccupied to lock the door as he withdrew.

As we entered the dim corridor, the sound of an argument filtered up the hallway towards us.

"By God, Wasser, what is all this twaddle? You told me it was dealt with."

"It was Sir Benton, it was."

"Then what is this?" The sound of something slamming down on a wooden desk echoed out. "Arrived this morning. Says that Markey has been found. At your pig farm."

"I received the same thing. I've no word myself, but I think someone's playing us like fools. Nobody that goes to the farm is ever found again. Mr. Bacon is very efficient."

"Well, he better be. If word about this gets out, then I won't be the only one suffering."

"Don't worry, Sir Benton. If I feel any heat, then I certainly won't be alone in Wandsworth."

"What do you mean?"

"Remember, you need me a lot more than I need you. That money you get for keeping things smooth with the law is only good while the drugs are legal. I don't care either way. If I have to go underground, then so be it. Risks are higher, but so is the profit."

"Why you – I've made things much easier for you over the years! Threatening me isn't going to end well!"

"Well, if this Dr. Markey has friends, then maybe I won't need your help much longer."

"You blackguard! I wouldn't be surprised if this was all your doing!"

"Now don't be stupid, sir. Why would I damage my operations like this? I don't know who did it, but I'd like to find them."

"Well, in that case," said Holmes, stepping through the office doorway, "here I am."

"Who the hell are you?" asked Wasser.

"Sherlock Holmes at your service." Stepping aside, he continued. "And this is Dr. Watson, along with Inspector Lestrade and Constable

Conway of Scotland Yard. I think they'll be very happy to talk with you after you virtually confessed to the murder of Dr. Dermid Markey."

The looks on both their faces were priceless.

***

"So this Sir Benton McBrough – what was his motivation?" I asked Holmes, as we both sat down to a wonderful meal at a local pub. We thought it fitting to have a small celebration. Holmes had brought both a local gangster passing himself off as an upright businessman, and a corrupt politician to justice.

"For the last two nights, I have spent many hours scouring the backstreets of Brixton and Camberwell and Peckham, talking with many of my contacts and piecing together an interesting narrative." He took a sip from the fine brandy we had ordered before continuing. "Our fine upstanding politician, Sir Benton, was deep in with Wasser. They share interests in much of the drug trade throughout the south of London – a trade that would only continue while the drugs were legitimate.

"Sir Benton became scared by Markey's success in last year's election. The margin wasn't close, but it represented a change in the electorate's opinions of him. If Sir Benton lost his place in Parliament, his lucrative side business of supporting the drug trade within south London would be lost. Worse, if Markey's popularity grew and more politicians paid attention to his stance, then there was the possibility of a movement growing within the Government and the medical industry. Which could lead to a loss of illicit income on his part."

"Money," I sighed.

"Yes, Watson, money. There are seven deadly sins, as outlined in the theology. Whenever the other six fail to account for a motive, always rely on greed to provide the solution."

The Demise of the Painted Devil

I had known Mrs. Hudson for the best part of two years, the same period spent under her roof as co-lodger with my colleague and friend Sherlock Holmes. To that point, I had always found her to be calm, stable, and almost stoic in her resolve, with an extreme level of reverence and what could almost be called love for Holmes.

But it was that morning in the autumn of 1883, that I first saw her in a highly emotional state, making her even more human, and indeed humane, in my eyes.

"I'm so sorry, Doctor," she said from our doorway, her face flushed red, and her eyes almost brimming with the expectation of tears, "Is Mr. Holmes awake? I do need to see him. Urgently."

"My dear Mrs. Hudson. Whatever can the matter be? Please come in. Sit, I'll stir Holmes from his slumber." I moved back, to allow Mrs. Hudson gress.

"Oh, it's not for me. I have a friend downstairs. A long-time friend that I've known almost all my life. Her world is crashing down, and I didn't know where to turn."

"In that case, bring her up. I'll rouse Holmes while you do."

Nodding, she disappeared quickly. The sound of her feet on the seventeen steps leading down to the landing, echoed as she fled.

"What was all that about?" asked a voice still rough from recent slumber. I "I have no idea, Holmes. Mrs. Hudson was all in a tizz. Make yourself comfortable, there may be something intriguing in all this for you."

My colleague moved across to the table and sat. Helping himself to a cup of coffee and rubbing the final rime of sleep from his eyes. "I do hope this will be stimulating. I spent several hours, last night, stalking the streets of Soho, without any hint of interest from the criminal world."

I smiled to myself. Over the last couple of years, I had become accustomed to my friend's strange activities, but even then some of his more obscure doings always brought a touch of humour to my thought patterns.

I opened my mouth to ask about his recent undertakings but was stopped when our door opened revealing Mrs. Hudson with a matronly woman of similar age, whose eyes were red-rimmed from a former tearful state.

When her sight fell on Holmes, Mrs. Hudson sighed with relief. "Oh, Mr. Holmes, I'm so glad you're awake." Ushering in her companion, she added, "This is my good friend, Mrs. Sonia Wengert, widowed. We've known each other since school and kept in touch for all these years."

The other woman nodded her head slightly. A pained expression crossed her face, one that I translated as either sorrow or embarrassment at placing her reliance on a virtual stranger.

Holmes stood and moved across to the doorway. He took Mrs. Wengert's hand in his own and ushered the unfortunate woman into our rooms, showing her to a comfortable chair. I could tell the gesture was to place the woman in as natural a position as possible, so that she would be assured enough to relate her story as thoroughly as possible. "It is a delight to meet you Mrs. Wengert."

The woman blurted out, "Oh, call me Sonia."

Bowing his head slightly, Holmes said, "Sonia." With the woman ensconced in the easy chair, he added. "Now, a friend of Mrs. Hudson's is a friend of mine, Sonia. What is it I can do for you?"

"Oh, I'm so sorry to be such a bother, Mr. Holmes. I've heard so much about you. I never believed I'd need your help. No. Never."

"That is fine. Please tell me what troubles you."

In her own inimitable way, Mrs. Hudson found a way to help the situation as well, bringing a fresh cup of tea to her good friend. Mrs. Wengert nodded as she took the cup and sipped at the hot brew. Her demeanour relaxed even further until she was ready to tell everything.

"It's the lady," she said, "They came this morning and arrested her."

"The Lady?"

"Yes, my Mistress. Mrs. Smartwood. Mrs. Rowena Smartwood. I have been their housekeeper for quite a few years. Lovely people."

Holmes turned and looked at me, a questioning glance, with one eyebrow raised. I shook my head. I'd never heard of the woman.

"Why would *they*, and by *they*, I assume you mean the police." The woman nodded. "Arrest her? Did they say what she is accused of?"

"Yes, yes, they did. Murder. They said she murdered Mr. Smartwood, but that's impossible."

"My word," I blurted out.

Holmes shot me a withering glance. Stifling any further utterances. Turning back to the woman he asked, "Take me back to the beginning. Is there anything to tell before the police arrested Mrs. Smartwood?"

"Oh, yes, yes there is." Holmes waited while Mrs. Wengert took another sip of tea. Finally, she took a deep breath and began to relate her tale. "I would say that it started last night. The Master, Mr. Frederick Smartwood, went out to his club, or group, or whatever he calls it."

"A regular occurrence, I would assume."

Mrs. Wengert nodded. "Yes. He's been spending more time there of late. Anyway, on some nights he retires to the room in the basement, instead of climbing the stairs to the master bedroom. The Mistress is a light sleeper and is possessed of a delicate disposition, so he has taken it on himself to leave her be if he knows he will return late."

"Was there anything different about his return last night?"

"Yes. That's why I mentioned it. He is normally as quiet as a mouse, but on his return last night, he was louder. Clattering into some furniture in the hallway. Knocking over a hatstand. Then he clambered down the stairs to his basement room. Worried, I had sprung from my bed, afraid that the Master had hurt himself, and found the Mistress upon the ground floor landing before the basement stairs."

"He's not a drinker?" I asked.

The woman looked horrified. "No. Never a drop above the sociable. I've seen him partake of a sherry or two at dinner with friends, but nothing more." She took another sip of tea before continuing. "I've never heard anything like what happened last night. It was late. Just before he returned, I heard the hallway clock strike twelve."

"What was Mrs. Smartwood's reaction?"

"Her face was a mask of fear. Like myself, she had never heard the Master in such a state. I lit a candle, and held it before us, as she pried open the basement door and we descended. The Master had flopped, fully clothed onto his bed. The Mistress moved over, prodding him slightly to see if he was alright."

"He was asleep, I would assume," said Holmes. "I don't wish to cast aspersions, but it does sound like he had imbibed."

Holding up a single finger, the woman simply said, "I know what a drunk's reaction would be in most cases. My late husband was one for the drink, but this was certainly not it." I noticed Mrs. Hudson nod at that, assumedly she well knew of the late Mr. Wengert.

"What happened next?" I asked.

"The Master virtually exploded in rage. As the Mistress laid a hand on his shoulder, he sprang up from the bed. His face, a mask of horror and rage. He lashed out, slapping the Mistress across the face with the back of his hand, before grasping her by the lapels of her dressing gown. The Mistress reacted in the same way I believe I would have. She slashed at his cheek with her nails extended. The pain drove the Master back far enough for the two of us to rush to the stairs and from the room. I locked the door, leaving the Master inside. For the next few minutes, we both cowered outside, listening for any response from within. When we finally felt safe, the tears flowing from both of us, I took the Mistress back to her bed-chamber, consoling her for all it was worth. We spent the next few hours in a fitful state of half-sleep because when the Mistress came down in the morning, she bore the darkened eyes of one who had not attained a good night's rest."

"What did you do next?" Holmes prompted, once the woman has stopped for a moment.

"The Mistress knocked on the door and called out to her husband, but there was no response. After a few moments, she asked me to unlock the door. I did not wish to, but after all, it was her husband.

Even my own Wilfred would have been as calm as a lamb by then, so I did as asked, and followed her down the stairs." Visibly disturbed, Mrs. Wengert took another sip of tea. "It was so quiet. I lit the gas lamp at the bottom of the stairs, and both of us gasped in horror. The Master was on the bed, lying on his back, his eyes open and staring at the ceiling, his skin a strange pallor with a blue tinge. The Mistress ran to him and tried to shake him awake, but he would not respond. Touching his brow, she withdrew her hand in terror. He was cold, she told me. It was then I knew the truth. He was dead. When I said I would send for a Doctor, the Mistress nodded, a look of loss growing on her face."

Mrs. Wengert pulled a kerchief from her sleeve and dabbed at the edges of her eyes. The telling was taking a toll on her.

"Within half an hour, Doctor Gibbison arrived on our doorstep. I took him straight down, but as soon as he laid eyes on the Master he simply shook his head. I've known the good Doctor for many years, and he did not disappoint. He was professional but careful to preserve the Master's dignity. Finally, he turned to the Mistress and declared that he was indeed dead. When asked how, he simply said, that is something I will need to discuss with the police. It was then the Mistress fainted. With the Doctor's help, we managed to take the Mistress to her room, and I put her in bed, while the Doctor arranged for the police to attend."

"Who?" asked Holmes.

"An Inspector Lanner arrived not long after."

"Lanner," I said, "Didn't we come across him on that Blessington business?"

"Yes," answered Holmes, "Young, diligent, ambitious. What did Lanner make of the scene?"

"That's where I can't tell you much more. Once the Inspector arrived, he and the Doctor made their way downstairs, while I went up to attend to the Mistress. About a half an hour after, they both presented at the Mistress's doorway. She invited them in, as she had recovered a little by then. But, when the Inspector said that the Master had been murdered, she began to grow faint once more. When he said that he was arresting her for that murder, she again fainted dead away."

"The blackguard," I blurted out, "How could he accuse a young woman of such a thing?"

"Well," said Holmes, "That is for us to find out, isn't it?"

***

After reassuring Mrs. Wengert, and indeed, Mrs. Hudson, that we would get to the bottom of it all, Holmes and I took a hansom to Ealing Police station to meet our old acquaintance, Inspector Lanner.

Even though I was slightly enraged and looking for confrontation, and I noticed Holmes was quiet and serious, which I presumed to be hiding a demeanour similar to mine, Lanner was anything but. The constable at the front desk found the Inspector quickly once he learned of our names and past association. The Inspector was as I had last seen him, keen of eye, clean of face, with just a slight touch of world-weariness about him.

"Mr. Holmes, Doctor Watson, how wonderful to see you."

"Hello Inspector," said Holmes, keeping things professional.

"What brings you to Ealing? A little out of your way isn't it?"

"I've taken on a case. One that you should be quite familiar with. It has only fallen into my lap, and I hope it can be cleared up quickly."

"If you're onto it, then I'm sure it won't take too long," said the eager young police officer.

"It concerns a young couple, who live not far from here. He is a solicitor, working out of his offices on the Ealing High Street, and his wife. She has been accused of his murder."

Lanner's face grew slightly dark as he realised what Holmes was talking about. "The Smartwoods? How did you find out about that so quickly?"

"The housekeeper is an old acquaintance of my landlady. In honour of her, I have taken the case. Now, why did you jump so quickly to a charge of murder against the wife?"

"That was on the evidence at the scene. It was pretty cut and dried. The husband came home, intoxicated from some substance still to be determined. He struck out at his wife. She retaliated but left quickly. When he fell into a stupor, she returned later and finished the job."

"What?" I stammered, "Finished the job? In what way?"

"Strangled him. In his sleep. She's a slight thing, but he messed her up, and she did him in. Cut and dried. The Doctor, Gibbinson, agreed. The local coroner is due to make his own assessment soon, and then it will be the gallows. No other explanation. There was no inference of a break-in, no evidence of a third party. Even the housekeeper had no motive, so I ruled her out straight away."

"Preposterous," I cried.

"Come Watson, no need to get emotional. We must simply look at the evidence and determine the facts as they come to hand." Turning to Lanner, Holmes added, "I would like to view the body, but first I think it would be best to talk with Mrs. Smartwood. I assume she is here."

"Yes, happy to escort you. I know it seems a little extraordinary, but I can see no other outcome."

***

Lanner led the two of us into the rear of the station, where several cells were located. They had the air of another age and were dark, damp and very dingy. I felt for the fair lady who sat within one of these horrors.

A small room sat at the end of the corridor, past the row of cells. We were shown inside and waited until Mrs. Smartwood, her face drawn in terror, her eyes red-rimmed from hours of crying, was shown inside.

"If I could interview her alone, Inspector, just to remove any aspect of the fear of retribution that your presence may inject."

"Of course," said Lanner, withdrawing from the room, and locking the door behind him. I looked through the small window and watched as he strode away, leaving a burly constable behind to ensure nothing untoward occurred.

Holmes led the poor woman to the only chair in the room and sat her down. Hunkering onto his knees, so that he was at her eye level before beginning his interview.

"I am so sorry that you have been treated this way, Mrs. Smartwood."

"Who are you?" she asked between sobs.

"My name is Sherlock Holmes; this is my colleague Doctor Watson. I am a consulting detective, and your housekeeper, Mrs. Wengert, has asked that I investigate the event of your husband's unfortunate demise to determine the truth of the matter.

"I had nothing to do with it," she cried out through a veil of tears. "The police. That Inspector, he said I strangled Frederick. How could I?" Holding out her hands, she said, "I would never do such a thing. I couldn't even if I tried." She indeed had a pair of delicate hands that I failed to imagine could even grasp a man's throat, let alone strangle the life from him.

"I can understand," said Holmes, "So, we must find out as many facts as we can. Until I see your husband, I cannot determine the likelihood of your involvement. Having seen Mrs. Wengert, I can't imagine that she would be able to do such a deed either. To strangle the life from a full-grown man takes a great deal of strength." He stood up for a moment, I could see his expression change to ponder some fact and remained quiet for a while. "Can you take me through the events of last night and this morning?"

Mrs. Smartwood began to relate her version of her husband's return and demise. Everything matched almost perfectly to Mrs. Wengert's story. The only differences were the points about Smartwood's entry into the house. The woman before us having been upstairs, heard slightly different noises to the housekeeper who would have been on the ground floor and much closer.

When she had finished, Holmes stared at her for a good while, waiting I feel, to see if anything else entered her mind, before asking, "This club that your husband frequented. Do you know what it was? Or indeed, its location."

Shaking her head, a look of confusion crossed her face. "No. He was ever so secretive about it. All I know is that he kept a collection of clothes in the basement room, that he took with him. He went there a good two to three times a week. Sometimes even more. I do know that it wasn't a normal gentlemen's club. There was no drinking. No smoking. It was altogether strange."

"Your husband was a solicitor." She nodded at this. "Where did he study?"

"Oxford. He was born near Stratford, studied hard and moved on to study in Oxford. He started reading history and the arts but switched to the law when he realised there would be no money in the other disciplines. We met in his final year. He undertook a position at my father's firm in Oxford, gaining experience and grounding in the law before graduating and becoming a full-time solicitor. We moved to London not long after. That was over five years ago."

"No children?" I asked.

Mrs. Smartwood dropped her head. I immediately regretted the question, especially when she answered, "No. I'm afraid I am barren. That is one thing Frederick always wanted, but something I could never give him."

"I... I'm so sorry for even asking."

Holmes continued. "What has the Inspector told you about the state of your husband? Or at least, has he told you why you were arrested?"

"Yes. He said I strangled Frederick. That there were marks on his neck, and that the scratches on his face meant I had the most motive."

Holmes shook his head and pursed his lips. "Flimsy at best. I am sorry to have troubled you, Mrs. Smartwood, and I assure you I will get to the bottom of this and have you out of this horrid place as quickly as possible."

Spinning, he thumped the door, which brought the constable quickly. Within a few minutes, we had said our goodbyes to Mrs. Smartwood and were on the high street and heading for the nearby hospital.

***

"I cannot believe that Lanner would incarcerate that woman for such a crime," I said, as we walked, "I do hope you can have her out of there as quickly as possible."

"Not too soon, Watson, " Holmes said. I noted a change in tone, which struck me as concerning.

"You don't think she had anything to do with it, do you?"

"I believe that the chances are slim that a lithe woman, such as Mrs. Smartwood, would have the strength to strangle a full-grown man to death, but," he held up a finger, "Until I have examined all the pertinent facts and clues, I will not pass judgement on anyone. At this stage, we only have Mrs. Smartwood, Mrs. Wengert, Mr. Smartwood, or some unknown villain as our perpetrator. Or it is not a simple murder as Inspector Lanner would have us believe. Our next destination should provide us with further information."

A few minutes stroll later, we came to the entrance of the Ealing Cottage Hospital. A quaint building that served the local community for most of its medical needs and was the location of the only morgue in the area.

It took us but a few minutes to find our way through the building and introduce ourselves to Doctor Langham, the long-time coroner of the area.

"I haven't had a chance to start the autopsy on the poor unfortunate Mr. Smartwood," he said, leading us to the gurney upon which the object of our interest lay. "I knew this poor man, you know. Had need of his expertise only a few months back. Some documents needed drafting for a property I was purchasing. Precise, articulate, well-kempt. The sort of person you feel comfortable leaving your legal dealings in the hands of." Pulling back the sheet, to reveal Smartwood's head and chest, he added, "Now, just another lump of meat, poor blighter."

I quickly ran my eyes over as much of Smartwood's body as I could. His neck was bruised and appeared to have swollen, such was the trauma visited upon it. I still couldn't justify Lanner's accusations of Mrs. Smartwood. Her husband was a large man, possibly six feet in height, and of considerable build. Her tiny hands would barely stretch to half his throat, rather than be able to reach around and choke the life from him.

"What is your opinion, Doctor Langham?" asked Holmes.

"Oh, initial observations agree with Inspector Lanner's summation." He pointed to the discolouration on the neck. "Bruising on the throat, and rear of the neck indicates possible strangulation."

"By someone's hands or other?"

"There's no burning or tearing of the skin, so I would not think it was a garrotte or rope or the like. Hands? Yes, possibly."

Holmes bent over the corpse, and taking out his glass, inspected the bruising and discolouration at length.

"A woman's hands, perhaps?"

The coroner stopped for a moment, stared at the cadaver, then at Holmes. "I think I will need to reserve my opinion on that point until I have completed my examination," he said, a tone of authority creeping into his voice.

It was at that point that an orderly poked his head into the room and requested Dr. Langham's assistance in another part of the hospital.

"If you would excuse me, gentlemen, it seems I am needed elsewhere." Removing his gloves, he moved towards the exit but stopped. "I'm happy for you to observe the corpse, but please do not disturb it in any way. I will begin my examination forthwith, and the Inspector will be the first to see the report. It was a pleasure meeting you, and I bid you adieu."

Holmes continued to peer at the corpse's face for a few moments, before answering. "Thank you, Doctor, we will see to your request and not disturb Mr. Smartwood here. I would be loath for anything to interfere with your work."

As the coroner withdrew, Holmes waited for a moment before moving to the door and peeking outside. Turning back, he strode across to Smartwood's body and withdrew a syringe from inside his coat.

"What do you intend to do with that?" I asked, watching Holmes screw a needle in place. "Draw blood?"

"No. It's not blood I'm after."

I was shocked as Holmes proceeded to pull back the sheet, revealing Smartwood's lower body, and plunged the needle into the cadaver. Instead of blood, a large volume of yellow liquid filled the glass tube.

"Holmes," I cried, "What in the blazes are you doing?"

"I feel that there is one particular angle that may not be within the coroner's field of vision and wish to conduct my own examination."

Once finished, Holmes disappeared the syringe into his coat, pulled the sheet back over the corpse and hurried to the door. I followed quickly behind.

***

As we arrived at 221B Baker Street, Holmes virtually leapt from the hansom and vaulted up the stairway. I paid off the surprised driver and wearily trudged my way upstairs to find Holmes bent over his chemistry equipment in the corner of our parlour.

Rather than ask questions, I left him to it and stripping off my coat and hat, hung them away and proceeded downstairs to inquire of Mrs. Hudson.

As her friend, Mrs. Wengert, had returned home, I told our landlady of all we knew, which I admitted wasn't much, before she offered to prepare a light luncheon. Glad for any food, I thanked her and made my way upstairs again, to find Holmes preparing to depart once more.

"Lunch is about to arrive," I said, "Mrs. Hudson informed me that her friend has left, but I feel we should eat before any further journeys."

Looking once at the chemistry equipment, where two spherical flasks were now bubbling merrily away, the acrid smell of ammonia filtering into my nostrils, Holmes said, "Well, this will take some time, and we have at least one more stop to make this afternoon. So, yes, let us eat then be on our way."

"I don't suppose you could open a window, could you?" I asked, eyeing the darkening yellow liquid as it boiled away.

Sniffing once, Holmes nodded. "Yes, boiling urine isn't the most pleasant smell, is it?"

***

After a wonderful lunch provided by Mrs. Hudson, and I couldn't help wonder if the level of quality had improved given Holmes's assistance in the case of the demise of Mr. Smartwood, we caught a cab back to Ealing, stopping outside a modest two-storey house in Culmington Road.

"This is the address that Mrs. Hudson gave us, and it has all the hallmarks of an up-and-coming solicitor," said Holmes, examining the

Smartwood's residence. "Also, it would seem that Mrs. Wengert is the only servant. Thus, eliminating any others who may present as suspects."

Indeed, it was Mrs. Wengert that greeted us once we had rung the bell.

"Oh, Mr. Holmes, Dr. Watson, have you any news?" she asked, a look of expectation writ large on her face.

"Not at this stage, I'm afraid I have nothing more to add. I felt I needed to visit the scene of Mr. Smartwood's demise to ascertain any other facts or clues that remain viable."

The old housekeeper's face descended into a look of confusion.

"Mr. Holmes merely wishes to see where Mr. Smartwood died. There may be some hidden clue that can help."

"Oh, I see," said the old woman, "Well, you better come in then."

Mrs. Wengert led us through the well-presented and modestly furnished house and stopped before a set of stairs leading down into the basement. The door was wide open, as it probably had been since the coroner removed the body. Lighting a nearby candle, she bid us to follow her into the gloom. "Now, watch your footing. I'll light the gas at the bottom."

The stairs opened into a smallish room, which would normally be used as a storage area, or previously as a coal cellar, but had been cleaned up and converted into a bedroom. Once, the gas light was lit, I could make out the single bed that lay near the centre, with a free-standing cupboard, and a bureau against the opposite wall.

"You mentioned that Mr. Smartwood used this as a bedroom when he arrived home late at night from his club."

Mrs. Wengert nodded. "Yes, he didn't want to wake the Mistress, so would often sleep down here. Many times, we needed to rouse him in the morning to ensure he was on time for his morning appointments. At times, he did arrive home at the strangest hour."

Holmes moved across to the bed and hunched over to examine the linen closely. Pulling out his glass, he became highly interested in some tiny detail. "How often do you change the bed linen?"

"Oh, every morning after the Master had slept here. I don't know what he gets up to, but it would be in a right state and need to be boiled to remove the stains."

Holmes murmured to himself as he straightened and moved across to the cupboard. Opening the door, he revealed all manner of brightly coloured clothing, not something I would have suspected a solicitor to possess. "I'm assuming this was not Mr. Smartwood's regular day clothes then?"

"No. I've never even looked in there. Mr. Smartwood was very insistent that I stay out of that cupboard."

"Really," said Holmes, "These may have played a part in whatever activities, Mr. Smartwood got up to at his club." Closing the cupboard door, Holmes slid open the top drawer of the bureau. It contained several thick books and loose leafed sheaves of paper. Intrigued, I joined Holmes and peered down at the papers.

"Are they plays?" I asked, seeing the top sheets of several bearing the names 'Romeo and Juliet," "Richard the Third," and "Timon of Athens."

"They do indeed appear to be," answered Holmes, as he flipped through several pages. "Do you remember, Mrs. Smartwood mentioned that her husband was born near Stratford?"

"Now that you mention it, yes, I do."

A wry grin came to Holmes's face. "From looking at these pages, I feel that he may have missed a calling in his home town."

"What do you mean?"

"Well, with the newly established theatre in Stratford, which is dedicated to the works of the bard, he could well have found a career in treading the boards, rather than reading the law."

"Quite, I suppose," I replied, "I assume that's something you have often aspired to as well."

Nodding, he added, "Well yes, but I have the advantage of plying my acting skills as part of my chosen career."

Before I could add anything further, Holmes turned to Mrs. Wengert and asked, "Does Mr. Smartwood have a study or office upstairs?"

***

Unlocking the heavy door, Mrs. Wengert proceeded to ignite a small gaslight in the study. It was fully enclosed with no exterior windows, and each wall was lined with bookcases, overflowing with legal texts and other leather-bound volumes.

A large mahogany desk sat in the centre of the room, opposite a small fireplace that assumedly provided warmth during the winter months.

"The Master doesn't let anyone else in here. I only come in to give the place a quick dust and clean once a week. I know he's gone, but I do have reservations about invading his privacy like this."

"I assure you, Madam, that I will be circumspect in my investigation. I merely wish to track down Mr. Smartwood's movements, and as he is a professional I can only assume that he would have a diary with his appointments well documented."

Nodding, the housekeeper turned, and with one last look around the room, left.

Holmes took no time in moving to the desk and rummaging through the drawers, whilst I went to the bookcases and searched for anything that looked like a diary. "Aha," I cried at my success when I pulled a thick volume nestled next to several of the same and opened it to find calendar entries dating back several months. I moved to the desk and placed it down on the last page with records.

Holmes plonked a similar volume down next to it. As he opened the book we saw lines of figures. "A ledger."

"Yes. Should be just as important as the diary."

Scanning both journals, side by side, our first sight was the previous night's appointment. It simply read "WS."

"WS? Perhaps, William Shakespeare?"

"Good, Watson, good thinking."

I pointed to an entry for this evening. Again, it simply read "WS."

"Another meeting? Tonight?"

"I agree," said Holmes, "That gives us only a few hours to ponder what this club is about, and to cogitate on the evidence so far." Scanning the diary further back, the entries for "WS" occurred twice a week, until recently, when a third and fourth night had been added.

The earliest appointment with that moniker had been twelve months previously. "We must check with Mrs. Wengert and determine when Mr. Smartwood began his nightly sojourns to this group."

Scanning the ledger, I found a payment that tied in with the evening appointments. "Look," I said, pointing at the entry. "There's a monthly payment of a pound made to someone called Winduss. Winduss? Could that be a club contribution or similar?"

"My word," said Holmes, "I wonder." After a moment, he shook his head and added, "It couldn't be surely?"

"What?"

"Riley Winduss. One of the premier authorities on the plays of William Shakespeare. He has played all the greats, Hamlet, Lear, Othello, Macbeth. Directed several plays for the Lyceum as well but disappeared off the map a few years back following a dalliance with his Lady Macbeth co-star."

"What was so wrong with that?"

"She just happened to be the wife of the primary benefactor of the Lyceum Theatre at the time."

"Oh."

"If this is the same Winduss," Holmes mused, striding from the room, and pausing his sentence until we stood in the basement once more, "Then it could be that our solicitor from Stratford has taken it upon himself to live a long-held dream."

"Of what?"

Holmes dropped the diary and ledger on the bed and moved to the cupboard, opening the door to reveal the sets of colourful clothing once more. Smiling to himself, he withdrew one that was various shades of green, then another that was virtually nothing but a close-fitting cloak.

"Of being an actor?" Holmes added. "If I was to guess, I would say that these costumes are Puck and perhaps Oberon."

Confused, I asked, "Why would a respectable solicitor be engaging in such?"

"Oh, come now Watson. Many a dignified professional has dreams of the stage, or of some other creative bent. I trod the boards in college on many occasions. You have your writings, something I assume has always been a burning desire. Fortunately for you, these cases we undertake have given you a focus and outlet."

I pursed my lips, suffering a slight chastisement of my documentation of Holmes's adventures. "Where does that leave us then?"

"We just need to find where Winduss is holed up and pay him a visit."

"I still don't see how this has anything to do with Smartwood's death."

Checking his pocket watch, Holmes smiled. "For that, we need to pop by Baker Street once more." Snatching up the journal and ledger, Holmes headed out of the basement.

***

As we stepped into our parlour, I rushed straight for the windows and threw them wide open. The rank odour of Holmes's experiment lingered within the confines of the room. When I turned around, I found Holmes hovering over his chemistry table. I noticed the gas flames beneath both flasks extinguished.

"Your experiment finished then?"

"Why yes, Watson. I do apologise for the noxious odour but come and look." Moving back from the table, so that I could join him, he added, "I think you'll find this interesting."

Joining Holmes, I glanced down at the two flasks. One contained a yellow-brown substance clumped on the base, in the other a white residue had collected across the surface.

"Interesting, you conducted two separate experiments it seems. What were you trying to prove?"

"Ah, that's where you are slightly wrong. It was the same experiment, just two different sources of the primary substance."

"Alright, from the horrid smell, I can only conclude that you withdrew a urine sample from Mr. Smartwood's corpse. Why? I have no idea, as yet, but what was the second source?"

"I needed a control to ensure my hypothesis was correct, and my experiment was conducted correctly, so I used my own."

I wrinkled my nose in disgust, "Oh, Holmes."

"It seemed the most convenient source. It was either that or request a sample from you."

"Fair point. What was the experiment? What were you looking for? Smartwood died from asphyxiation, why investigate his urine?"

"From your extensive medical knowledge, what are the symptoms that come to mind when you consider arsenic poisoning?"

"Arsenic poisoning?" He nodded his head indicating I'd heard correctly. I thought for a moment. "The immediate effects are, cramping, nausea, muscle pains, diarrhoea."

"Yes. Immediate high-level ingestion or exposure will often then lead to cardiac arrest and death. What about longer-term exposure? Have you ever come across any cases or literature in that area?"

"It's not something that happens very often any more. Once the dangers of arsenic were identified in many common products, its use was stopped."

"True. There are records of long-term exposure resulting in sudden mood changes, delirium, swelling, and skin discolouration, especially around the throat and neck region."

My eyes grew wide as Holmes spoke. "My word, Holmes, are you saying that Smartwood died from prolonged arsenic poisoning?"

"Well, given the symptoms, I wanted to be sure, hence my surreptitious gathering of the urine sample. I didn't think it was something that the coroner would even contemplate searching for." Pointing at the two flasks before us, he added, "That's where this experiment comes in."

"What did you mix with the urine samples?"

"Magnesium Nitrate. It has been used of late to bond with the arsenic in urine to create arsenic nitrate, such as we find here." Holmes indicated the yellow-brown substance. "Smartwood's urine was filled with a high concentration of arsenic." Picking up the flask, he jostled it around, causing the flaky substance to break up. "A concentration this high could never have come from a single ingestion of the poison. Smartwood would simply have collapsed in excruciating pain and died straight away before the arsenic could be passed into his urine. This indicates that our poor victim has been exposed for quite some time. The poison accruing in his system until he finally succumbed." He replaced the flask on its stand. "I can only conclude that his inebriation of last night was the culmination of the poisoning, and the stress caused by his argument with his wife resulted in his body finally succumbing."

"The poor fellow." I almost choked on my next words, as I realised the importance of Holmes's findings. "But that means that Mrs. Smartwood is innocent." I turned to leave, taking two strides towards the door. "We must tell Lanner and have her released."

"Wait a moment, my friend, we have simply identified a probable cause of death. Before we can declare Mrs. Smartwood innocent, we must locate the source of the poison. The good inspector would still be quite prepared to lay the blame on his current suspect unless we can shed more light on the circumstances of Mr. Smartwood's demise."

Stopping I nodded, resigned to leave the poor woman incarcerated at Ealing police station for the time being. I hoped it wouldn't be for long.

***

The earliest entry in the diary, which luckily seemed to be the very first, included an address. Holmes had suggested that it may be Winduss's actual address, or where the club met.

The hansom stopped at the address on Park Street in Camden. The building was nondescript, with boarded-up windows, as if it hadn't been used for several years. "Are you sure this is the place," I asked.

"Oh, yes, Watson. You don't realise what this building is, do you?"

"No. A hangout for the destitute if anyone actually inhabits it."

"This, my dear Watson," Holmes said, waving one arm across the faded façade. "Is the Park Theatre, once known as the Royal Alexandria Theatre. It opened back in 1873 and hosted many wonderful productions through to the early part of this decade. Sadly, the owners had to sell up, and I believe it is destined to be demolished." He stepped up to the double entry doors. "I do hope it has retained some of its former grandeur."

The inside foyer would have appeared elaborate in its prime, but after several years of neglect, it was one step up from the back alleys of Brixton. A thick layer of dust covered the carpet and fittings. Vandals had broken in, or more likely walked in like the two of us, and broken or removed seats, counters, and anything that wasn't nailed down. "It has seen better days."

"Quite so. Though if someone were to rescue it, I'm sure it could be brought back to once again join other great London theatres."

"I'm afraid that is not likely. The group of men that bought this poor old place have their minds set on tearing her down within the next year or two."

We both turned to see an older gentleman, who I picked to be in his sixties, though his posture was as straight and true as any I had seen. As he walked towards us, I was struck by his impressively handsome face, untouched by wrinkles, but framed with a shock of steel-grey hair.

"Riley Winduss, if I'm not mistaken."

At Holmes's statement, the man stopped and slowly eyed us both. "Do I know you, Sir?"

"Like my knowledge of yourself, you may have heard of me. I am Sherlock Holmes, and this is my colleague Doctor John Watson."

"My word, to what do I owe this honour? Do you wish to join our little group? To relive your past successes on the stage?"

"You know of Holmes's past acting performances?"

"Yes, I do. It has been some years though hasn't it? There was a time that I caught as many university performances as I could, to recruit for my troupe. Now that I think of it, I should have approached you."

Holmes nodded, a wry grin and a twinkle in his eye, to which I presumed was his mind running through some of his memories. "The draw of the stage never leaves the soul. You will always find ways of revisiting it." Moving past Winduss, Holmes approached a large set of double doors and threw them open revealing a dark voluminous hall beyond. "This little group, as you called it, I presume you perform on the stage down here."

"Why, yes." Winduss floated past Holmes, firing up several gas lights inside the auditorium and casting a dull yellow pall across the area. "The new owners have allowed me to rent the place until they finally bring down the roof, so to speak."

"What is it that your group does here?"

"Ah, my boy, we explore all things concerning the bard."

"Shakespeare?" I asked, just confirming. My knowledge of the stage was far less than that of Holmes.

"Yes, yes. The one and only." We followed as Winduss strode down the aisle. He deftly climbed onto the stage and took up a position in the centre. To my eye, it seemed to be his natural habitat. "We read. We speak. We perform the plays of the bard."

"We?" asked Holmes.

"Men." He threw his arms wide. "In the spirit of the Elizabethan theatre, I have gathered a troupe of men together for the sole purpose of revitalising the Bard's work as it would have been performed in his time. The troupe contains only men. And there are only a few, so each actor plays several parts where possible."

"In full costume?"

"Oh, yes, with changes conducted at lightning speed, as would have been the case when these wonderful plays were performed before her majesty."

"Are there audiences?"

"Sometimes but always limited. We have had the odd occasion where members of the actors' families or close associates attend, but most of my actors prefer the solitude of an empty theatre."

"These men in your company, who are they?"

"Oh, we have many from all walks of life. From dustmen to scholars. Even a lawyer. All have a simple yearning for the stage."

My ears pricked up at the last occupation. "This lawyer? What was his name?"

"Oh, I couldn't. Most of the actors don't even know each other's names. When we are in character, we go by that name alone."

"Would it be a Mr. Frederick Smartwood?"

Winduss's jaw dropped open in shock, though I felt he was still in character and simply overplaying his role. "How? How did you know of Frederick's attendance?"

"Well, you may know me as an actor, but I am actually a consulting detective. Mr. Smartwood's housekeeper has requested that I investigate his sudden and sad demise."

This time Winduss's face became a mask of horror, though I wasn't so sure he was still acting. He dropped to the stage, sliding his legs over the edge, and sat, his head bowed and shaking. "Oh, my poor Frederick." Growing silent for a moment, I half expected another explosion of emotion, but instead, he mumbled, "Who will play Caliban now?"

Not believing my ears, I felt compelled to accost the man. "Did you just ask who would replace Smartwood in your play?" I admit I was livid. "A man has died, and that's all you can question?"

Lifting his head to stare into my eyes, he answered, "Of course, you're right. I can worry about that later. How did he die? Was it sudden?" His answer did nothing to calm my unrest.

"The police say that it was strangulation, but I will present an argument to the coroner that it was indeed arsenic poisoning."

"My word, poisoned, strangled. Who would murder poor Frederick? He was a lamb of a man. Such a wonderful actor. No part was too small, and he delved into each with all his soul. Even in the first readings, he would appear in full costume and makeup. Such commitment. I truly feel that within him was a sense of loss at pursuing a career in the law. His wish was a life on the stage, which was evident in his attitude and decorum."

"Admirable, but like myself, he probably felt that life would not afford him the level of comfort to which he wished."

"True. It is not a highly paid career. I do it just for the love. This little group is simply a sideline to pay the bills."

"You mentioned that Smartwood appeared in costume and makeup on every occasion."

"Yes. The dressing rooms are still intact, so the actors use them at their leisure."

***

Within moments, we stood inside the large and once lavish dressing rooms. Now, simply a series of stalls for the actors to apply their makeup and store their costumes.

Winduss led us across to one corner and lit the gaslight above. "This was Frederick's spot. He had made it his own for quite a while now."

Two costumes hung from hooks next to a large, stained mirror. Holmes took one look and said, "Ah, Caliban, as you have already alluded, and." He ran his fingers across a more ornate costume of white silk and feathers. "Ariel, if I were to take a guess."

"Very good, Sir. You know your Shakespeare. When I handed out the assignments, Frederick was extra effusive at being handed the dual roles of Caliban, the painted devil, and Ariel, the angel. He designed and had these costumes made at his own expense."

Staring down at the makeup table, Holmes picked up a large jar and lifted the lid. It contained a thick white concoction. The pot looked as if it came from another age. The label had faded, and parts were sloughing off as the glue disintegrated. The jar itself was an opaque colour and reminded me more of ceramic than glass, while the lid was of the same material, simply sitting on top loose as opposed to a tight-fitting cork or rubber stopper.

"This makeup," asked Holmes, "Where did it come from?"

"Again, that was something Frederick procured for his own use," said Winduss, going quiet for a moment as he pondered. "He told me that he had found it in an antique shop in Stratford. I remember a bright smile on his face, as he said it was the same type of foundation used by the original Stratford Shakespeare players. I admit I did scoff at the notion, but he seemed genuine and proud of his find."

"The original players," said Holmes, staring at the pot of cream once more. "If that's true then this could contain an arsenic-based concoction. Something that was outlawed over a century ago." He sniffed at the cream, then shrugged. "How long did Smartwood use this?"

"Oh, for well over three months." Leaning in towards Holmes, Winduss nodded. "Yes. Over half has gone. It was full when he first showed it to me."

Frederick was extra effusive at being handed the dual roles of Caliban, the painted devil, and Ariel, the angel.

"My word, Holmes," I said, "If he's been using this several times a week for months, then…"

"Precisely Watson, the arsenic would have leached in through his skin. That ties in with the white remnants I chanced across deep in the pores of his face when I viewed his corpse, and the stains upon his sheets." Holding up the jar towards Winduss, "Sir, I need to take this with me. The life of Mr. Smartwood's wife could depend on it."

"By all means, good Sir. But remember us here. As much as I am saddened by Frederick's passing, we could well do with another performer now."

"I will consider it," said Holmes.

I caught a slight glint in his eye and chastised him as we left. "Surely, you're not considering his offer of replacing Smartwood?"

"Why not? Caliban and Ariel are two of the more challenging roles in *The Tempest*. I understand the sorrow you feel at poor Mr. Smartwood's unfortunate death, but as they say, the show must go on."

***

It was four weeks later that I found myself once more in the auditorium of the virtually derelict Park Theatre. The main room was dimly lit, but the stage was ablaze with gaslights.

The Park Theatre Shakespeare troupe, as the esteemed Riley Winduss had decided to call them, was presenting their production of *The Tempest* to an audience of one. Me. Holmes had failed to tell me that they were performing, but Mr. Winduss had sent a telegram to 221B Baker Street with the sole intention of inviting me. I kept this from Holmes and snuck in while the preparations were underway. Luckily, Holmes was otherwise engaged, probably preparing his costume and makeup.

The day after our first meeting with Winduss, Mrs. Rowena Smartwood was released from Ealing station. Holmes, with myself in tow, returned directly to Baker Street and ran tests on the makeup that Smartwood had used. Within an hour it was confirmed that the makeup was the type outlawed over a century previously. It was riddled with arsenic, and users of an older age had dropped dead with great regularity before the authorities had finally outlawed its use.

Once the evidence was presented to the coroner, he, in turn, conducted his own tests on Smartwood's corpse and came to agree with Holmes's assessment. The cause of Smartwood's death was changed to long term exposure to arsenic, not strangulation.

Lanner's reaction was one of suppressed rage at having his conclusions found to be incorrect. Reluctantly, he apologised profusely to Mrs. Smartwood and allowed her to leave. My final view of Lanner, was his crestfallen posture as he dropped his head and moped back into the bowels of the police station. Holmes's only comment was, "Hopefully, he learns a lesson not to jump to the first conclusion, but to examine all the evidence and information presented. Only then, if the evidence doesn't fit your postulation, re-examine all you know until your conclusion is irrefutable or you change it to fit the facts."

Understandably, Mrs. Hudson was extremely effusive, showering both of us with thanks and later that evening as sumptuous a supper as I had devoured in many a year.

As I mused, the house lights dimmed, followed by the sounds of thunder and a remarkably effective flash of lightning.

"Boatswain!" the first actor called, and the play commenced.

The Adventure of the Great Wyrley Outrages

An adapted chronicle of an event from Arthur Conan Doyle's life.

It was a cold, crisp morning that saw me delivered unto the very steps of St. Mark's church in the tiny coal-mining town of Great Wyrley. I had an appointment with Reverend Shapurji Edalji, admittedly an odd name for that locale, but my understanding was he had emigrated from India many years before and converted from Parsee to the Church of England and taken on the ministry of St. Mark's.

I had long held the belief that our country could only benefit from the thoughts, opinions, and experiences of those born and raised from across the world. Reverend Edalji would be one such, and I hoped I could help he and his family in the matter that had come to my attention. Though I doubted if all my fellow countrymen held the same view, especially those whose lives were confined and entrenched in a tiny town such as this.

There was no one in the church itself, and I realised that at the hour of my visit, the Reverend would still be in his house at the rear of the property. A short walk found me before the modest house, and a quick knock brought the smiling face of my host to the door. "Mr. Arthur Conan Doyle, I am so pleased to make your acquaintance," said Reverend Edalji, his dark complexion broken by a wide grin showing pearly white teeth. Stepping aside, he allowed me entry and introduced his wife, Charlotte.

I was led to a small parlour, set with three places, and bade to sit, with the Reverend joining me, and Charlotte disappearing into the kitchen, I presumed. Within a moment, she re-joined us, placing a wonderful array of foods on the table for our breakfast.

"My word, I didn't expect anything this extravagant, so I thank you most humbly."

"Think nothing of it, Sir. You have expressed a wish to help our son, George, so nothing is too much trouble."

At the mention of her son's name, I noticed a sad look cross Charlotte's face. "I will do all I can to assist. His story is shocking and smacks of more than a simple misunderstanding," I said.

"Oh, you do not know the half of it," said the Reverend.

***

It had been when I read the headline *The Great Wyrley Ripper* that my initial interest in what became known as the *Great Wyrley Outrages* began. Four years earlier, in 1903, this quaint little village had become the centre of a series of horrid crimes. On numerous occasions, the residents would awake to find horses, cows, and pit ponies from the mines, mutilated and left to die in excruciating pain. Many were in such a state that their innards littered the clay soil, and the villages needed to put the poor animals out of their misery.

Great Wyrley became known as *the village of fear*, as the residents never knew what fresh horror may await them at the dawn of a new day.

From my reading, I realised that the local police were clueless. The attacks occurred in the dead of night, with the killer slashing the animals and leaving as silently as they came. No trace or piece of evidence was found that could conclusively lead to a single assailant.

The police issued orders for farmers to lock up their livestock, and for children to remain indoors after dark. Even with an increase in surveillance, the Ripper carried on with his deeds.

It wasn't until the 18th of August, when a young miner, Henry Garrett, was walking to begin his shift at the colliery and noticed a horse limping in a nearby field. His caring nature overcoming his desire to be punctual at work led him to find that the poor beast had been slashed. Raising the alarm, the villagers rushed to assist the animal, with the police soon pouncing on their only suspect, George Edalji, the Reverend's son.

***

"They put him away for three years," said the Reverend, his cup of coffee halfway to his lips. Replacing the cup, he shook his head in despair as the memories flooded back. "My poor boy, three years for crimes he didn't commit."

"Yes, I do agree with you. The whole trial was a sham. The evidence they presented was circumstantial at best. False at worst."

"He didn't even use a razor. George always attended the local barber, but the police didn't want to know."

The poor boy had suffered at the hands of the legal system. Something I was thoroughly disgusted about.

It had been chance that brought me into the story and convinced me to pursue the truth.

At the time of his arrest, George Edalji was forging a career as a solicitor in nearby Birmingham. Every morning he would make the journey to the larger town, only to return to the village in the evening. The police raided the vicarage where he still lived with his parents, finding a coat, supposedly with horsehair on it, a pair of muddied boots and a straight razor.

I hadn't established whether the police had sought legal permission to search the vicarage, or whether the Reverend and his wife had allowed it, having full faith in the constabulary.

George had been quickly arrested at his office in Birmingham, and then put on trial in nearby Stafford. The process lasted four days, with a jury finding him guilty of all charges after only fifty minutes of deliberation. He had been sentenced to seven years, and naturally, his career was destroyed.

Even though my interest at the time of the trial was purely in passing, minds more interested in the legal aspects of the trial took up the cause. Citing that the process was flawed, a petition was raised that gathered over ten thousand signatures. On presentation to the court, it was considered on its merits and George was released on parole. However, the spectre of guilt still hung over his head and barred him from practising the law, something in which he had spent years building up his proficiency and expertise.

By this stage, my own life had taken a dark turn. Touie, my darling wife, had recently died from tuberculosis. I was not myself, lost in guilt and despair, for while my wife succumbed to the dreaded disease, I had met and fallen in love with another. I know in my heart that Touie would never begrudge me a new love, but I could not shake the thoughts of betrayal within my own mind.

It was by chance that I happened upon George Edalji's letter amongst my usual sacks of mail from fans of the great detective. Reading his story, I realised taking up his cause was just the stimulant that my life required.

Writing to and meeting George at the Grand Hotel in Charing Cross was a tonic to my mind. Here was a man that had been wronged, by the very system I had supported for all my years. The system that my greatest creation reinforced throughout all of his dauntless exploits. George had read all of my novels and stories, and begged me, the creator of the world's premier consulting detective, to use his powers as if they were my own to prove his innocence. I have had many people write and tell me how much they love my stories, but there was something in George's appeal that piqued my interest.

As soon as I spotted George Edalji waiting for me in the hotel lobby, my heart went out to him. He was the only Indian in the room, a fact which drew several stares from other patrons and reinforced my thoughts on the matter, but it was the second pertinent fact that made me realise this man could never have undertaken such atrocious acts.

"He's extremely myopic," I mentioned to the Reverend and his wife. "When I met with him, he held his newspaper so close to his face that there was no other conclusion to be drawn. He confessed that he had read all of my stories but considering his condition I find that even more incredible."

"Yes. Sadly, our George does suffer with his eyesight. Something that tormented him for all those years in prison. Reading became his only relief."

"Before meeting George, I revisited the facts of the case. The night in question, the 17th of August was miserable. A virtual torrent ran through the county. In heavy rain, a man with George's eyesight would never have been able to cross the darkened fields safely."

"My word, that's true. George struggles to navigate the trip to the train station. I'm sure we told this to the police, but nothing came of it."

"I've also found, through my readings, that the killings continued after George was imprisoned."

Nodding his head sadly, "Yes, again another fact we brought up with the police, but by then they simply washed their hands of the incident. Some of the locals just put it down to someone copying George's acts."

I reached into my bag and drew out an old local paper that I had procured from the library. Turning to a particular article, I pointed at the horrid headline "Dark Oriental Killing Frenzy Stopped."

Charlotte gasped. The Reverend simply shook his head once more. "Yes. We have had to live with these lies and slanders for many years, even before George's arrest." He stood and walked from the room, returning momentarily with a handful of letters and placing them before me. "That article is mild compared to these."

I leafed through the letters and found myself shocked and disgusted at the contents. Each successive letter contained horrible accusations against the family, stemming from their conversion from the esoteric Parsee religion. They were accused of blood sacrifices and of virtually being part of some satanic cult.

"Did you show these to the police?"

"Oh, yes, many times. Ever since we started receiving them, which has been almost two decades now."

"How do you put up with this?" I asked, sliding the letters back across to the Reverend, and wishing to have nothing more to do with the filth they contained.

"I am a man of faith. I place my fate in the hands of God, and with that, I absolve these poor people of their sins."

I had to admire the Reverend's beliefs, but this was not something that could be swept away in the name of faith. A wrong had been committed and a man's future crushed.

Standing I said, "I have one more person to visit before returning to London, but rest assured I am thoroughly disgusted by everything that has occurred in this case. I will use whatever means I have at my disposal to see that justice is finally served."

With that, I bid the couple adieu and strolled back into town.

***

"Look, I don't care if he was blind as a bat. And I don't care what that Hindoo vicar says neither, he's just protecting his son. The evidence is clear. The little bugger did it. We arrested him, he was convicted and sent to prison. If a judge wants to let him out, then so be it. I done my job, and I won't be lectured to by some jumped-up little johnny that thinks he's a policeman just 'cause he had a few detective stories published."

I stared at Captain Anson, the head of the Staffordshire police, and took slow deep breaths to calm myself. This was the man that headed up the investigation that brought about the eventual conviction against George Edalji. He was a great beast of a man, and bull-headed in nature, and if I might say, not just a little racist.

It was becoming clearer in my mind that this entire affair smacked of ineptitude and incompetence, with a slathering of prejudice thrown in. Where little evidence existed, the police had fabricated, overlooked, or simply amplified what there was.

"Either the man is innocent and deserves exoneration and compensation, or he is guilty and deserves punishment," I thundered, my temper getting the better of me. "Your incompetence in this matter, Sir, has seen neither. But you have effectively destroyed his life and left him hanging by his thumbs in the eyes of the public."

"Pah," shouted Anson, "He's guilty. He wrote all those letters himself."

"Even those that arrived when he was merely twelve years old?"

"Then it was his father. No matter. His coat had horse hair on it. His boots were muddy. He had a razor."

"He has astigmatism. He can barely see one foot in front of himself. He could hardly navigate an open field on a dark and stormy night. As to the supposed evidence, all circumstantial and should have been thrown out before presentation."

The large man's face grew enraged. There was nothing further that could be gained from speaking with him. I simply left him to it

224

and returned to London, convinced that a grave injustice had been played out.

***

I may not be the detective that I made famous, but I have my own abilities. Starting with an article in the Daily Telegraph, the name and story of George Edalji spread across the nation. Even appearing in the new world.

Keeping up my articles and protestations at this travesty for many months, I soon had others of my ilk on George's side. My friends J.M. Barrie, Bram Stoker and George Bernard Shaw joined my cause and lauded my articles far and wide.

So loud was the roar of disapproval, that the Home Office reneged and appointed a committee to look into the case.

Finally, after many months, they issued a full pardon to Mr. George Edalji, but no compensation.

This development angered me such that I pestered them continuously, making many enemies within the Office itself, and a lifelong enemy of Captain Anson. Neither worried me, my only concern was justice.

My harassment led to George's readmittance to the Solicitors' Roll, and with that he moved to London to begin practising law once more, never to return home to Great Wyrley, the town he had come to accept hated him simply for his heritage and appearance.

Although George never received the proper respect or remuneration for the court's bumbling, my pursuits found success with the establishment of what would become known as the Court of Criminal Appeal. In the future, this institution would allow those that could prove they had been wrongly accused and convicted of crimes, an avenue to have their cases revisited and hopefully, their verdicts overturned.

The entire affair left me with a resounding feeling of satisfaction and I found that my own bereavement and guilt were assuaged through my dedication to George's cause, for later that year I married my new love, Jean Elizabeth Leckie. We were fortunate enough to have three wonderful children and many years together.

I believe that Touie would have approved.

It was by chance that I happened upon George Edalji's letter amongst my usual sacks of mail from fans of the great detective.

www.ingramcontent.com/pod-product-compliance
Lightning Source LLC
Chambersburg PA
CBHW071148260626
47162CB00003B/965

*9 7 8 1 8 0 4 2 4 5 7 6 7 *